THE
ROMANCE OF ELAINE
A DETECTIVE NOVEL
Sequel to the "Exploits"
BY
ARTHUR B. REEVE

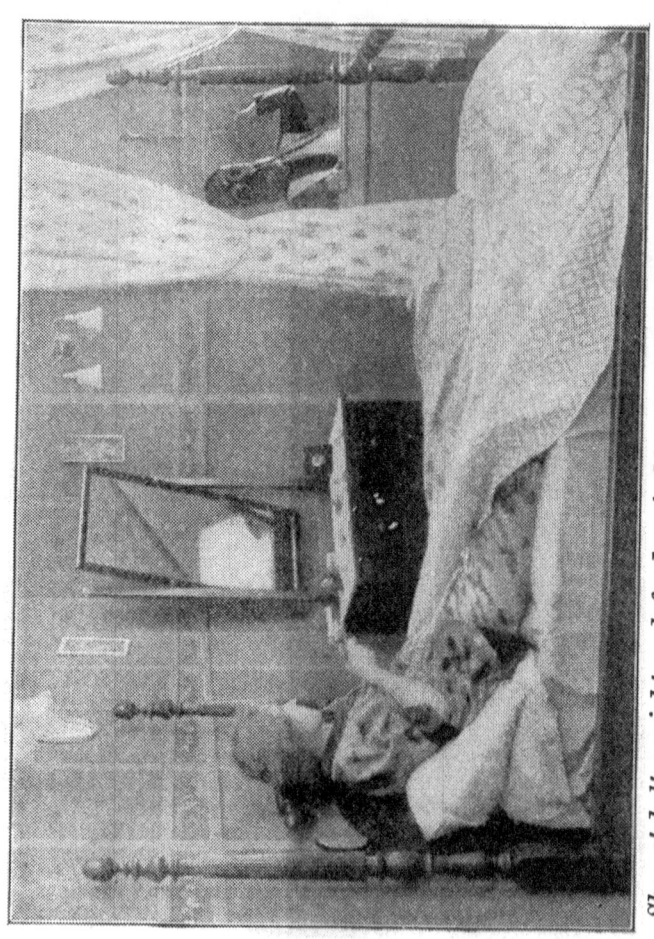

She sat bolt upright and fired, pointblank, at the window, shivering the glass.

(page 8)

THE ROMANCE
OF ELAINE

BY
ARTHUR B. REEVE

WITH FRONTISPIECE

WILDSIDE PRESS
BERKELEY HEIGHTS • NEW JERSEY

Another great publication from...

Wildside Press
PO Box 45
Gillette, NJ 07933-0045
www.wildsidepress.com

First Wildside Press edition:
September 2000

CONTENTS

The Romance of Elaine

CHAPTER I

THE SERPENT SIGN

RESCUED by Kennedy at last from the terrible incubus of Bennett's persecution in his double life of lawyer and master criminal, Elaine had, for the first time in many weeks, a feeling of security.

Now that the strain was off, however, she felt that she needed rest and a chance to recover herself and it occurred to her that a few quiet days with " Aunt " Tabitha, who had been her nurse when she was a little girl, would do her a world of good.

She sent for Aunt Tabby, yet the fascination of the experiences through which she had just gone still hung over her. She could not resist thinking and reading about them, as she sat, one morning, with the faithful Rusty in the conservatory of the Dodge house.

I had told the story at length in the *Star,* and the heading over it caught her eye.

It read:

THE CLUTCHING HAND DEAD

Double Life Exposed by Craig Kennedy

I

Perry Bennett, the Famous Young Lawyer, Takes
Poison—Kennedy Now on Trail of Master Criminal's Hidden Millions.

———

As Elaine glanced down the column, Jennings announced that Aunt Tabby, as she loved to call her old
friend, had arrived, and was now in the library with
Aunt Josephine.

With an exclamation of delight, Elaine dropped
the paper and, followed by Rusty, almost ran into the
library.

Aunt Tabby was a stout, elderly, jolly-faced
woman, precisely the sort whom Elaine needed to
watch over her just now.

"Oh, I'm so glad to see you," half laughed Elaine
as she literally flung herself into her nurse's arms.
"I feel so unstrung—and I thought that if I could
just run off for a few days with you and Joshua in
the country where no one would know, it might
make me feel better. You have always been so good
to me. Marie! Are my things packed? Very well.
Then, get my wraps."

Her maid left the room.

"Bless your soul," mothered Aunt Tabby stroking
her soft golden hair, "I'm always glad to have you in
that fine house you bought me. And, faith, Miss
Elaine, the house is a splendid place to rest in but I
don't know what's the matter with it lately. Joshua
says its haunts—"

"Haunts?" repeated Elaine in amused surprise.
"Why, what do you mean?"

Marie entered with the wraps before Aunt Tabby

could reply and Jennings followed with the baggage.

"Nonsense," continued Elaine gaily, as she put on her coat, and turned to bid Aunt Josephine good-bye. "Good-bye, Tabitha," said her real aunt. "Keep good care of my little girl."

"That I will," returned the nurse. "We don't have all these troubles out in the country that you city folks have."

Elaine went out, followed by Rusty and Jennings with the luggage.

"Now for a long ride in the good fresh air," sighed Elaine as she leaned back on the cushions of the Dodge limousine and patted Rusty, while the butler stowed away the bags.

The air certainly did, if anything, heighten the beauty of Elaine and at last they arrived at Aunt Tabby's, tired and hungry.

The car stopped and Elaine, Aunt Tabby and the dog got out. There, waiting for them, was "Uncle" Joshua, as Elaine playfully called him, a former gardener of the Dodges, now a plain, honest countryman on whom the city was fast encroaching, a jolly old fellow, unharmed by the world.

Aunt Tabby's was an attractive small house, not many miles from New York, yet not in the general line of suburban travel.

. . . .

Kennedy and I had decided to bring Bennett's papers and documents over to the laboratory to examine them. We were now engaged in going over the great mass of material which he had collected, in the hope of finding some clue to the stolen millions

which he must have amassed as a result of his vil-
lainy. The table was stacked high.

A knock at the door told us that the expressman
had arrived and a moment later he entered, deliver-
ing a heavy box. Kennedy signed for it and started
to unpack it.

I was hard at work, when I came across a large
manila envelope carefully sealed, on which were written the figures " $7,000,000." Too excited even to
exclaim, I tore the envelope open and examined the
contents.

Inside was another envelope. I opened that. It
contained merely a blank piece of paper!

With characteristic skill at covering his tracks,
Bennett had also covered his money. Puzzled, I
turned the paper over and over, looking at it carefully. It was a large sheet of paper, but it showed
nothing.

"Huh!" I snorted to myself, "confound him."

Yet I could not help smiling at my own folly, a
minute later, in thinking that the Clutching Hand
would leave any information in such an obvious place
as an envelope. I threw the paper into a wire basket
on the desk and went on sorting the other stuff.

Kennedy had by this time finished unpacking the
box, and was examining a bottle which he had taken
from it.

"Come here, Walter," he called at length. "Ever
see anything like that?"

"I can't say," I confessed, getting up to go to
him. "What is it?"

"Bring a piece of paper," he added.

I went back to the desk where I had been working and looked about hastily. My eye fell on the blank sheet of paper which I had taken from Bennett's envelope, and I picked it up from the basket.

"Here's one," I said, handing it to him. "What are you doing?"

Kennedy did not answer directly, but began to treat the paper with the liquid from the bottle. Then he lighted a Bunsen burner and thrust the paper into the flame. The paper did not burn!

"A new system of fire-proofing," laughed Craig, enjoying my astonishment.

He continued to hold the paper in the flame. Still it did not burn.

"See?" he went on, withdrawing it, and starting to explain the properties of the new fire-proofer.

He had scarcely begun, when he stopped in surprise. He had happened to glance at the paper again, bent over to examine it more intently, and was now looking at it in surprise.

I looked also. There, clearly discernible on the paper, was a small part of what looked like an architect's drawing of a fireplace.

Craig looked up at me, nonplussed. "Where did you say you got that?" he asked.

"It was a blank piece of paper among Bennett's effects," I returned, as mystified as he, pointing at the littered desk at which I had been working.

Kennedy said nothing, but thrust the paper back again into the flame. Slowly, the heat of the burner seemed to bring out the complete drawing of the fireplace.

We looked at it, even more mystified. "What is it, do you suppose?" I queried.

"I think," he replied slowly, "that it was drawn with sympathetic ink. The heat of the burner brought it out into sight."

What was it about?

.   .   .   .

Elaine had gone to bed that night at Aunt Tabby's in the room which her old nurse had fixed up especially for her. It was a very attractive little room with dainty chintz curtains and covers and for the first time in many weeks Elaine slept soundly and fearlessly.

Down-stairs, in the living-room, Rusty also was asleep, his nose between his paws.

The living-room was in keeping with everything at Aunt Tabby's, plain, neat, homelike. On one side was a large fireplace that gave to it an air of quaint hospitality.

Suddenly Rusty woke up, his ears pointed at this fireplace. He stood a moment, listening, then, with a bark of alarm he sped swiftly from the living-room, up the stairs at a bound, until he came to Elaine's room.

Elaine felt his cold nose at her hand and stirred, then awoke.

"What is it, Rusty?" she asked, mindful of the former days when Rusty gave warning of the Clutching Hand and his emissaries.

Rusty wagged his tail. Something was wrong.

Elaine followed him down to the living-room. She went over and lighted the electric lamp on the table, then turned to Rusty.

"Well, Rusty?" she asked, almost as if he were human.

She had no need to repeat the question. Rusty was looking straight at the fireplace.

Elaine listened. Sure enough, she heard strange noises. Was that Aunt Tabby's "haunt"? Whatever it was, it sounded as if it came up from the very depths of the earth.

She could not make out just what it sounded like. It might have been some one striking a piece of iron, a bolt, with a sledge.

What was it?

She continued to listen in wonder, then ran to Aunt Tabby's bedroom door, on the first floor, and knocked.

Aunt Tabby woke up and shook Joshua.

"Aunt Tabby! Aunt Tabby!" called Elaine.

"Yes, my dear," answered the old nurse, now fully awake and straightening her nightcap. "Joshua!"

Together the old couple came out into the living-room, still in their nightclothes, Joshua yawning sleepily still.

"Listen!" whispered Elaine.

There was the noise again. This time it was more as though some one were beating a rat-tat-tat with something on a rock. It was weird, uncanny, as all stood there, none knowing where the strange noises came from.

"It's the haunts!" cried Aunt Tabby, trembling a bit. "For three nights now we've been hearing these noises."

Around and around the room they walked, still trying to locate the strange sounds. Were they under the floor? It was impossible to say. They gave it up and stood there, looking blankly at each other. Was it the work of human or superhuman hands?

Finally Joshua went to a table drawer and opened it. He took out a huge, murderous-looking revolver.

"Here, Miss Elaine," he urged, pressing it on her, "take this—keep it near you!"

The noises ceased at length, as strangely as they had begun.

Half an hour later, they had all gone back to bed and were asleep. But Elaine's sleep now was fitful, a constant procession of faces flitted before her closed eyes.

Suddenly, she woke with a start and stared into the semi-darkness. Was that face real, or a dream face? Was it the hideous helmeted face that had dragged her down into the sewer once? That man was dead. Who was this?

She gazed at the bedroom window, holding the huge revolver tightly. There, vague in the night light, appeared a figure. Surely that was no dream face of the oxygen helmet. Besides, it was not the same helmet.

She sat bolt upright and fired, pointblank, at the window, shivering the glass. A second later she had leaped from the bed, switched on the lights and was running to the sill.

Down-stairs, Aunt Tabby and Uncle Joshua had heard the shot. Joshua was now wide awake. He seized his old shotgun and ran out into the living-room. Followed by Aunt Tabby, he hurried to Elaine.

"Wh-what was it?" he asked, puffing at the exertion of running up-stairs.

"I saw—a face—at the window—with some kind of thing over it!" gasped Elaine. "It was like one I saw once before."

Uncle Joshua did not wait to hear any more. With the gun pointed ahead of him, ready for instant action, he ran out of the room and into the garden, beneath Elaine's window.

He looked about for signs of an intruder. There was not a sound. No one was about, here.

"I don't see any one," he called up to Elaine and Aunt Tabby in the window.

He happened to look down at the ground. Before him was a small box. He picked it up.

"Here's something, though," he said.

Joshua went back into the house.

"What is it?" asked Elaine as he rejoined the women.

She took the curious little box and unfastened the cover. As she opened it, she drew back. There in the box was a little ivory figure of a man, all hunched up and shrunken, a hideous figure. She recoiled from it—it reminded her too much of the Chinese devil-god she had seen,—and she dropped the box.

For a moment all stood looking at it in horrified amazement.

.   .   .   .

It was the afternoon following the day of our strange discovery of the fireplace done in sympathetic

ink on the apparently blank sheet of paper in Bennett's effects, when the speaking-tube sounded and I
answered it.

"Why—it's Elaine," I exclaimed.

Kennedy's face showed the keenest pleasure at the
unexpected visit. "Tell her to come right up," he
said quickly.

I opened the door for her.

"Why—Elaine—I'm awfully glad to see you," he
greeted, "but I thought you were rusticating."

"I was, but, Craig, it seems to me that wherever I
go, something happens," she returned. "You know,
Aunt Tabby said there were haunts. I thought it was
an old woman's fear—but last night I heard the
strangest noises out there, and I thought I saw a face
at the window—a face in a helmet. And when Joshua
went out, this is what he found on the ground under
my window."

She handed Kennedy a box, a peculiar affair which
she touched gingerly and only with signs of the greatest aversion.

Kennedy opened it. There, in the bottom of the
box, was a little ivory devil-god. He looked at it curiously a moment.

"Let me see," he ruminated, still regarding the
sign. "The house you bought for Aunt Tabby, once
belonged to Bennett, didn't it?"

Elaine nodded her head. "Yes, but I don't see what
that can have to do with it," she agreed, adding with
a shudder, "Bennett is dead."

Kennedy had taken a piece of paper from the desk
where he had put it away carefully. "Have you ever

seen anything that looks like this?" he asked, handing her the paper.

Elaine looked at the plan carefully, as Kennedy and I scanned her face. She glanced up, her expression showing plainly the wonder she felt.

"Why, yes," she answered. "That looks like Aunt Tabby's fireplace in the living-room."

Kennedy said nothing for a moment. Then he seized his hat and coat.

"If you don't mind," he said, "we'll go back there with you."

"Mind?" she repeated. "Just what I had hoped you would do."

.   .   .   .

Wu Fang, the Chinese master mind, had arrived in New York.

Beside Wu, the inscrutable, Long Sin, astute though he was, was a mere pigmy—his slave, his advance agent, as it were, a tentacle sent out to discover the most promising outlet for the nefarious talents of his master.

New York did not know of the arrival of Wu Fang, the mysterious—yet. But down in the secret recesses of Chinatown, in the ways that are devious and dark, the oriental crooks knew—and trembled.

Thus it happened that Long Sin was not permitted to enjoy even the foretaste of Bennett's spoils which he had forced from him after his weird transformation into his real self, the Clutching Hand, when the China-man had given him the poisoned draught that had put him into his long sleep.

He had obtained the paper showing where the

treasure amassed by the Clutching Hand was hidden, but Wu Fang, his master, had come.

Wu had immediately established himself in the most sumptuous of apartments, hidden behind the squalid exterior of the ordinary tenement building in China-town.

The night following his arrival, Wu Fang was re-clining on a divan, when his servant announced that Long Sin was at the door.

As Long Sin entered, it was evident that, cunning and shrewd though he was himself, Wu was indeed his master. He approached in fear and awe, cringing low.

" Have you brought the map with you? " asked Wu.

Long Sin bowed low again, and drew from under his coat the paper which he had obtained from Ben-nett. For a moment the two, master and slave in guile, bent over, closely studying it.

At one point in the map Long Sin's bony finger paused over a note which Bennett had made:

BEWARE POISONED GAS UPON OPENING
COMPARTMENT.

" And you think you can trace it out? " asked Wu.

" Without a doubt," bowed Long Sin.

He went over to a bag near-by, which he had al-ready sent up by another servant, and opened it. In-side was an oxygen helmet. He replaced it, after showing it to Wu.

" With the aid of the science of the white devil, we shall overcome the science of the white devil," purred Long Sin subtly.

Outside, Wu had already ordered a car to wait, and together the two drove off rapidly. Into the country, they sped, until at last they came to a lonely turn in a lonely road, somewhat removed from the section that was rapidly being built up as population reached out from the city, but on a single-tracked trolley line.

Long Sin alighted and disappeared with a parting word of instruction from Wu who remained in the car. The Chinaman carried with him the heavy bag with the oxygen helmet.

Along this interurban trolley the cars made only half-hourly trips at this time of night. Long Sin hurried down the road until he came to a trolley pole, then looked hastily at his watch. It was twenty minutes at least before the next car would pass.

Quickly, almost monkey-like, he climbed up the pole, carrying with him the end of a wire which he had taken from the bag.

Having thrown this over the feed wire, he slid quickly to the ground again. Then, carrying the other end of the wire in his rubber-gloved hands, he made his way through the underbrush, in and out, almost like the serpent he was, until he came to a passageway in the rough and uncleared hillside—a small opening formed by the rocks.

It was dark inside, but he did not hesitate to enter, carrying the wire and the bag with him.

.   .   .   .

It was nightfall before we arrived with Elaine at Aunt Tabby's. We entered the living-room and Elaine introduced us both to Aunt Tabby and her husband.

It was difficult to tell whether Elaine's old nurse

was more glad to see her than the faithful Rusty who almost overwhelmed her even after so short an absence.

In the midst of the greetings, I took occasion to look over the living-room. It was a very cozy room, simply and tastefully furnished, and I fancied that I could see in the neatness of Aunt Tabby a touch of Elaine's hand, for she had furnished it for her faithful old friend.

I followed Kennedy's eyes, and saw that he was looking at the fireplace. Sure enough, it was the same in design as the fireplace which the heat had so unexpectedly brought out in sympathetic ink on the blank sheet of paper.

Kennedy lost no time in examining it, and we crowded around him as he went over it inch by inch, following the directions on the drawing.

At one point in the drawing a peculiar protuberance was marked. Kennedy was evidently hunting for that. He found it at last and pressed the sort of lever in several ways. Nothing seemed to happen. But finally, almost by chance, he seemed to discover the secret.

A small section at the side of the fireplace opened up, disclosing an iron ladder, leading down into one of those characteristic hiding-places in which the Clutching Hand used to delight.

Kennedy looked at the mysterious opening some time, as if trying to fathom the mystery.

"Let's go down and explore it," I suggested, taking a step toward the ladder.

Kennedy reached out and pulled me back. Then

without a word he pressed the little lever and the door closed.

"I think we'd better wait a while, Walter," he decided. "I would rather hear Aunt Tabby's haunts myself."

He carefully went over not only the rest of the house but the grounds about it, without discovering anything.

Aunt Tabby, with true country hospitality, seemed unable to receive guests without feeding them, and, although we had had a big dinner at a famous roadhouse on the way out, still none of us could find it in our hearts to refuse her hospitality. Even that diversion, however, did not prevent us from talking of nothing else but the strange noises, and I think, as we waited, we all got into the frame of mind which would have manufactured them even if there had been none.

We were sitting about the room when suddenly the most weird and uncanny rappings began. Rusty was on his feet in a moment, barking like mad. We looked from one to another.

It was impossible to tell where the noises came from, or even to describe them. They were certainly not ghostly rappings. In fact, they sounded more like some twentieth century piece of machinery.

We listened a moment, then Kennedy walked over to the fireplace. "You can explore it with me now, Walter," he said quietly, touching the lever and opening the panel which disclosed the ladder.

He started down the ladder and I followed closely.

Elaine was about to join us, when Kennedy paused on the topmost round and looked up at her.

" No, no, young lady," he said with mock severity, " you have been through enough already—you stay where you are."

Elaine argued and begged but Kennedy was obdurate. It was only when Aunt Tabby and Joshua added their entreaties that she consented reluctantly to remain.

Together, Craig and I descended into the darkness about eight or ten feet. There we found a passageway, excavated through the earth and rock, along which we crept. It was crooked and uneven, and we stumbled, but kept going slowly ahead.

Kennedy, who was a few feet in front of me, stopped suddenly and I almost fell over him.

" What is it? " I whispered.

.   .   .   .

Long Sin had made his way from the opening of the cave to the point on the plan which was marked by a cross, and there he had set up his electric drill which was connected to the trolley wire. He was working furiously to take advantage of the fifteen minutes or so before the next car would pass.

The tunnel had been widened out at this point into a small subterranean chamber. It was dug out of the earth and the roof was roughly propped up, most of the weight being borne by one main wooden prop which, in the dampness, had now become old and rotten.

On one side it was evident that Long Sin had already been at work, digging and drilling through the earth and rock. He had gone so far now that he had disclosed what looked like the face of a small safe set directly into the rock.

As he worked he would stop from time to time and consult the map. Then he would take up drilling again.

He had now come to the point on which Bennett had written his warning. Quickly he opened the bag and took out the oxygen helmet, which he adjusted carefully over his head. Then he set to work with re-doubled energy.

It was that drill as well as his pounding on the rock which had so alarmed Elaine and Aunt Tabby the night before and which now had been the signal for Kennedy's excursion of discovery.

.   .   .   .

Our man, whoever he was, must have heard us approaching down the tunnel, for he paused in his work and the noise of the drill ceased.

He looked about a moment, then went over to the prop and examined it, looking up at the roof of the chamber above him. Evidently he feared that it was not particularly strong.

From our vantage point around the bend in the passageway we could see this strange and uncouth figure.

" Who is it, do you think? " I whispered, crouching back against the wall for fear that he might look even around a corner or through the earth and discover us.

As I spoke, my hand loosened a piece of rock that jutted out and before I knew it there was a crash.

" Confound it, Walter," exclaimed Kennedy.

2

Down the passageway the figure was now thoroughly on the alert, staring with his goggle-like eyes into the blackness in our direction. It was not the roof above him that was unsafe. He was watched, and he did not hesitate a minute to act.

He seized the bag and picked his way quickly through the passage as if thoroughly familiar with every turn of the walls and roughness of the floor.

We were discovered and if we were to accomplish anything, it was now or never.

Kennedy dashed forward and I followed close after him.

We were making much better time than our strange visitor and were gaining on him rapidly. Nearer and nearer we came to him, for, in spite of his familiarity with the cavern he was hampered by the outlandish head-gear that he wore.

It was only another instant, when Kennedy would have laid his hands on him.

Suddenly he half turned, raised his arm and dashed something to the earth much as a child explodes a toy torpedo. I fully expected that it was a bomb; but, as a moment later, I found that Kennedy and I were still unharmed, I knew that it must be some other product of this devilish genius.

The thickest and most impenetrable smoke seemed to pervade the narrow cavern!

"A Chinese smoke bomb!" sputtered and coughed Kennedy, as he retreated a minute, then with renewed vigor endeavored to penetrate the dense and opaque fumes.

We managed to go ahead still, but the intruder had

exploded one after another of his peculiar bombs, always keeping ahead of the smoke which he created, and we found that under its cover he had made good his escape, probably reaching the entrance of the cave in the underbrush.

At the other end of the passageway, up in the living-room of the cottage, the draught had carried large quantities of the smoke. Elaine, Aunt Tabby and Joshua coughing and choking, saw it, and opened a window, which seemed to cause a current of air to sweep through the whole length of the passageway and helped to clear away the fumes rapidly.

Long Sin, meanwhile, had started to work his way through the bushes to reach the waiting car, with Wu, then paused and listened. Hearing no sound, he replaced the helmet which he had taken off.

Pursuit was now useless for us. With revolvers drawn, we crept back along the passageway until we came again to the chamber itself. There, on the floor, lay a bag of tools, opened, as though somebody had been working with them.

"Caught red-handed!" exclaimed Kennedy with great satisfaction.

He looked at the tools a minute and then at the electric drill, and finally an idea seemed to strike him. He took up the drill and advanced toward the safe. Then he turned on the current and applied the drill.

The drill was of the very latest design and it went quickly through the steel. But beyond that there was another thin steel partition. This Kennedy tackled next.

The drill went through and he withdrew it.

Instantly the most penetrating and nauseous odor seemed to pervade everything.

Kennedy cried out. But his warning was too late. We staggered back, overcome by the escaping gas and fell to the ground.

.   .   .   .

Long Sin, with his oxygen helmet on again, had returned to the passageway and was now stealthily creeping back.

He came to the chamber and there discovered us lying on the ground, overcome. He bent down and, to his great satisfaction, saw that we were really unconscious.

Quickly he moved over to the safe and pried open the last thin steel plate.

Inside was a small box. He picked it up and tried to open it, but it was locked. There was no time to work over it here, and he took it under his arm and started to leave.

He paused a moment to look at us, then took out a piece of paper and a pencil and on the paper wrote, " Thanks for your trouble."

Beneath, it was signed by his special stamp—the serpent's head, mouth open and fangs showing.

Long Sin looked at us a moment, then a subtle smile seemed to spread over his face. At last he had us in his power.

He drew out a long, wicked-looking Chinese knife and stuck it through the note.

Then he felt the edge of the knife. It was keen.

.   .   .   .

In the sitting-room, Elaine, Aunt Tabby and Joshua had been listening intently at the fireplace but heard nothing.

They were now getting decidedly worried. Finally, the fumes which we had released made their way to the room. They were considerably diluted by fresh air by that time, but, although they were nauseous, were not sufficient to overcome any one. Still, the smell was terrible.

"I can't stand it any longer," cried Elaine. "I'm going down there to see what has become of them."

Aunt Tabby and Joshua tried to stop her, but she broke away from them and went down the ladder. Rusty leaped down after her.

Joshua tried to follow, but Aunt Tabby held him back. He would have gone, too, if she had not managed to strike the spring and shut the door, closing up the passageway.

Joshua got angry then. "You are making a coward of me," he cried, beating on the panel with the butt of his gun and struggling to open it.

He seemed unable to fathom the secret.

Elaine was now making her way as rapidly as she could through the tunnel, with Rusty beside her.

.   .   .   .

It was just as Long Sin had raised his knife that the sound of her footsteps alarmed him.

He paused and leaped to his feet.

There was no time for either to retreat. He started toward Elaine, and seized her roughly.

Back and forth over the rocky floor they struggled. As they fought,—she with frantic strength, he craftily,

—he backed her slowly up against the prop that upheld the roof.

He raised his keen knife.

She recoiled. The prop, none too strong, suddenly gave way under her weight.

The whole roof of the chamber fell with a crash, earth and stone overwhelming Elaine and her assailant.

. . . .

By this time Joshua had left the house and had gone out into the garden to get something to pry open the fireplace door.

Of a sudden, to his utter amazement, a few feet from him, it seemed as if the very earth sank in his garden, leaving a yawning chasm.

He looked, unable to make it out.

Before his very eyes a strange figure, the figure of Long Sin in his oxygen helmet, appeared, struggling up, as if by magic from the very earth, shaking the debris off himself, as a dog would shake off the water after a plunge in a pond.

Long Sin was gone in a moment.

Then again the earth began to move. A paw appeared, then a sharp black nose, and a moment later, Rusty, too, dug himself out.

Joshua had run into the house to get a spade when Rusty, like a shot, bolted for the house, took the window at a leap and all covered with earth landed before Joshua and Aunt Tabby.

"See!—he went down there—now he's here!" cried Aunt Tabby, pointing at the fireplace, then looking at the window.

Rusty was running back and forth from Joshua to the window.

" Follow him! " cried Aunt Tabby.

Rusty led the way back again to the garden, to the cave-in.

" Elaine! " gasped Aunt Tabby.

By this time Joshua was digging furiously. Rusty, too, seemed to understand. He threw back the earth with his paws, helping with every ounce of strength in his little body.

At last the spade turned up a bit of cloth.

" Elaine! " Aunt Tabby cried out again.

She was in a sort of little pocket, protected by the fortunate formation of the earth as it fell, yet almost suffocated, weak but conscious.

Aunt Tabby rushed up as Joshua laid down the spade and lifted out Elaine.

They were about to carry her into the house, when she cried weakly, but with all her remaining strength.

" No—no—Dig! Craig—Walter! " she managed to gasp.

Rusty, too, was still at it. Joshua fell to again. Man and dog worked with a will.

" There they are! " cried Elaine, as all three pulled us out, unconscious but still alive.

Though we did not know it, they carried us into the house, while Elaine and Aunt Tabby bustled about to get something to revive us.

At last I opened my eyes and saw the motherly Aunt Tabby bending over me. Craig was already revived, weak but ready now to do anything Elaine ordered, as she held his hand and stroked his forehead softly.

.   .   .   .

Meanwhile Long Sin had made his way to the automobile where his master, Wu, waited impatiently.

"Did you get it?" asked Wu eagerly.

Long Sin showed him the box.

"Hurry, master!" he cried breathlessly, leaping into the car and struggling to take off the helmet as they drove away. "They may be here—at any moment."

The machine was off like a shot and even if we had been able to follow, we could not now have caught it.

Back in Wu's sumptuous apartment, later, Wu and his slave, Long Sin, after their hurried ride, dismissed all the servants and placed the little box on the table. Wu rose and locked the door.

Then, together, they took a sharp instrument and tried to pry off the lid of the box.

The lid flew off. They gazed in eagerly.

Inside was a smaller box, which Wu seized eagerly and opened.

There, on the plush cushion lay merely a round knobbed ring!

Was this the end of their great expectations? Were Bennett's millions merely mythical?

The two stared at each other in chagrin.

Wu was the first to speak.

"Where there should have been seven million dollars," he muttered to himself, "why is there only a mystic ring?"

CHAPTER II

THE CRYPTIC RING

KENNEDY had been engaged for some time in the only work outside of the Dodge case which he had consented to take for weeks.

Our old friend, Dr. Leslie, the Coroner, had appealed to him to solve a very ticklish point in a Tong murder case which had set all Chinatown agog. It was, indeed, a very bewildering case. A Chinaman named Li Chang, leader of the Chang Wah Tong, had been poisoned, but so far no one had been able to determine what poison it was or even to prove that there had been a poison, except for the fact that the man was dead, and Kennedy had taken the thing up in a great measure because of the sudden turn in the Dodge case which had brought us into such close contact with the Chinese.

I had been watching Kennedy with interest, for the Tong wars always make picturesque newspaper stories, when a knock at the door announced the arrival of Dr. Leslie, anxious for some result.

" Have you been able to find out anything yet? " he greeted Kennedy eagerly as Craig looked up from his microscope.

Kennedy turned and nodded. " Your dead man was murdered by means of aconite, of which, you know, the active principle is the deadly alkaloid aconitine."

25

Craig pulled down from the shelf above him one of his well-thumbed standard works on toxicology. He turned the pages and read:

"Pure aconite is probably the most actively poisonous substance with which we are acquainted. It does not produce any decidedly characteristic post-mortem appearances, and, in fact, there is no reliable chemical test to prove its presence. The chances of its detection in the body after death are very slight."

Dr. Leslie looked up. "Then there is no test, none?" he asked.

"There is one that is brand new," replied Kennedy slowly. "It is the new starch-grain test just discovered by Professor Reichert, of the University of Pennsylvania. The peculiarities of the starch grains of various plants are quite as great as those of the blood crystals, which, you will recall, Walter, we used once.

"The starch grains of the poison have remained in the wound. I have recovered them from the dead man's blood and have studied them microscopically. They can be definitely recognized. This is plainly a case of aconite poisoning—probably suggested to the Oriental mind by the poison arrows of the Ainus of Northern Japan."

Dr. Leslie and I both looked through the microscope, comparing the starch grains which Kennedy had discovered with those of scores of micro-photographs which lay scattered over the table.

"There are several treatments for aconite poisoning," ruminated Kennedy. "I would say that one of the latest and best is digitalin given hypodermically."

He took down a bottle of digitalin from a cabinet, adding, " only it was too late in this case."

. . . .

Just what the relations were between Long Sin and the Chong Wah Tong I have never been able to determine exactly. But one thing was certain: Long Sin on his arrival in New York had offended the Tong and now that his master, Wu Fang, was here the offence was even greater, for the criminal society brooked no rival.

In the dark recesses of a poorly furnished cellar, serving as the Tong headquarters, the new leader and several of his most trusted followers were now plotting revenge. Long Sin, they believed, was responsible for the murder, and, with truly Oriental guile, they had obtained a hold over Wu Fang's secretary.

Their plan decided on, the Chinamen left the headquarters and made their way separately up-town. They rejoined one another in the shelter of a rather poor house, before which was a board fence, in the vicinity of a fashionable apartment house. A moment's conference followed, and then the secretary glided away.

. . . .

Wu had taken another apartment up-town in one of the large apartment houses near a parkway; for he was far too subtle to operate from his real headquarters back of the squalid exterior of Chinatown.

There Long Sin was now engaged in making all possible provisions for the safety of his master. Any one who had been walking along the boulevard and had happened to glance up at the roof of the tall apartment building might have seen Long Sin's figure silhouetted against the sky on the top of the mansard roof near a flagpole.

He had just finished fastening to the flagpole a stout rope which stretched taut across an areaway some twenty or thirty feet wide to the next building, where it was fastened to a chimney. Again and again he tested it, and finally with a nod of satisfaction descended from the roof and went to the apartment of Wu.

There, alone, he paused for a few minutes to gaze in wonder at the cryptic ring which had been the net result so far of his efforts to find the millions which Bennett, as the Clutching Hand, had hidden. He wore it, strangely enough, over his index finger, and as he examined it he shook his head in doubt.

Neither he nor his master had yet been able to fathom the significance of the ring.

Long Sin thought that he was unobserved. But outside, looking through the keyhole, was Wu's secretary, who had stolen in on the mission which had been set for him at the Tong headquarters.

Long Sin went over to a desk and opened a secret box in which Wu had placed several packages of money with which to bribe those whom he wished to get into his power. It was Long Sin's mission to carry out this scheme, so he packed the money into a bag, drew his coat more closely about him and left the room.

No sooner had he gone than the secretary hurried into the room, paused a moment to make sure that Long Sin was not coming back, then hurried over to a closet near-by.

From a secret hiding-place he drew out a small bow and arrow. He sat down at a table and hastily wrote a few Chinese characters on a piece of paper, rolling up the note into a thin quill which he inserted into a prepared place in the arrow.

Then he raised the window and deftly shot the arrow out.

Down the street, back of the board fence, where the final conference has taken place, was a rather sleepy-looking Chinaman, taking an occasional puff at a cigarette doped with opium.

He jumped to his feet suddenly. With a thud an arrow had buried itself quivering in the fence. Quickly he seized it, drew out the note and read it.

In the Canton vernacular it read briefly: " He goes with much money."

It was enough. Instantly the startling news overcame the effect of the dope, and the Chinaman shuffled off quickly to the Tong headquarters.

They were waiting for him there, and he had scarcely delivered the message before their plans were made. One by one they left the headquarters, hiding in doorways, basements and areaways along the narrow street.

.   .   .   .

Long Sin was making his rounds, visiting all those whom the glitter of Wu's money could corrupt.

Suddenly from the shadows of a narrow street, lined with the stores of petty Chinese merchants, half a dozen lithe and murderous figures leaped out behind Long Sin and seized him. He struggled, but they easily threw him down.

Any one who has visited Chinatown knows that at every corner and bend of the crooked streets stands a policeman. It was scarcely a second before the noise of the scuffle was heard, but it was too late. The half dozen Tong men had seized the money which Long Sin carried and had deftly stripped him of everything else of value.

The sound of the approaching policeman now alarmed them. Just as the new Tong leader had raised an axe to bring it down with crushing force on Long Sin's skull a shot rang out and the axe fell from the broken wrist of the Chinaman.

In another moment the policeman had seized him. Then followed a sharp fight in which the Tong men's knowledge of jiu-jitsu stood them in good stead. The policeman was hurled aside, the Tong leader broke away, and one by one his followers disappeared through dark hallways and alleyways, leaving the policeman with only two prisoners and Long Sin lying on the sidewalk.

But the ring and the money were gone.

"Are you hurt much?" demanded the burly Irish officer, assisting Long Sin to his feet, none too gently.

Long Sin was furious over the loss of the precious ring, yet he knew to involve himself in the white man's law would end only in disaster both for him and his master. He forced a painful smile, shook his head and managed to get away down the street muttering.

He made his way up-town and back to the apartment of Wu, and there, pacing up and down in a fury, attended to his wounds.

His forefinger, from which the ring had been so

ruthlessly snatched, was a constant reminder to him of the loss. Any one who could have studied the vengefulness of his face would have seen that it boded ill for some one.

. . . .

It was the day after her return from Aunt Tabby's that Kennedy called again upon Elaine to find that she and Aunt Josephine were engaged in the pleasant pastime of arranging an entertainment.

Jennings announced Craig and held back the portieres as he entered.

"Oh, good!" cried Elaine as she saw him. "You are just in time. I was going to send you this, but I should much rather give it to you."

She handed him a tastefully engraved sheet of paper which he read with interest:

Miss Elaine Dodge
requests the honor of your presence
at an Oriental Reception
on April 6th, at 8 o'clock.

"Very interesting," exclaimed Craig enthusiastically. "I shall be delighted to come."

He looked about a moment at the library which Elaine was already rearranging for the entertainment.

"Then you must work," she cried gaily. "You are just in time to help me buy the decorations. No objections—come along."

She took Kennedy's arm playfully.

"But I have a very important investigation for the Coroner that I am——"

" No excuses," she cried, laughingly, dragging him out.

Among the many places which Elaine had down on her shopping list was a small Chinese curio shop on lower Fifth avenue.

They entered and were greeted with a profound bow by the proprietor. He was the new Tong leader, and this up-town shop was his cover. In actual fact, he was what might have been called a Chinese fence for stolen goods.

In their interest in the wealth of strange and curious ornaments displayed in the shop they did not notice that the Chinaman's wrist was bound tightly under his flowing sleeve.

Elaine explained what it was she wanted, and with Kennedy's aid selected a number of Chinese hangings and decorations. They were about to leave the shop when Elaine's eye was attracted by a little show case in which were many quaint and valuable Chinese ornaments in gold and silver and covered ivory.

" What an odd looking thing," she said, pointing out a nobbed ring which reposed on the black velvet of the case.

" Quite odd," agreed Kennedy.

The subtle Chinaman stood by the pile of hangings on the counter which Elaine had bought, overjoyed at such a large sale. Praising the ring to Elaine, he turned insinuatingly to Kennedy. There was nothing else for Craig to do—he bought the ring, and the Chinaman proved again his ability as a merchant.

From the curio shop where Elaine had completed her purchases they drove to Kennedy's laboratory.

I had been at work on a story for the *Star* when they entered.

"You will be there, too, Mr. Jameson?" coaxed Elaine, as she told of their morning's work.

I needed no urging.

We were in the midst of planning the entertainment when a slight cough behind me made me start and turn quickly.

There stood Long Sin, the astute Chinaman who had delivered the bomb to Kennedy and had betrayed Bennett. We had seen very little of him since then.

Long Sin bowed low and shuffled over closer to Kennedy. I noticed that Elaine eyed Long Sin sharply. But as yet we had seen no reason to suspect him, so cleverly had he covered his tracks. Kennedy, having used him once to capture Bennett, was still not unwilling to use him in attempting to discover where Bennett's hidden millions lay.

"I am in great trouble, Professor Kennedy," began Long Sin in a low tone. "You don't know the Chinese of the city, but if you did you would know what blackmailers there are among them. I have refused to pay blackmail to the Chong Wah Tong, and since then it has been trouble, trouble, trouble."

Kennedy looked up quickly at the name Chong Wah Tong, thinking of the investigation which the Coroner had asked him to make into the murder. He and Long Sin moved a few steps away, discussing the affair.

Elaine and I were still talking over the entertainment.

She happened to place her hand on the desk near Long Sin. My back was toward him and I did not
2

see him start suddenly and look at her hand. On it was the ring—the ring which, unknown to us, Long Sin had found in the passageway under Aunt Tabby's garden, of which he had been robbed, and which now, by a strange chance, had come into Elaine's possession.

It was a peculiar situation for Long Sin, although as yet we did not know it. He could not lay claim to the mystic ring, for then Kennedy would make him prove his ownership, and the whole affair of which we still knew nothing would be exposed.

He acted quickly. Long Sin decided to recover the ring by stealth.

Elaine was still talking enthusiastically about her party, when Long Sin turned from Kennedy and moved toward us with a bow.

"The lady speaks of an Oriental reception, he remarked. "Would she care to engage a magician?"

Elaine turned to him surprised. "Do you mean that you are a magician?" she asked, puzzled.

Long Sin smiled quietly. He reached over and took a small bottle from Kennedy's laboratory table. Holding it in his hand almost directly before us, he made a few sleight-of-hand passes, and, presto! the bottle had disappeared. A few more passes, and a test tube appeared in its place. Before we knew it he had caused the test tube to disappear and the bottle to reappear. We all applauded enthusiastically.

"I don't think that is such a bad idea after all," nodded Kennedy to Elaine.

"Perhaps not," she agreed, a little doubtfully. "I hadn't intended to have such a thing, but—why, of course, that would interest everybody."

.   .   .   .

It was the night of the reception. The Dodge library was transformed. The Oriental hangings which Elaine and Kennedy had purchased seemed to breathe mysticism. At the far end of the room a platform had been arranged to form a stage on which Long Sin was to perform his sleight-of-hand. The drawing-room also was decorated like the library.

At the other end of the room Elaine and Aunt Josephine, in picturesque Oriental costume, were greeting the guests. Every one seemed to be delighted with the novelty of the affair.

We came in just a bit ahead of Long Sin, and Elaine greeted us.

Almost everybody had arrived when Elaine turned to the guests and introduced Long Sin with a little speech. Long Sin bowed and every one applauded. He made his way to the platform in the library and mounted it.

I shall not attempt to describe the amazing series of tricks which he performed. His hands and fingers seemed to move like lightning. Among other things, I remember he took up a cover from a table near-by. He held it up before us. Instantly it seemed that a flock of pigeons flew out of it around the room. How he did it I don't know. They were real pigeons, however, and the trick brought down the house.

Long Sin bowed.

Another of his feats which I recall was nothing less than kindling a fire on a small bit of tin and, as the flames mounted, he deliberately stepped into them, apparently as unharmed as a salamander.

So it went from one thing to another. The entertainment was brilliant in itself, but Long Sin seemed to put the finishing touch to it. In fact, I suppose that it was a couple of hours that he continued to amuse us.

He had finished and every one crowded about him to congratulate him on his skill. His only answer, however, was his inscrutable smile.

" This is wonderful, wonderful," I repeated as I happened to meet Elaine alone. We walked into the conservatory while the guests were crowding around Long Sin. She seated herself for the first time during the evening.

" May I get you an ice? " I suggested.

She thanked me, and I hurried off. As I passed through the drawing-room I did not notice that Long Sin had managed to escape further congratulations of the guests. Just then a waiter passed through with ices on a tray. I called to him and he stopped.

A moment later Long Sin himself took an ice from the tray and retreated back of the portieres. No one was about, and he hastily drew a bottle from his pocket. On the bottle was a Chinese label. He palmed the bottle, and any one who had chanced to see him would have noticed that he passed it two or three times over the ice, then, lifting the portieres, entered the drawing-room again.

He had made the circuit of the rooms in such a way as to bring himself out directly in my path. With a smile he stopped before me, rubbing both hands together.

" It is for Miss Elaine? " he asked.

I nodded.

By this time several of the guests who were fascinated with Long Sin gathered about us. Long Sin
fluttered open a Chinese fan which he had used in his
tricks, passed it over my hand, and in some incompre-
hensible way I felt the plate with the ice literally disappear from my grasp. My face must have shown my
surprise. A burst of laughter from the other guests
greeted me. I looked at Long Sin, half angry, yet
unable to say anything, for the joke was plainly on me.
He smiled, made another pass with the fan, and instantly the plate with the ice was back in my
hand.

There was nothing for me but to take the joke in
the spirit in which the other guests had taken it. I
laughed with them and managed to get away.

Meanwhile Kennedy had been moving from one to
another of the guests seeking Elaine. He had already taken an ice from the waiter and was going in
the direction of the conservatory. There he found
her.

" Won't you take this ice? " he asked, handing it
to her.

" It is very kind of you," she said, " but I have already sent Walter for one.

Kennedy insisted and she took it.

She had already started to eat it when I appeared
in the doorway. I was rather vexed at Long Sin for
having delayed me, and I mumbled something about it.

Kennedy laughed, rather pleased at having beaten
me.

" Never mind, Walter," he said with a smile, " I'll
take it. And er—I don't think that Elaine will object

if you play the host for a little while with Aunt Josephine," he hinted.

I saw that three was a crowd and I turned to retrace my steps to the drawing-room.

Kennedy, however, was not alone. Back of the palms in the conservatory two beady black eyes were eagerly watching. Long Sin had noted every movement as his cleverly laid plan miscarried.

Chatting with animation, Kennedy tasted the ice. He had taken only a couple of spoonfuls when a look of wonder and horror seemed to spread over his face.

He rose quickly. A cold sweat seemed to break out all over him. His nerves almost refused to respond. His tongue seemed to be paralyzed and the muscles of his throat seemed to be like steel bands.

He took only a few steps, began to stagger, and finally sank down on the floor.

Elaine screamed.

We rushed in from the library and drawing-room. There lay Kennedy on the floor, his face most terribly contorted. We gathered around him and he tried to raise himself and speak, but seemed unable to utter a sound.

He had fallen near the fountain and one hand drooped over into the water. As he fell back he seemed to have only just enough strength to withdraw his hand from the fountain. On the stone coping, slowly and laboriously, he moved his finger.

"What's the matter, old man?" I asked, bending over him.

There was no answer, but he managed to turn his head, and I followed the direction of his eyes.

With trembling finger he was tracing out, one by one, some letters. I looked and it flashed over me what he meant. He had written with the water:

" Digitalin—lab—"

I jumped up and almost without a word dashed out of the conservatory, down the hall and into the first car waiting outside.

" To the laboratory," I directed, giving the driver the directions, " and drive like the deuce! "

Fortunately there was no one to stop us, and I know we broke all the speed laws of New York. I dashed into the laboratory, almost broke open the cabinet, and seized the bottle of digitalin and a hypodermic syringe, then rushed madly out again and into the car.

Meanwhile some of the guests had lifted up Kennedy, too excited to notice Long Sin in his hiding-place. They had laid Craig down on a couch and were endeavoring to revive him. Some one had already sent for a doctor, but the aconite was working quickly on its victim, and he was slowly stiffening out. Elaine was frantic.

I scarcely waited for the car to stop in front of the house. I opened the door and rushed in.

Without a word I thrust the antidote and the syringe into the hands of the doctor and he went to work immediately. We watched with anxiety. Finally Kennedy's eyes opened and gradually his breathing seemed to become more normal.

The antidote had been given in time.

.   .   .   .

Kennedy was considerably broken up by the narrow

escape which he had had, and, naturally, even the next morning, did not feel like himself.

In the excitement of leaving Elaine's we had forgotten the bottle of digitalin. As for myself, I had been so overjoyed at seeing my old friend restored that I would have forgotten anything.

Kennedy looked rather wan and peaked, but insisted on going to the laboratory as usual.

"Do you remember what became of the bottle of digitalin?" he asked, fumbling in the closet.

Mechanically I felt in my own pockets; it was not there. I shook my head.

"I don't seem to remember what became of it— perhaps we left it there. In fact, we must have left it there."

"I don't like to have such things lying around loose," remarked Kennedy, taking up his hat and coat with forced energy. "I think we had better get it."

Elaine had spent rather a sleepless night after the attempt to poison her which had miscarried and resulted in poisoning Kennedy.

To keep her mind off the thing, she had already started to take down the decorations. Jennings and Marie, as well as a couple of workmen, were restoring the library to its normal condition under the direction of Aunt Josephine.

The telephone rang and Elaine answered it. Her face showed that something startling had happened.

"It was Jameson," she cried, almost dropping the receiver, overcome.

They all hurried to her. "He says that Mr. Kennedy and he were visiting that Chinaman this morning and Mr. Kennedy suffered a relapse—is dying there, in the Chinaman's apartment. He wants us to come quickly and bring that medicine that they used last night. He says it is on the tabaret in the library. Marie, will you look for it? And, Jennings, get the car right away."

Jennings hurried from the room, and a moment later Marie had found the bottle behind some ornaments on the tabaret and came back with it.

Scarcely knowing what to do, Elaine, followed by Aunt Josephine, had rushed from the house, hatless and coatless, just as the car swung around from the garage in the rear. Jennings went out with the wraps. They seized them and leaped into the car, which started off swiftly.

It was only a matter of minutes when they pulled up before the apartment house where Wu had taken the suite from which Long Sin had telephoned the message in my name. Together Elaine and Aunt Josephine hurried in.

.   .   .   .

Kennedy went directly from the laboratory to the Dodge house.

I don't think I ever saw such an expression of surprise on anybody's face as that on Jennings's when he opened the door and saw us. He was aghast. Back of him we could see Marie. She looked as if she had seen a ghost.

"Is Miss Elaine in?" asked Kennedy.

Jennings was even too dumfounded to speak.

"Why, what's the matter?" demanded Kennedy.

"Then—er—you are not ill again?" he managed to blurt out.

"Ill again?" repeated Kennedy.

"Why," explained Jennings, "didn't Mr. Jameson just now telephone that you had had a relapse in the apartment of that Chinaman, and for Miss Elaine to hurry over there right away with that bottle of medicine?"

Kennedy waited to hear no more. Seizing me by the arm, he turned and dashed down the steps and back again into the taxicab in which we had come.

.   .   .   .

In Wu's apartment Long Sin was giving his secretary and another Chinaman the most explicit instructions. As he finished each nodded and showed him a Chinese dirk concealed under his blouse.

Just then a knock sounded at the door. The secretary opened it, and Aunt Josephine and Elaine almost ran in. Before they knew it, the secretary had locked the door.

Long Sin rose and bowed with a smile.

"Where is Mr. Kennedy?" demanded Elaine. Long Sin bowed again, spreading out his hands, palm outward.

"Mr. Kennedy? He is not here."

Then, straightening up, he faced the two women squarely.

"You have a ring that means much to me," he said quickly. "The only way to get it from you was to bring you here."

He was pointing now at the ring on Elaine's finger. She looked at it a moment in surprise, then at the

menacing Chinaman, and turned quickly. She ran to
the door. It was locked.

Long Sin, motionless, smiled. " There is no way
to get out," he murmured.

Aunt Josephine was standing now with her back to
the door leading into another room. She happened to
look up and saw the secretary, who was near her and
half turned away. From where she was standing
she could see the murderous dirk up his sleeve.

She acted instantly. Without a word she summoned
all her strength and struck him. The secretary stumbled.

" Elaine," she cried, " look out! they have knives."

Before Elaine knew it Aunt Josephine had taken her
by the arm, had pulled her into the back room, and,
although Long Sin and the others had rushed forward,
managed to slam the door and lock it.

The Chinamen set to work immediately to pry it
open.

While they were at work on the door, which was
already swaying, Aunt Josephine and Elaine were running about, trying to find an outlet from the room.

There seemed to be no way out. Even the windows
were locked.

" I don't know why they want the ring," whispered
Aunt Josephine, " but they won't get it. Give it to me,
Elaine."

She almost seized the ring, hiding it in her waist.
As she did so the door burst open and Wu, Long Sin
and the other Chinamen rushed in.

A second later they seized Elaine and Aunt Josephine.

. . . .

Kennedy and I dashed up before the apartment house in which we knew that Long Sin lived, leaped out of the car and hurried in.

It was on the second floor, and we did not wait for the elevator but took the steps two at a time. Kennedy found the door locked. Instantly he whipped out his revolver and shot the lock in pieces. We threw ourselves against the door, the broken lock gave way and we rushed in through the front room.

No one was there, but in a back room we could hear sounds. It was Elaine and Aunt Josephine struggling with the Chinamen. Long Sin and the others had seized Elaine and Aunt Josephine was trying to help her just as we rushed in. With a blow Kennedy knocked out the secretary, while I struggled with the other Chinamen who blocked the way.

Then Kennedy went directly at Long Sin. They struggled furiously.

Long Sin, with his wonderful knowledge of jiu-jitsu, might not have been a match for six other Chinamen, but he was for one white man. With a mighty effort he threw Kennedy, rushed for the door and, as he passed through the outside room, seized a Tong axe from the wall.

Afraid of the wonderful jiu-jitsu, I had picked up the first thing handy, which was a tabaret. I literally broke it over the head of my Chinaman, then turned and dashed out after Long Sin just as Kennedy picked himself up and followed.

I caught up with the Chinaman and we had a little struggle, but he managed to break away and raised his axe threateningly. A shout from Kennedy caused him to turn and run down the flight of stairs, Kennedy closely behind him.

In the main hall of the apartment house were two elevator shafts facing the street entrance, some twenty-five or thirty feet away. Through the street door the janitor and two or three other men were running in. They had heard the noise of the fighting above.

Escape to the street was cut off. We were behind him on the flight of stairs.

Long Sin did not hesitate a moment. He ran to the elevator, the door of which was open, seized the elevator boy and sent him sprawling on the marble floor. Then he slammed the door and the elevator shot up.

Kennedy was only a few feet behind, and he took in the situation at a glance. He leaped into the other elevator, and before the surprised boy could interfere shot it up only a few feet behind Long Sin.

Up the two elevators rose, Kennedy firing as best he could at Long Sin, while the shots reverberated through the elevator shaft like cannon.

It was a wild race to the roof. Long Sin had the start, and as the elevator reached the top floor he flung it open, dashed out and through a door up to the roof itself.

A second later Kennedy's elevator stopped. Craig leaped out and fired his last shot at the legs of Long Sin as he disappeared at the top of the flight of stairs to the roof. He flung the revolver from him and followed.

Without a moment's hesitation Kennedy threw himself at Long Sin. They struggled with each other. Finally Long Sin managed to wrench one arm lose and raise the Tong axe over Kennedy's head.

Kennedy dodged back. As he did so he tripped on the very edge of the roof and went sliding down the slates of the mansard.

Fortunately he was able to catch himself in the gutter.

It was the opportunity that Long Sin wanted. He started across the rope, which he had stretched from this apartment house to the building across the court, with all the deftness of the most expert Chinese acrobat.

By this time I had reached the roof, followed by the janitor and the elevator boys.

Kennedy was now crawling up the mansard, helping himself as best he could by some of the ornamental ironwork. I hurried over with the janitor, and together we pulled him out of danger.

Long Sin had reached the roof on the opposite side as we ran across in the direction of the taut rope.

A moment later he returned and bowed at us mockingly, then disappeared behind a skylight.

Kennedy did not stop an instant.

" You fellows go down to the street and see if you can head him off that way," he cried. " Stay here, Walter."

Before I knew it he had seized the rope and was going across to the other building, hand over hand. It was a perilous undertaking, but his blood was up.

Kennedy had almost reached the other roof when suddenly from behind the skylight stepped Long Sin.

With a wicked leer, he advanced to the edge of the roof, his axe upraised. I looked across the yawning chasm, horrified.

Slowly Long Sin raised the axe above his head, gathering all the strength which he had, waiting for Kennedy to approach closer. Kennedy stopped. Swiftly the axe descended, slashing the rope at one blow.

Like the weight of a pendulum Kennedy swung back against our own building, managing to keep his hold on the rope with superhuman strength.

I bent far over the edge of the roof, fully expecting to see him dashed to pieces at the bottom of the court.

There was a tremendous shattering of glass.

The rope had been just long enough to make him strike a window and he had gone crashing through the glass three floors below.

I dashed down the stairs and into the apartment. Kennedy was lying on the floor badly cut. I raised him up. He was dazed and considerably overcome; but as he staggered to his feet with my help I saw that no bones were broken.

" Help me, quick, Walter," he urged, moving toward the elevators.

Meanwhile Long Sin had quickly dived down into the next building. A few moments later he had come out on the ground floor at the rear.

Gazing about to see whether he was followed, he disappeared.

.   .   .   .

Back in the apartment, Elaine and Aunt Josephine were just about to run out when the two Chinamen who had been knocked out recovered. One of them threw himself on Elaine. Aunt Josephine tried to ward him off, but the other one struck her and threw her down.

Before she could recover they had seized Elaine.

With a hasty guttural exclamation they picked her up and ran out. Instead of going down-stairs they crossed the hallway, slamming the door behind them.

As Kennedy and I reached the ground floor we saw the janitor and one of the elevator boys on either side of Aunt Josephine.

"Elaine! Elaine!" she cried.

"What's the matter?" demanded Kennedy, leaning heavily on me.

"They have kidnapped her," cried Aunt Josephine.

Kennedy pulled himself together.

"Tell me, quick—how did it happen?" he demanded of Aunt Josephine.

"It was the ring," she cried, handing it to him.

Kennedy took the ring and looked at it for a moment. Then he turned to us blankly.

All the rooms were empty.

Elaine had been spirited away.

CHAPTER III

THE WATCHING EYE

Not a clue was left by the kidnappers when they so mysteriously spirited Elaine away from the apartment of Wu Fang. She had disappeared as completely as if she had vanished into the thin air.

Kennedy was frantic. Wu and Long Sin themselves seemed to have vanished, too. Where they held her, what had happened to her was a sealed book. And yet, no move of ours was made, no matter how secret, that it did not seem to be known to them. It was as though a weird, uncanny eye glared at us, watching everything.

Craig neglected no possibility in his eager search. He even visited the little house in the country which Elaine had given to Aunt Tabby, and spent several hours examining the collapsed subterranean chamber in the vain hope that it might yield a clue. But it had not.

It was half filled with debris from above, where the pillar had given way that night when we had all so nearly lost our lives. Still, there was enough room in what remained of the cavern so that we could move about.

Kennedy had even dug away some of the earth and rock, in the hope of discovering some trace of the strange visitor whom we had surprised at work. But here, also, he had found nothing.

It was maddening. What might at any moment be happening to Elaine—and he powerless to help her?

Unescapably, he was forced to the conclusion that not only Elaine's amazing disappearance, but the tragic succession of events which had preceded it, had been caused, in some way, by the curiously engraved ring which Aunt Josephine had taken from Elaine.

Craig had taken possession of the mystic ring himself, and now, forced back on this sole clue, it had occurred to him that if the ring were so valuable, other attempts would, without doubt, be made to get possession of it.

I came into the laboratory, one afternoon, to find Kennedy surrounded by jeweler's tools, hard at work making an exact copy of the ring.

"What do you think of it, Walter?" he asked, holding up the replica.

"Perfect," I replied, admiringly. "What are you going to do with it?"

"I can't say—yet," answered Kennedy, forlornly, "but if I understand these Chinese criminals at all, I know that the only way we can ever track them is through some trick. Perhaps the replica will suggest something to us later."

He placed the copy in a velvet-lined box closely resembling that in which the real ring lay, and dropped both into his pocket.

"Let's see if Aunt Josephine has received any word," he remarked abruptly, putting on his hat and coat, and nodding to me to follow.

. . . .

Kennedy and I were not the only visitors to the subterranean chamber where it had seemed that the clue to the Clutching Hand's millions might be found.

It was as though that hidden, watching eye followed us. The night after our own unsuccessful search, Wu Fang, accompanied by Long Sin, made his way into the cavern.

As they flashed their electric bull's-eyes about the place, they could see readily that we had already been digging there.

Wu examined the safe which had been broken into, while Long Sin repeated his experiences there.

"And you say there was nothing else in it?" demanded Wu.

"Nothing but the ring which they got from me," replied Long Sin, ruefully.

"Strange—very strange," ruminated Wu, still regarding the empty strong box.

Long Sin was now going over the walls of the cavern minutely, his close-set, beady black eyes examining every square inch of it.

A sudden low guttural exclamation caused Wu to turn to him quickly. Long Sin had discovered, back of the debris, a small oblong slot, cut into the rock. Above it were some peculiar marks.

Wu hurried over to his henchman, and together they tried to decipher what had been scratched on the rock.

As Long Sin's slender and sinister forefinger traced over the inscription, Wu suddenly caught him by the elbow.

"The ring!" he cried, as at last he interpreted the meaning of the cryptic characters.

But what about the ring? For a moment Wu looked at the slot in deep thought. Then he reached down and withdrew a ring from his own finger and dropped it through the slot.

They listened a moment. They could hear the ring tinkle as though it were running down some sort of track-like declivity inside the rock. Then, faintly, they could hear it drop. It had fallen into a little cup of a compartment below at their feet.

Nothing happened. Wu recovered his ring. But he had hit at last upon the Clutching Hand's secret!

Bennett had devised a ring-lock which would open the treasure vault. No other ring except the one which he had so carefully hidden was of the size or weight that would move the lever which would set the machinery working to open the treasure house.

Again Wu tried another of his own rings, and a third time Long Sin dropped in a ring from his finger. Still there was no result.

"The ring which we lost is the key to the puzzle—the only key," exclaimed Wu Fang finally. "We must recover it at all hazard."

To his subtle mind a plan of action seemed to unfold almost instantly. "There is no good remaining here," he added. "And we have gained nothing by the capture of the girl, unless we can use her to recover the ring."

Long Sin followed his master with a sort of intuition. "If we have to steal it," he suggested deferentially, " it can be accomplished best by making use of Chong Wah Tong."

The Tong was the criminal band which they had offended, which had in fact stolen the ring from Long Sin and sold it to Elaine. Yet in a game such as this enmity could not last when it was mutually disadvantageous. Wu took the suggestion. He decided instantly to make peace with his enemies—and use them.

Later that night, in his car, Wu stopped near the little curio shop kept by the new Tong leader.

Long Sin alighted and entered the shop, while the Tong man eyed him suspiciously.

" My master has come to make peace," he began, saluting the Tong leader behind the counter.

Nothing, in reality, could have pleased the Tong men more, for in their hearts they feared the masterlike subtlety of Wu Fang. The conference was short and Long Sin with a bow left quickly to rejoin Wu, while the Tong leader disappeared into a back room of the shop where several of the inner circle sat.

" All is well, master," reported Long Sin when he had made his way back to the car around the corner in which Wu was waiting.

Wu smiled and a moment later followed by his slave in crime entered the curio shop and passed through with great dignity into the room in the rear.

As the two entered, the Tong men bowed with great respect.

" Let us be enemies no more," began Wu briefly. " Let us rather help each other as brothers."

He extended his right hand, palm down, as he spoke. For a moment the Tong leader parleyed with the others, then stepped forward and laid his own hand, palm down, over that of Wu. One by one the others did the same, including Long Sin, the aggrieved.

Peace was restored.

Wu had risen to go, and the Tong men were bowing a respectful farewell. He turned and saw a large vase. For a moment he paused before it. It was an enormous affair and was apparently composed of a mosaic of rare Chinese enamels, cunningly put together by the deft and patient fingers of the oriental craftsmen. Extending from the widely curving bowl below was an extremely long, narrow, tapering neck.

Wu looked at it intently; then an idea seemed to strike him. He called the Tong leader and the others about him.

Quickly he outlined the details of a plan.

. . . .

"Have you received any word yet?" asked Aunt Josephine anxiously, when Jennings had ushered us into the Dodge library.

Kennedy shook his head sadly. There was no need to repeat the question to Aunt Josephine. The tears in her eyes told only too plainly that she herself had heard nothing, either.

Craig bent over and placed his hand on her shoulder. For the moment, none of us could control our emotions.

A few minutes later, Jennings entered the room softly again. "The expressmen are outside, ma'am, with a large package," he said.

"A package?" inquired Aunt Josephine, looking up, surprised. "For me—are you sure?"

Jennings bowed and repeated his remark. Aunt Josephine followed him out into the hall.

There, already, the delivery men had set down a huge oriental vase with a remarkably long and narrow neck. It was, as befitted su n a really beautiful object of art, most carefully crated. But to Aunt Josephine it came as a complete surprise. " I can't imagine who could have sent it," she temporized. " Are you quite sure it is for me? "

The expressman, with a book, looked up from the list of names down which he was running his finger. " This is Mrs. Dodge, isn't it? " he asked, pointing with his pencil to the entry with the address following it. There seemed to be no name of a shipper.

" Yes," she replied dubiously, " but I don't understand it. Wait just a moment."

She went to the library door. " Mr Kennedy," she said, " may I trouble you and Mr. Jameson a moment? "

We followed her into the hall and there stood gazing at the mysterious gift while she related its recent history.

" Why not set it up in the library? " I suggested, seeing that the expressmen were getting restive at the delay. " If there is any mistake, they will send for it soon. No one ever gets anything for nothing."

Aunt Josephine turned to the expressmen and nodded. With the aid of Jennings they carried the vase into the library and there it was uncrated, while Kennedy continued to question the man with the book, without eliciting any further information than that he thought it had been reconsigned from another express company. He knew nothing more than that it had been placed on his wagon, properly marked and pre-paid.

When Kennedy rejoined us, the vase had been completely uncrated, Aunt Josephine signed for it, and, grumbling a bit, the expressmen left. There we stood, nonplussed by the curious gift.

Craig walked around the vase, looking at it critically. I had a feeling of being watched, one of those sensations which psychologists tell us are utterly baseless and unfounded. I was glad I had not said anything about it when he tapped the vase with his cane, then stuck it down the long narrow neck, working it around as well as he could. The neck was so long and narrow, however, that his stick could not fully explore the inside of the vase, but it seemed to me to be quite empty.

"Well, there's nothing in it, anyhow," I ventured.

I had spoken too soon. Kennedy withdrew his cane and on the ferrule, adhering as though by some sticky substance, was a note. Kennedy pulled it off and unfolded it, while we gathered about him.

"Maybe it's from Elaine," cried Aunt Josephine, grasping at a straw.

We read:

DEAR AUNT JOSEPHINE,

This is a token that I am unharmed. Have Mr. Kennedy give the ring to the man at the corner of Williams and Brownlee Avenues at midnight to-night, and they will surrender me to him.—ELAINE.

P. S. Have him come alone or my life will be in danger.

We looked at each other in amazement.

"I thought something like this would happen," remarked Craig at length.

"Oh," cried Aunt Josephine, "it's too good to be true."

"We'll do it," exclaimed Kennedy quickly, "only this is the ring that we'll give them."

He drew from his pocket the replica of the ring which he had made and showed it to Aunt Josephine. Then he drew from another pocket the real ring, replacing the replica.

"Here's the real one," he said in a low tone. "Guard it as you would guard your life."

She took the ring, almost fearfully. It seemed as if nothing but misfortune had followed it. Still, she realized that it was necessary that she should take care of it, if the plan was to work.

"And, oh, Mr. Kennedy," she implored, as we rose to go, "please get back my little girl for me."

Craig clasped her hand. "I'll try my best," he replied fervently, patting her shoulder to cheer her up, as she sank into a chair.

Aunt Josephine was worn out with the sleepless nights of worry since Elaine's disappearance. After we had gone, she tried to eat dinner, but found that she had no appetite.

All the evening she sat in the library, with a book at which she stared, though she scarcely read a page. However, as the hours lengthened, she found herself nodding through sheer exhaustion.

It was getting late and her thoughts were still on Elaine. At the desk in the library, she was examining the curious ring, which she had taken from her jewel case, thinking of the terrible train of events that had followed it.

Although she had intended to sit up until she received some word from Kennedy that night, the long strain had told on her and in spite of her worry about Elaine, she decided, at length, to retire. She replaced the ring in the case, locked the case, and turned out the lights.

"Good night, Jennings," she said, as she passed the faithful old butler in the hall.

"Good night, ma'am," he replied, pausing on his rounds to see that the doors and windows were locked.

Aunt Josephine, clasping the jewel case tightly, mounted the stairs and entered her room. She locked the door carefully and put the jewelry case under her pillow. Then she switched off the light.

The moment Jennings's footsteps ceased down-stairs in the library, a small piece of the vase seemed to break away from the rest of the mosaic, as though it were knocked out from the inside. Then a large piece fell out, and another.

At last from the strange hiding-place a lithe figure, as shiny as though bathed in oil, naked except for a loin-cloth, seemed to squirm forth like a serpent. It was Wu Fang—the watchful eye which, literally as well as figuratively, had been leveled at us in one form or another ever since the kidnapping of Elaine.

Silently he tiptoed to the doorway and listened. There was not a sound. Just as noiselessly then he went back to the library table and, muffling the telephone bell, took down the receiver. He whispered a number, waited, then whispered some directions.

A moment later he wormed his way out of the library and into the drawing-room. On he went cautiously, snake-like, up the stairs until he came to the door of Aunt Josephine's room.

He bent down and listened. There was no sound except Aunt Josephine's breathing. Silently he drew from a fold in the loin-cloth a screwdriver and removed the screws from the hinges of the door. Quietly he pushed the bedroom door open, pivoting it on the lock, just far enough open so that he could slip through.

Creeping along the floor, like a reptile whose sign he had assumed, he came nearer and nearer Aunt Josephine's bed. As he paused for a moment his quick eye seemed to catch sight of the bulging lump under her pillow. His long thin hand reached out for it.

Aunt Josephine moved restlessly in her sleep. Instantly he seized a murderous-looking Chinese dirk fastened to his side and raised it above her head ready to strike on the slightest outcry. She moved slightly, and relapsed into sound sleep again.

Holding the knife above her, Wu slowly and quietly removed the jewel-case from under her pillow.

.   .   .   .

In a country road-house Long Sin was waiting patiently. The telephone rang and the proprietor answered. Long Sin was at his side almost before he could hand over the receiver. It was Long Sin's master, Wu.

"Beware," came the whispered message over the wire. "Kennedy has made a false ring. I'll get the real one. By the great Devil of Gobi, you must cut him off."

"It is done," returned Long Sin, hanging up the receiver in great excitement.

He hurried out of the room and left the road-house. Down the road in an automobile, bound between two Chinamen, one at her head and the other at her feet, was Elaine, wrapped around in blankets, not even her face visible. The guards looked up startled as Long Sin streaked out ot the shadow to the car.

"Quick!" he ordered. "The master will get the ring himself. I will take care of Kennedy."

An instant and they were gone, while Long Sin slunk back into the shadows from which he had come.

Through the underbrush the wily Chinaman made his way to an old barn, which stood back some distance from the road, and entered the front door. There was another door in the rear, and one quite large window.

In the dim light of a lantern hanging from a rafter could be seen several large barrels in a corner. Without a moment's hesitation, Long Sin seized a bucket and placed it under the spiggot of one of the barrels. The liquid poured forth into the bucket and he emptied the contents on the floor, filling the bucket again and again and swinging it right and left in every direction until the barrel had finally run dry.

Then he moved over to the window, which he examined carefully. Satisfied with what he had done, he drew a slip of paper from his pocket and hastily wrote a note, resting the paper on an old box. When he had finished writing, he folded up the note and thrust it into a little hollow carved Chinese figure which he took also from his pocket.

These were, apparently, his emergency preparations which he was ready to execute in case he received such a message from his master as he had actually received.

With a final hasty glance about he extinguished the lantern, letting the moonlight stream fitfully through the single window. Then he left the barn, with both front and rear doors open.

Taking advantage of every bit of shelter, he made his way across the field in the direction of the cross-roads, finally dropping down behind a huge rock some yards from the finger post that pointed each way to Williams and Brownlee Avenues.

. . . .

Late that night, Kennedy left his apartment prepared to follow the instructions in the note which had been so strangely delivered in the vase.

As he climbed into a roadster, he tucked the robe most carefully into a corner under the leather seat.

"For heaven's sake, Craig," I gasped from under the robe, "let me have a little air."

I had taken my place under the robe before the car was driven up before the apartment, lest some emissary of Wu Fang might be watching to see that there was no such trick.

"You'll get air enough when we get started, Walter," he laughed back under his breath, apparently addressing the engine.

Kennedy was a hard driver when he wanted to be and enough was at stake to-night to make him drive hard. He whizzed along in the roadster, and I was indeed glad enough to huddle up under the robe.

We had reached a point in the suburbs which was deserted and I did not recognize a thing when he pulled up by the side of the road with a jerk. I peered through a crease in the corner of the robe, and saw him slide out from under the wheel and stand by the side of the car, looking up and down. Ahead of us the road curved sharply and I had no idea what was there, though Kennedy seemed to know the place.

A moment later he pulled the robe partly off me, and bent down as though examining the batteries on the side of the car.

"Get out on the other side in the shadow of the car, Walter," he whispered hoarsely. "Go down the road a bit—only cut in and keep under cover. This is Williams Avenue. You'll see a big rock. Hide behind it. Ahead you'll see Brownlee Avenue. Be prepared for anything. I shall have to trust the rest to you. I don't know myself what's going to happen."

I slid out and went along the edge of the road, as Craig had directed, and finally crouched behind a huge rock, feeling on as much tension as if I had been a boy playing at Wild West. Only this might at any moment develop into the reality of a Wild Far East.

After a moment to give me a chance, Craig himself left the car pulled up close by the side of the road and went ahead on foot. At last he came to the cross-roads just around the bend, where in the moonlight he could read the sign: "Williams Avenue" and "Brownlee Avenue." He stood there a moment, then glanced at his watch which registered both hands approaching the hour of twelve. He gazed about at the deserted country. Had the appointment been a hoax, after all, a scheme to get him away from the city for some purpose?

Suddenly, at his feet in the dust of the road something heavy seemed to drop. He looked about quickly. No one was in sight.

He reached down and picked up a little Chinese figure. Tapping it with his knuckle, he examined it curiously. It was hollow.

From the inside he drew out a piece of paper. He strained his eyes in the moonlight and managed to make out:

The Serpent is all-wise, and his fang is fatal. You have signed the white girl's death warrant.

Beneath this sinister warning was stamped the serpent sign of Wu Fang.

It was not a hoax, and Kennedy stood there a moment gazing about in tense anxiety. Had that uncanny watching eye observed his every action? Was it staring at him now in the blackness?

.   .   .   .

Meanwhile, I had made my way stealthily, peering into the bushes and careful not even to step on anything that would make a noise and was now, as I have said, crouched behind the big rock to which Craig had directed me. I heard him go along the road and looked about cautiously, but could hear and see nothing else.

I had begun to wonder whether Kennedy might not have made a mistake when, suddenly, from behind the shadow of another rock, ahead of me, but toward

Brownlee Avenue, I saw a tall, gaunt figure of a man
rise in the moonlight, almost as if it had sprung from
the very earth.

My heart gave a leap, as he quickly raised his right
arm and hurled something as far as he could in the
direction that Kennedy had taken. If it had been a
bomb, followed by an explosion, I would not have been
surprised.   But no sound followed as the figure
dropped back, as if it had been a wraith.

I stole out from my own hiding-place in the shadow
of my rock and darted quickly to the shelter of a bush,
nearer the figure.

The figure was no wraith. It turned to steal away.
I remembered Kennedy's parting words. If the man
ever gained the darkness of a clump of woods, just
beyond us, he was as good as safe. This was the time
to act.

I leaped at him and we went down, rolling over and
over in the underbrush and stubble. We fought
fiercely, but I could not seem to get a glimpse of his
face which was muffled.

He was powerful and stronger than I and after a
tough tussle he broke loose. But I had succeeded,
nevertheless. I had delayed him just long enough.
Kennedy heard the sound of the struggle and was now
crashing through the hedge at the cross-roads in our
direction.

I managed to pick myself up, just as Kennedy
reached my side and, together, we followed the retreating figure, as it made its way among the shadows.
Across the open space before us we followed him and
at last saw him dive into an old barn.

A moment later we followed hot-foot into the barn. As we entered, we could hear a peculiar grating noise, as though a door was swung on its rusty hinges. The front door was open. Evidently the man had gone through and closed the back door.

We threw ourselves against the back door. But it did not yield. There was no time to waste and we turned to rush out again by the way we had come, just as the front door was slammed shut.

The man had trapped us. He had left both doors open, had run through, braced the back door, then had rushed around outside just in time to brace the front door also.

We could hear his feet crunching the dry leaves and twigs as he went around the side of the barn again. Together we threw ourselves against the front door, but, although it yielded a little he had barred it so that it would resist our united strength for some time.

Again and again we threw ourselves against it. It was horribly dark in there, except for an oblong spot where the moonlight streamed in through a window. Suddenly the pale silver of the moonlight on the floor reddened.

The man had struck a match and thrown it into a mass of oil-soaked straw and gunpowder which protruded through one of the weather-beaten boards, near the floor.

It was only a matter of a second or so now when the fire swept into the barn itself. There was no beating it out. Some one had literally soaked the straw and the floor with oil. It seemed as though the whole place burst into a sudden blaze of tinder. Outside,

5

we could hear footsteps rapidly retreating toward the shelter of the clump of woods.

For a second I looked dismayed at the rapidly-mounting flames.

"A very pretty situation," I forced with a laugh. "But I hope he doesn't think we'll stay here and burn, with a perfectly good window in full view."

I took a step toward the window, but before I could take another, Kennedy yanked me back.

"Don't think for a moment that he overlooked that," he shouted.

Craig looked around hastily. In a corner, just back of us was a long pole. He snatched it up and moved cautiously toward the window, keeping the pole as level as possible as he endeavored to get a leverage on the sash. The flames were mounting faster and higher, licking up everything.

"Keep back, Walter," he muttered, "just as far as you can."

He had scarcely raised the window a fraction of an inch when an old rusty, heavy anvil and a bent worn plowshare crashed down to the floor directly over the spot where I should have been if he had not dragged me away. I started back, aghast. Nothing had been overlooked to finish us off.

"I think you may try it safely now, all right," smiled Kennedy coolly.

We climbed out of the window, not an instant too soon from the raging inferno about us.

Having gained the clump of woods, the gaunt figure had paused long enough to gloat over his clever scheme. Instead, he saw us making good our escape. With a gesture of intense fury he turned. There was nothing more for him to do but to zigzag his way to safety across country.

The barn was now burning fiercely and it was almost as light as day about us. Kennedy paused only long enough to look down at the ground where the fire had been started.

"See, Walter," he exclaimed pointing to a square indention in the soft soil. "No white man ever made a footprint like that."

I bent over. The prints had the squareness of those paper-layered soles of a Chinaman.

"Long Sin," came the name involuntarily to my lips, for I knew that Wu would delegate just such a job to his faithful slave.

Kennedy did not pause an instant longer, but in the light of the burning barn, as best he could, started to follow the trail in a desperate endeavor either to overtake Long Sin, or at least to find the final direction in which he would go.

. . . .

At the entrance of the passageway which led to the little underground chamber in which we had sought the treasure hidden by the Clutching Hand, Wu Fang was seated on a rock waiting impatiently, though now and then indulging in a sinister smile at the subtle trick by which he had recovered the ring.

The sound of approaching footsteps disturbed him. He was far too clever to leave anything to chance and, like a serpent, he wriggled behind another rock and waited. It was only a glance, however, that he needed to allay his suspicions. It was Long Sin, breathless.

Wu stepped out beside him so quietly that even the acute Long Sin did not hear. " Well? " he said in a guttural tone.

Long Sin drew back in fear. " I have failed, oh, master," he replied in an imploring tone. " Even now they follow my tracks."

It was bad enough to confess defeat without the fear of capture.

Wu frowned. " We must work quickly, then," he muttered.

He picked up a dark lantern near-by, indicating another to Long Sin. They entered the cave, flashing the lights ahead of them.

" Be careful," ordered Wu, proceeding gingerly from one stepping-stone to another. " We shall be followed no further than this."

He paused a moment and pointed his finger at the earth. Everywhere, except here and there where a stone projected, was a sticky, slimy substance. It was an old trick of primitive races.

" Bird lime," hissed Wu, pointing at the viscid substance made of the juice of the holly bark, extracted by boiling, and mixed with a third part of nut oil and grease.

They passed on from stone to stone until they came to the subterranean chamber itself. Without a moment's hesitation, Wu made his way toward the rock in which they had found the slot with its cryptic inscription.

Long Sin watched his master in silent admiration as, at last, he drew forth the mystic ring for which they had dared all.

Without a word, Wu dropped it in the slot. It tinkled down the runway, a protuberance hit a trigger and pushed it a hair's breadth.

A noise behind them caused the two to turn startled. Even Wu had not expected it.

On the other side of the chamber, a great rock in the ground slowly turned, as though on a pivot. They watched, fascinated. Even then Wu did not forget the precious ring, but as the rock turned, reached down quickly and recovered it from the cup at the floor.

Inch by inch the pivoted rock moved on its axis. They flashed their lanterns full on it and, as it moved, they could see disclosed huge piles of gold and silver in coins and bars and ornaments, a chest literally filled with brilliants, set and unset, rubies, emeralds, precious stones of every conceivable variety, a cave that would have staggered even Aladdin—the rich reward of the countless marauding operations of Bennett's other personality.

For a moment they could merely stand in avaricious exultation.

.   .   .   .

Painfully and slowly, we managed to trail Long Sin's footprints, until we came to a road where they were lost in the hard macadam. There was no time to stop. We must follow the road on the chance that he had taken it. But which way?

Kennedy chose the most likely direction, for the trail had been at an angle to the road and Long Sin was not likely to double back. We had not gone many rods before Kennedy paused a minute and looked about in the moonlight.

"It's right, Walter," he cried. "Do you recognize it?"

I looked about. Then it flashed over me. This was the back road that led past the entrance to the treasure vault at Aunt Tabby's.

We went on now more quickly, listening carefully to catch any sounds, but· heard nothing. At last Kennedy stopped, then plunged among the rocks and bushes beside the road. We were at the cave.

"You go in this way, Walter," he directed. "I'll go around and down where it caved in."

I groped my way along through the darkness.

I had gone only a yard or two, when it seemed as though something had grasped my foot.

With a great wrench I managed to pull it loose. But the weight on my other foot had imbedded it deeper. I struggled to free this foot and got the other caught. My revolver, which I had drawn, was jarred from my hand and in the effort to recover it, I lost my balance. Unable to move a foot in time to catch myself, I fell forward. My hands were now covered by the slimy, sticky stuff, and the more I struggled, the worse I seemed to get entangled.

.   .   .   .

Wu and Long Sin paused only a minute in astonishment. Then they literally fell upon the wealth that lay before them, gloating over the gold, stuffing their hands into the jewels, lifting them up and letting the priceless gems run through their fingers.

Suddenly they paused. There was the slight tinkle of a Chinese bell.

Kennedy had reached Aunt Tabby's garden, outside

the roof of the subterranean chamber where it had given way, had gone down carefully over the earth and rock, and in doing so had broken a string stretched across the passageway. The tinkle of a bell attached to it aroused his attention and he stopped short, a second, to look about. Wu Fang had arranged a primitive alarm.

Quickly, Wu and Long Sin blew out their lanterns while Wu gave the rock a push. Slowly, as it had opened, it now closed and they stood there listening.

I was still struggling in the bird lime, getting myself more and more covered with it, when the reverberation of revolver shots reached me.

Wu and Long Sin had opened fire on Kennedy, and Kennedy was replying in kind. In the cavern it sounded like a veritable bombardment. As they retreated, they came nearer and nearer to me and I could see the revolvers spitting fire in the darkness. So intent were they on Kennedy that they forgot me.

I watched them fearfully as they hopped deftly from one stone to another to avoid the lime—and were gone.

"Craig! Craig!" I managed to cry feebly. "Be careful. Keep to the stones."

He strained his eyes toward the ground in the darkness, at the sound of my voice. Then he struck a match and instantly took in the situation which, to me, under any other circumstances, would have been ludicrous.

Stepping from stone to stone, he followed the retreating Chinamen. But they had already reached the mouth of the cave and were making their way rapidly down the road to a bend, in the opposite direction from which we had come. There, Wu's automobile was waiting. They leaped into it and the driver, without a word, shot the car off into the darkness of early dawn.

A moment later, Kennedy appeared, but they had made their getaway. Baffled, he turned and retraced his steps to the cave.

I don't think that I ever welcomed him more sincerely than I did as, finally, I crawled slowly out from the bird lime, exhausted by the effort that I had made to free myself from the sticky mess.

"They got away, Walter," he said, lighting a lantern they had dropped. "By George," he added, I think a little vexed that I had not been able to stop them, "you are a sight!"

He was about to laugh, when I fainted. I can remember nothing until I woke up over by the wall of the chamber where he dragged me.

Kennedy had been working hard to revive me, and, as I opened my eyes, he straightened up. His eye suddenly caught something on the rock beside him. There was a little slot carved in it, and above the slot was a peculiar inscription.

For several minutes, Kennedy puzzled over it, as Wu had done. Then he discovered the little cup near the ground.

"The ring!" he suddenly cried out.

I was too muddled to appreciate at once what he meant, but I saw him reach into his fob pocket and draw forth the replica of the trinket which had caused so much disaster, as if it had been cursed by the Clutching Hand himself. He dropped it into the slot.

Struggling to my feet, I saw across from me the

very rock itself moving. Was it an hallucination, born of my nervous condition?

"Look, Craig!" I cried involuntarily, pointing.

He turned. No, it was not a vision. It actually moved. Together we watched. Slowly the rock turned on a pivot. There were disclosed to our astonished eyes the hidden millions of the Clutching Hand.

I looked from the gold and jewels to Kennedy, in speechless amazement.

"We have beaten them, anyhow," I cried.

Slowly Craig shook his head sadly.

"Yes," he murmured, " we have found the Clutching Hand's millions, but we have lost Elaine."

CHAPTER IV

THE VENGEANCE OF WU FANG

ELAINE was still in the power of Wu Fang.

Kennedy had thwarted the Chinese master criminal in his search for the millions amassed by the Clutching Hand. But any joy that we might have derived from this success was completely obscured by the fear that Wu might wreak some diabolical vengeance on Elaine.

It was a ticklish situation. In fact, I doubt whether Craig would have discovered the treasure at all, if our pursuit of Wu and Long Sin the night before had not literally forced us into doing so.

Nor were Kennedy's fears unfounded. Wu and Long Sin had scarcely reached the secret apartment back of the deceptive exterior of the Chinatown tenement, when the subtle Chinaman began to contemplate his revenge.

Long Sin was smoking a Chinese pipe, resting after their hurried flight, while Wu, the tireless, was seated at a table at the other end of the room. At last Wu Fang took up a long Chinese dirk from the table before him, looked at it, turned it over, felt its edge. It was keen and the point was sharp. He rose and deliberately walked across to a door leading into a back room.

On a couch lay Elaine and with her, as a guardian, was Weepy Mary whom the Clutching Hand had used to lure her to the church where the faked record of her father's marriage was supposed to be. Indeed, though Wu had lost the Clutching Hand's millions, he had seen his chance and had fallen heir to what was left of Bennett's criminal organization.

As Wu, the Serpent, entered and advanced slowly towards Elaine, she crouched back from him in deadly fear. He stopped before her without a word and his menacing eye seemed to read her very thoughts.

Slowly he drew from under his robe the Chinese dirk. He felt the edge of it again and gazed significantly at Elaine. She shrank back even further, as far as the divan would permit.

It was a critical moment.

Just then Long Sin entered. "One of the five millions waits outside," he reported simply, with a bow.

Wu understood. It had been a pleasant fiction of his that although he did not, of course, absolutely control such a stupendous organization he could, by his subtle power, force almost unlimited allegiance from the simple coolies in that district of China from which he came.

Out in the front room, just a moment before, a knock at the door had disturbed Long Sin, and a Chinese servant had announced a visitor. Long Sin had waved to the servant to usher him in and a poorly clad coolie had entered.

He bowed as Long Sin faced him. "Where is the master?" he had asked.

Long Sin had not deigned to speak. With a mere

wave of his hand, he indicated that he would be the bearer of the message, and had followed Wu through the door of the back room.

So, almost by chance, Wu was interrupted in the brutal vengeance which had first come to his mind. He sheathed the knife and, still without a word, went back into the main room, giving a nod to Weepy Mary to guard Elaine closely.

Wu eyed the coolie until the newcomer could almost feel the master's penetrating gaze, although his head was bowed in awe. Quickly the coolie thrust his hand under his blouse and drew forth a package. With another bow, he advanced.

"For your enemies, oh master," he said, handing the package over to Wu.

For the first time since the loss of the treasure, Wu Fang seemed to take an interest in something besides revenge. The coolie started to open the package, removed the paper wrapper, and then a silk wrapping inside. Finally he came to a box, from which he drew a leather pouch, each operation conducted with greater care as it became evident that the contents were especially precious in some way. Then he took from the pouch a small vial.

"What is it?" demanded Wu Fang, as the coolie displayed it.

The coolie drew forth now a magnifying glass and a glass slide. Opening the vial with great care he shook something out on the slide, then placed it under the lens.

"Look!" he said simply.

Wu bent over and looked. Under the lens what had

formerly seemed to be merely a black speck of dirt became now one of the most weird and uncanny little creatures to be found in all the realm of nature. It seemed to be all legs and feelers moving at once. A normal person would have looked at the creature only with the greatest repugnance. Wu regarded it with a sort of unholy fascination.

"And it is?" he queried.

"What the white man calls the African tick which carries the recurrent fever," answered the coolie deferentially.

A flash of intense exultation seemed to darken Wu Fang's sinister face. Several times he paced up and down the room, as he contemplated the sight which he had just seen. Then he came to a sudden determination.

"Wait," he said to the coolie, as he moved slowly again into the back room.

Long Sin had remained there. With Weepy Mary he was guarding Elaine when Wu Fang reentered. Elaine was thoroughly aroused by this time. Even the fact that Wu no longer held the murderous dirk did not serve to reassure her, for the look on his face was even more terrible than before.

He smiled cunningly to himself.

"Suffering is a state of mind," he said in a low tone, "and I have decided that it would be poor revenge for me to harm you. You are free."

Nothing could have come as a greater surprise to Elaine. Even Long Sin had not expected any such speech as this. Elaine, however, was wonder-stricken.

"Do you—do you really mean it?" she asked, scarcely able to believe what her ears heard.

Wu merely nodded, and with a wave of his hand to Long Sin indicated that Elaine was to be released.

Long Sin, the slave, did not stop to question his master, but merely moved over to a closet and took out the hat and wraps which Elaine had worn when she had been kidnapped in the up-town apartment. He handed them over to her and she put them on with trembling hands.

No one stopped her and she nerved herself to take several steps toward the door. She had scarcely crossed half the room.

"Wait!" ordered Wu sharply.

Was he merely torturing her, as a cat might torture a mouse? She stopped obediently, afraid to look at him.

"This will be the vengeance of Wu Fang," he went on impressively. "Slowly, one by one, your friends will weaken and die, then your family, until finally only you are left. Then will come your turn."

He stopped again and raised his long lean forefinger. "Go," he hissed. "I wish you much joy."

He turned to Long Sin and whispered a word to him. A moment later, Long Sin drew forth a large silken handkerchief and tied it tightly over Elaine's eyes. Then he took her hand and led her out. There was to be no chance by which she could lead a raiding party back to the den in which she had been held.

.   .   .   .

I don't think that in all our friendship I have ever

seen Kennedy so utterly depressed as he was when we returned after the discovery of the vast fortune which Bennett had cleverly secreted. I came upon him in the laboratory the next morning while he was trying to read. He had laid aside his scientific work, and now he had even laid aside his book.

There seemed to be absolutely nothing to do until some new clue turned up. I placed my hand on his shoulder, but the words that would encourage him died on my lips. Several times I started to speak, but each time I checked myself. There did not seem to be anything that would be appropriate for such an occasion.

A sharp ring at the telephone made both of us fairly jump, so nervous had we become. Kennedy reached over instantly for the instrument in the vague hope that at last there was some news.

As I watched his face, it changed first from despair to wonder, and finally it seemed to light up with the most remarkable look of relief and happiness that one could imagine.

" I shall be right over," he cried, jamming the receiver down on the hook, and in the same motion reaching for his hat and coat. " Walter," he cried, " it is Elaine! They have let her go! "

I seized my own hat and coat in time to follow him and we dashed out of the laboratory.

The suspense under which Aunt Josephine had been living had told on her. Her niece, Elaine's cousin, Mary Brown, who lived at Rockledge, had come into the city to comfort Aunt Josephine and they had been sitting, that morning, in the library. Marie, the maid was busy about the room, while Aunt Josephine talked sadly over Elaine's strange disappearance. She was on the verge of tears.

Suddenly a startled cry from Jennings out in the hall caused both ladies to jump to their feet. They could scarcely believe what they heard as the faithful old butler cried out the name.

"Why—Miss Elaine!" he gasped.

An instant later Elaine herself burst into the room and flung herself into Aunt Josephine's arms. All talking and half crying from joy at once, they crowded about her. Breathlessly she answered the questions that flew thick and fast.

In the excitement Aunt Josephine had seized the telephone and called our number. She did not even wait to break the good news, but handed the telephone to Elaine herself.

We left the laboratory on the run, too fast to notice that just around the building line at the corner stood a limousine with shades drawn. Even if we had paused to glance back, we could not have seen Wu Fang and Long Sin inside, gazing out through the corner of the curtains. They were in European dress now and had evidently come prepared for just what they knew was likely to happen.

In all the strange series of events, I doubt whether we had ever made better time from the laboratory over to the Dodge house than we did now. We were admitted by the faithful Jennings and almost ran into the library.

"Oh, Craig!" cried Elaine, as Kennedy, almost speechless, seized her by both hands.

For a few seconds none of us could speak. Then followed a veritable flood of eager conversation.

I watched Elaine carefully, in fact we all did, for she seemed, in spite of the excitement of her return, to be almost a complete nervous wreck from the terrible experiences she had undergone.

"Won't you come and stay with me a few days up in the country, dear?" urged Mary at last.

Elaine thought a moment, then turned to Aunt Josephine.

"Yes," considered her aunt, "I think it would do you good."

Still she hesitated; then shyly looked at Kennedy and laughed. "You, too, Craig, must be fagged out," she said frankly. "Come up there with us and take a rest."

Kennedy smiled. "I shall be delighted," he accepted promptly.

"You, too, Mr. Jameson," she added, turning to me.

I hesitated a moment and Kennedy tried to catch my eye. I was just about to speak when he brought his heel down sharply on my toe. I looked at him again and caught just the trace of a nod of his head. I saw that I was *de trop*.

"No, thank you," I replied. "I'm afraid I'd better not go. Really, I have too much work staring at me. I can't get away—but it's very kind of you to think of asking me."

We chatted, then left a few moments later so that Kennedy could pack.

   .   .   .   .

Around the corner from the laboratory, as we dashed out, had been, as I have said, Wu Fang and Long Sin looking out from the limousine. No sooner had we disappeared across the campus than their driver started up the car and they sped around to our apartment.

Cautiously they alighted and walked down the street. Then making sure they were not observed, they entered and mounted the stairs to our doorway. Long Sin was stationed down the hall on guard while Wu Fang drew from his pocket a blank key, a file and a candle. He lighted the candle and held the key in its flame until it was covered with soot.

Then he inserted the key in the keyhole, turned it and took the key out. Working quickly now, he examined the key sharply. In the soot were slight scratches indicating where it struck and prevented the turning of the lock. He filed the key, trying it again and again. Finally he finished, and opened the door. Beckoning Long Sin, he entered our rooms.

As they stood there, Wu Fang gazed about our living-room, keenly. He was evidently considering where to place something, for, one after another, he picked up several articles on the desk and examined them. Each time that he laid one down he shook his head.

Finally his eye rested on the telephone. It seemed to suggest an idea to him and he crossed over to it. Carefully holding down the receiver on the hook, he unscrewed the case which holds the diaphragm, while with his clever fingers he held the rest of the instrument intact. Then he removed from his pocket the vial which the coolie had given him and placed its contents on the diaphragm itself. Quickly now he re-placed the receiver, and, having finished their work, Long Sin and Wu Fang stealthily crept out.

A second time, as we approached our apartment after the visit to Elaine, we were too excited to notice the limousine in which were Wu and Long Sin. But no sooner had we entered than Long Sin left the car with a final word of instruction from his master.

Up-stairs, in the apartment, Kennedy began hur-riedly to pack, and I helped him as well as I could. We were in the midst of it when the telephone rang and I answered it.

"Hello!" I called.

There was no response.

"Hello, Hello!" I repeated, raising my voice.

Still there was no answer. I worked the hook up and down but could get no reply. Finally, disgusted, I hung up.

A moment later, I recall now, it seemed to me as though some one had stuck a pin into the lobe of my ear. Still, I thought nothing of it in the excitement of Kennedy's departure, and went to work again to help him pack.

We had scarcely got back to work, when the tele-phone bell jangled again, and a second time I an-swered it.

"Is Mr. Kennedy there?" came back a strange voice.

I handed the instrument to Craig.

"Hello," he called. "Who is this?"

No response.

"Hello, hello," he shouted, working the hook as I

had done and, as in my case, there was still no answer.

"Some crank," he exclaimed, jamming down the receiver in disgust and returning to his packing.

Neither of us thought anything of it at the time, but now I recall that I did see Kennedy once or twice press the lobe of his ear as though something had hurt it.

We did not know until later that in a pay station down the street our arch enemy, Long Sin, had been calling us up and then, with a wicked smile, refusing to speak to us.

.   .   .   .

It was about a week later that I came home late one night from the *Star,* feeling pretty done up. Whatever it was, a violent fever seemed to have come on me suddenly. I thought nothing of it, at first, because I soon grew better. But while it lasted, I had the most intense shivering, excruciating pains in my limbs, and delirious headache. I recall, too, that I felt a peculiar soreness on the ear. It was all like nothing I had ever had before.

Indeed the next morning when I woke up, I felt a lassitude that made it quite hard enough even to lounge about in my bath-robe. Finally, feeling no better, I decided to see a doctor. I put on my clothes with a decided effort and went out.

The nearest doctor was about half a block away and we scarcely knew him, for neither Kennedy nor I were exactly sickly.

"Well," asked the doctor, as he closed the door of

his office and turned to me. "What seems to be the matter?"

I tried to smile. "I feel as though I had been celebrating not wisely but too well," I replied, trying to cheer up, "but as a matter of fact I have been leading the simple life."

He sounded me and pounded me, .looked at my tongue and my eyes, listened to my heart and lungs, though I don't think he treated my symptoms very seriously.   In fact, I might have known what he would do.   He talked a little while on generalities, diet and exercise then walked over to a cabinet, and emptied out a few pills into a little paper box.

"Take one every hour," he said, handing them to me, and carefully returning the bottle to the cabinet so that I could not see what was on the label. "Cut your cigarettes to three a day, and don't drink coffee. Four dollars, please."

I suppose I ought to have been cured, and in fact I was cured—of going to that doctor.   I paid him and went back to the apartment, my head soon in a whirl from a new onset of the fever.

I managed to get back into my bath-robe, and threw myself down on the divan, propped up with pillows. I had taken the pills but they had no more effect than sugar of milk.   By this time, I was much more delirious and was crying out.

I saw faces about me, but I did not see the faces which were actually out by our hall door. Wu Fang and Long Sin had waited patiently for their revenge. Now that they thought sufficient time had elapsed, they had stolen stealthily to the apartment door. While Long Sin watched, Wu listened.

"The white devil has it," whispered Wu Fang, as he rejoined his fellow conspirator.

How long I should have remained in this state, and in fact how long I did remain, I don't know. Vaguely, I recall that our acquaintance, Johnson, who had the apartment across the hall, at last heard my cries and came out to his own door. He needed only a moment to listen at ours to know that something was wrong.

"Why, what's the matter, Jameson?" he asked, poking his head in and looking anxiously at me.

I could only rave some reply, and he tried his best to quiet me. "What's the matter, old man?" he repeated. "Tell me. Shall I send for a doctor?"

Somehow or other I knew the state I was in. I knew it was Johnson, yet it all seemed ureal to me. With a great effort I gathered all my scattered wits and managed to shout out, "Telegraph Kennedy—Rockledge."

By this time Johnson himself was thoroughly alarmed. He did not lose a second in dictating a telegram over the telephone.

.   .   .   .

At about the same time, up at Rockledge, Kennedy and Elaine, with her cousin Mary Brown, were starting out for a horseback ride through the hills. They were chatting gaily, but Kennedy was forcing himself to do so.

In fact, they had scarcely gone half a mile when Kennedy, who was riding between the two and fighting off by sheer nerve the illness he felt, suddenly fell

over in half a faint on the horse's neck.   Elaine and
Mary reined up their horses.

"Why, Craig," cried Elaine, startled, "what's the
matter?"

The sound of her voice seemed to arouse him.   He
braced up.   "Oh, nothing, I guess," he said with a
forced smile.   "I'm all right."

It was no use, however.   They had to cut short the
ride, and Kennedy returned to the house, glad to
drop down in an easy chair on the porch, while Elaine
hovered about him solicitously.   His head buzzed, his
skin was hot and dry, his eyes had an unnatural look.
Every now and then he would place his hand to his
ear as though he felt some pain.

They had already summoned the country doctor, but
it took him some time to get out to the house.   Suddenly a messenger boy rode up on his bicycle and
mounted the porch steps.   "Telegram for Mr. Kennedy," he announced, looking about and picking out
Craig naturally as the person he wanted.

Kennedy nodded and took the yellow envelope while
Elaine signed for it.   Listlessly he tore it open.   It
read:

CRAIG KENNEDY,
   c/o Wellington Brown,
    Rockledge, N. J.
Jameson very ill.   Wants you.   Better come.
                              JOHNSON.

The message seemed to rouse Kennedy in spite of
his fever.   His face showed keen alarm, which he en-

deavored to conceal from Elaine. But her quick eye had caught the look.

"I must see Walter," he exclaimed, rising rather weakly and going into the house.

How he ever did it is still, I think, a mystery to him, but he managed to pack up and, in spite of the alternating fever and chills, made the journey back to the city.

When at last Craig arrived at our apartment, it must have seemed to him that he found me almost at death's door. I was terribly ill and weak by that time, but had refused to see the doctor again and Johnson had managed to get me into bed.

Ill himself, Kennedy threw himself down for a moment exhausted. "When did this thing come on Walter?" he asked of Johnson.

"Yesterday, I think, at least as nearly as I can find out," replied our friend.

Craig was decidedly worried. "There's only one person in New York to call on," he murmured, pulling himself out of bed and getting into the living-room as best he could.

"Is that you, Godowski?" he asked over the telephone. "Well, doctor, this is Kennedy. Come over to my apartment, quick. I've a case—two cases for you."

Godowski was a world-famous scientist in his line and had specialized in bacteriology, mainly in tropical diseases.

As Kennedy hung up the receiver, he made his way back again to the bedroom, scratching his ear. He noticed that I was doing the same in my delirium.

"Has Walter been scratching his ear?" he asked of Johnson.

Johnson nodded. "That's strange," considered Craig thoughtfully. "I've been doing the same."

He turned back into the living-room and for a moment looked about. Finally his eye happened to fall on the telephone and an idea seemed to occur to him.

He went over to the instrument and unscrewed the receiver. Carefully he looked inside. Then he looked closer. There was something peculiar about it and he picked up a blank sheet of white paper, dusting off the diaphragm on it. There, on the paper, were innumerable little black specks.

Just then, outside, Dr. Godowski's car drew up and he jumped out, swinging his black bag. Not being acquainted with what we were going through, Godowski did not notice the almond-eyed Chinaman who was watching down the street.

"How do you do, doctor," greeted Craig faintly, at the door.

"What seems to be the difficulty?" inquired the doctor eagerly.

"I don't know," returned Craig, "but I have my suspicions. I'm too ill to verify them myself. So I've called on you. Look at Jameson first," he added.

While Godowski was examining me, Craig managed to get out his microscope and was looking through it at the strange black specks on the paper. There, under the lens, he could see the most remarkable, almost microscopic creature, all legs and feelers, a most vicious object.

Weak though he was, he could not help an exclamation of exultation at his discovery, just as Godowski had finished with me.

"Look!" he cried, calling the doctor. "I know what the trouble is, Godowski."

He had started to tell, but the excitement of the journey and the exertion were so great that he could hardly mumble.

"Here—look—on this paper," he cried. "From the telephone—"

He had risen and was handing the paper to the scientist when his weakness overcame him. He fell flat on his face on the floor and dropped the paper, spilling the contents.

Godowski, now thoroughly alarmed, bent over Craig. But the delirium had overcome Kennedy, too.

Unable to make any sense out of Craig's broken wanderings, Godowski lost no time in taking samples of our blood.

Then he hurried away to his laboratory in his car. As he did so, however, Long Sin leaped into a taxicab which was waiting and followed.

.   .   .   .

In Godowski's laboratory, where he was studying tropical diseases, the bacteriologist set to work at once to confirm his own growing suspicions.

From a monkey which he had there for experimental purposes, he drew off some blood samples. Then, with the aid of his assistant, he took the blood samples he had obtained from us. The monkey's blood, under the microscope, seemed full of rather elongated wriggling germs of a peculiar species. In and out they made their way among the blood corpuscles each like a dart aimed at life itself.

Then he took the samples of our blood. In them were the same germs—carried by that gruesome tick!

"The spirillum!" he muttered. "They are infected with African recurrent fever. The only remedy is atoxyl, administered intravenously, after the manner of Professor Ehrlich's famous '606'."

Godowski had rung the call box hastily for a messenger, when Long Sin, who had managed stealthily to creep up to the doctor's laboratory window, scowled through at the action—then moved away.

While his assistant gathered the apparatus, the doctor wrote:

MISS ANNE SEPTIX,
    301 W. —th St.
Please go at once to the apartment of Craig Kennedy,—Claremont Ave. Surgical case.

GODOWSKI, M. D.

The boy arrived finally and the doctor gave him a generous tip to hurry with the note.

He had not turned the corner, however, when Long Sin appeared. Subtly he played on the boy's cupidity to get him to deliver a note of his own, even offered to deliver the boy's note for him. The flash of a five dollar bill made the rest easy.

As the boy disappeared on a fake errand, Long Sin, with the real note hurried down-town, smiling wickedly.

"They have discovered the fever, Master," he reported in the den.

Wu was beside himself with rage. Before he could speak, however, Long Sin spread out Godowski's message. "But I have this," he added.

It took merely a glance to suggest to Wu a new plan of action. He rose and moved quickly into the back room. "Come," he ordered Weepy Mary. "You must dress up as a nurse—immediately."

Quickly she donned one of the numerous disguises while Wu planned his campaign.

"Here," he directed when she was ready, handing her a little vial. "You must infect every instrument the doctor uses on Kennedy and Jameson,—see?"

She nodded and a moment later was on her way uptown.

.   .   .   .

Meanwhile Godowski himself had arrived at our apartment, much to the relief of our friend Johnson, and was unpacking his instruments.

Quickly he improvised two operating tables, and placed one of us on each. Then, with his assistant, he put on his white robes, mask, gloves and other precautions for asepsis, setting out the apparatus for the intravenous administration of the drug that would kill the spirillum.

Godowski was busy with the atoxyl, mixing it in a normal salt solution. He would drop in a few drops of an acid, then a few drops of an alkaline solution, so as to keep the mixture neutral. Finally, he poured the solution into a container, to the bottom of which was attached a long tube. This container he raised high over our heads, clamping the tube.

Then he fastened a tiny needle to the end of the tube, so that it could be inserted in our arms, catching skillfully a vein—a very difficult piece of work in which he excelled. The liquid would then flow by the force of gravity from the container down through the tube, through the hollow needle and into the vein where it would act on the germs of the fever.

They had finished their preparations and were waiting for Miss Septix. "She ought to be here, now," muttered Godowski impatiently, looking at his watch.

Just then a cab drove up outside.

"Perhaps that is she," he exclaimed. "It must be."

A few moments later the door of the apartment opened. His face showed his disappointment. It was a stranger.

"Miss Septix is ill," she introduced, "and sent me to take her place."

The doctor looked about. "Very well, then," he said briskly, seeing his preparations. "Are you ready to go ahead?"

She nodded and threw off her coat that covered her immaculate white uniform.

The specialist plunged whole-heartedly into his work of saving us now. "Hand me that needle, please," he directed the false nurse.

She moved over to the table near-by and took it up, pausing only long enough to dip it secretly into a vial she carried with her.

"Please hurry," repeated the doctor.

She turned from the table and handed it to him. He adjusted it and already held it poised for the thrust which was not to cure but to poison us further.

"Weepy Mary!" cried a frightened voice at our door.

.   .   .   .

Elaine had been deeply alarmed by the sudden illness of Kennedy and the message from Jameson. No sooner had Kennedy gone, than it flashed over her that Wu Fang had predicted something like this.

"The threat!" she exclaimed, seeking her cousin. "Mary, I must go to the city—right away."

On the next train, then, she had been speeding back to New York, and, arriving at the station, she realized that there was not a moment to lose. She called a cab, drove directly to our apartment, and hurried in, without even ringing the bell.

One glance at the improvised hospital was enough to alarm her. But the sight that had transfixed her was of a woman whose face she remembered only too well, though Kennedy and I had never seen her.

"Please, Miss," began Godowski's assistant, trying to quiet Elaine, while Godowski turned in vexation to his work.

"No, no!" repeated Elaine. "This woman is no nurse. She is a criminal!"

Godowski paused. It was true he did not know the woman. He gazed from Elaine to Weepy Mary in doubt.

The game was up. Weepy Mary dropped a piece of gauze which she had soaked in the solution from the vial which Wu had given her and bolted for the door.

So sudden was her flight that no one was quick enough to stop her. She managed to reach the hall and slam the door. Down she rushed to the street, Godowski's assistant after her.

There, awaiting, was Long Sin's car. She leaped in and was off in a moment. The assistant had just time to dive at the running-board. But his grip was poor and Long Sin easily threw him off.

"You—you fool!" he hissed at Mary, as soon as the danger of pursuit was over and the assistant had gone back into the apartment.

"Oh, sir," she begged, "it was not my fault. Miss Dodge came in—unexpectedly—she recognized me. If I had not fled, they would have caught me—perhaps you, too."

Long Sin was furious. He threatened her and she cowered back. However, there was nothing to be gained by that and he subsided and drove quickly down-town.

The excitement more than ever alarmed Elaine now. "Tell me," she appealed to Dr. Godowski, "what is the matter?"

"In some way," he replied quickly, "they have become infected by the bite of an African tick which carries spirillum fever."

"She got away, in a cab," panted the assistant, returning.

Godowski raised his hands in despair. "I was just about to start," he cried. "Everything is ready. I can't send for another nurse. Every minute counts."

Elaine had thrown off her coat and hat. Her sleeves were up in a moment and before the doctor knew what she was about she was scrubbing her hands in the antiseptic wash.

"Only—show me—what to do," she cried. "I will be the nurse!"

.   .   .   .

Several days later, when we had recovered sufficiently from the diabolical attack that had been made upon us, Kennedy was again at work in the laboratory, while I was writing. We still felt rather weak, but Godowski's skill had pulled us out all right.

Our speaking-tube sounded and I knew that it was Elaine and Aunt Josephine.

" How do you feel? " inquired Elaine anxiously, as she almost ran across the laboratory to Craig.

" Fine! " he exaggerated, brightly.

" Really? " she repeated anxiously.

" Look! " he said, turning to his microscope.

He took some blood from a test tube in our electric incubator and placed a drop on a slide. It was some of the blood infected by the germs carried by the tick.

" That is how our blood looked—before the new nurse arrived," he smiled, while Elaine looked at it in horror.

Then he pricked his arm and let a drop smear on another slide.

" Now look at that—perfectly normal," he added.

" Oh—I'm so glad," she exclaimed radiantly.

" Normal—thanks to you. You saved us. You were just in time," cried Craig taking both her hands in his.

He was about to kiss her, when she broke away. " Craig," she whispered, blushing and looking hastily at us.

Aunt Josephine and I could only smile at the disgusted glance Craig gave us, as he thrust his hands in his pockets and wished us a thousand miles away at that moment.

CHAPTER V

For a long time Kennedy had, I knew, been at work at odd moments in the laboratory secretly. What it was that he was working on, even I was unable to guess, so closely had he guarded his secret. But that it was something momentous, I was assured.

Long Sin had already been arrested and it was a day or two after the escape of Wu himself who had come just in time to prevent the confession by one of his emissaries of the whereabouts of his secret den. Kennedy had Chase and another detective whom he frequently employed on routine matters at work over the clues developed by his use of the sphygmograph. Elaine, anxious for news, had dropped in on us at the laboratory just as Kennedy was hastily opening his mail.

Craig came to a large letter with an official look, slit open the envelope, and unfolded the letter. " Hurrah! " he cried, jumping up and thrusting the letter before us. " Read that."

Across the top of the paper were embossed in blue the formidable words:

United States Navy Department,
Washington, D. C.

The letter was most interesting:

PROFESSOR CRAIG KENNEDY,
  The University, New York City.
DEAR SIR,
  Your telautomatic torpedo model was tested yester-
day and I take great pleasure in stating that it was
entirely successful.   There is no doubt that the United
States is safe from attack as long as we retain its
secret.
                    Very sincerely yours,
                              DANIEL WATERS,
                                    Ass't Sec'y.

  " Oh, Craig," congratulated Elaine, as she handed
back the note. " I'm so glad for your sake.   How
famous you will be! "
  " When are we going to see the wonderful invention, Craig? " I added as I grasped his hand and, in
return, he almost broke the bones in mine wringing it.
  " As soon as you wish," he replied, moving over to
the safe near-by and opening it.   " Here's the only
other model in existence besides the model I sent to
Washington."
  He held up before us a cigar-shaped affair of steel,
about eight inches long, with a tiny propeller and rudder of a size to correspond.   Above was a series of
wires, four or five inches in length, which, he explained, were the aerials by which the torpedo was
controlled.
  " The principle of the thing," he went on proudly,
" is that I use wireless waves to actuate relays on the

torpedo. The power is in the torpedo; the relay releases it. That is, I send a child with a message; the grown man, through the relay, does the work. So, you see, I can sit miles away in safety and send my little David out anywhere to strike down a huge Goliath."

It was not difficult to catch his enthusiasm over the marvellous invention, though we could not follow him through the mazes of explanation about radio-combinators, telecommutators and the rest of the technicalities. I may say, however, that on his radio-combinator he had a series of keys marked "Forward," "Back," "Start," "Stop," "Rudder Right," "Rudder Left," and so on.

He had scarcely finished his brief description when there came a knock at the door. I answered it. It was Chase and his assistant, whom Kennedy had employed in the affair.

"We've found the place on Pell Street that we think is Wu Fang's," they reported excitedly. "It's in number fourteen, as you thought. We've left an operative disguised as a blind beggar to watch the place."

"Oh, good!" exclaimed Elaine, as Craig and I hurried out after Chase and his man with her. "May I go with you?"

"Really, Elaine," objected Craig, "I don't think it's safe. There's no telling what may happen. In fact, I think Walter and I had better not be seen there even with Chase."

She pouted and pleaded, but Craig was obdurate. Finally she consented to wait for us at home provided we brought her the news at the earliest moment and demonstrated the wonderful torpedo as well. Craig was only too glad to promise and we waved good-bye as her car whisked her off.

Half an hour later we turned into Chinatown from the shadow of the elevated railroad on Chatham Square, doing our best to affect a Bowery slouch.

We had not gone far before we came to the blind beggar. He was sitting by number fourteen with a sign on his breast, grinding industriously at a small barrel organ before him on which rested a tin cup.

We passed him and Kennedy took out a coin from his pocket and dropped it into the cup. As he did so, he thrust his hand into the cup and quickly took out a piece of paper which he palmed.

The blind beggar thanked and blessed us, and we dodged into a doorway where Kennedy opened the paper: " Wu Fang gone out."

"What shall we do?" I asked.

" Go in anyhow," decided Kennedy quickly.

We left the shelter of the doorway and walked boldly up to the door. Deftly Kennedy forced it and we entered.

We had scarcely mounted the stairs to the den of the Serpent, when a servant in a back room, hearing a noise, stuck his head in the door. Kennedy and I made a dash at him and quickly overpowered him, snapping the bracelets on his wrists.

"Watch him, Walter," directed Craig as he made his way into the back room.

.   .   .   .

In the devious plots and schemes of Wu Fang, his

nefarious work had brought him into contact not only with criminals of the lowest order but with those high up in financial and diplomatic circles.

Thus it happened that at such a crisis as Kennedy had brought about for him Wu had suddenly been called out of the city and had received an order from a group of powerful foreign agents known secretly as the Intelligence Office to meet an emissary at a certain rocky promontory on the Connecticut shore of Long Island Sound the very day after Kennedy's little affair with him in the laboratory and the day before the letter from Washington arrived.

Though he was mortally afraid of Kennedy's pursuit, there was nothing to do but obey this imperative summons. Quietly he slipped out of town, the more readily when he realized that the summons would take him not far from the millionaire cottage colony where Elaine had her summer home, which, however, she had not yet opened.

There, on the rocky shore, he sat gazing out at the waves, waiting, when suddenly, from around the promontory, came a boat rowed by two stalwart sailors. It carried as passengers two dark-complexioned, dark-haired men, foreigners evidently, though carefully dressed so as to conceal both their identity and nationality.

As the boat came up to a strip of sandy beach among the rocks, the sailors held it while their two passengers jumped out. Then they rowed away as quickly as they had come.

The two mysterious strangers saluted Wu.

" We are under orders from the Intelligence Office,"

introduced one who seemed to be the leader, " to get this American, Kennedy."

A subtle smile overspread Wu's face. He said nothing but this adventure promised to serve more than one end.

" Information has just come to us," the stranger went on, " that Kennedy has invented a new wireless automatic torpedo. Already a letter is on its way informing him that it has been accepted by the Navy."

The other man who had been drawing a cigar-shaped outline on the wet sand looked up. " We must get those models," he put in, adding, " both of them—the one he has and that the government has. Can it be done? "

" I can get them," answered Wu sinisterly.

And so, while Kennedy was drawing together the net about Wu, that wily criminal had already planned an attack on him in an unexpected quarter.

Down in Washington the very morning that our pursuit of Wu came to a head, the officials of the navy department, both naval and civil, were having the final conference at which they were to accept officially Kennedy's marvellous invention which, it was confidently believed, would ultimately make war impossible.

Seated about a long table in one of the board rooms were not only the officers but the officials of the department whose sanction was necessary for the final step. By a window sat a stenographer who was transcribing, as they were taken, the notes of the momentous meeting.

They had just completed the examination of the torpedo and laid it on the end of the table scarcely an arm's length from the stenographer. As he finished a page of notes he glanced quickly at his watch. It was exactly three o'clock.

Hastily he reached over for the torpedo and with one swift, silent movement tossed it out of the window.

Down below, in a clump of rhododendrons, for several moments had been crouching one of the men who had borne the orders to Wu Fang at the strange meeting on the promontory.

His eyes seemed riveted at the window above him. Suddenly the supreme moment for which this dastardly plot had been timed came. As the torpedo model dropped from the window, he darted forward, caught it, turned, and in an instant he was gone.

.   .   .   .

Wu Fang himself had returned after setting in motion the forces which he found necessary to call to aid the foreign agents in their plots against Kennedy's torpedo.

As Wu approached the door of his den and was about to enter, his eye fell on our outpost, the blind beggar. Instantly his suspicions were aroused. He looked the beggar over with a frown, thought a moment, then turned and instead of entering went up the street.

He made the circuit of the block and now came to an alley on the next street that led back of the building in which he had his den. Still frowning, he gazed about, saw that he was not followed, and entered a doorway.

Up the stairs he made his way until he came to an empty loft. Quickly he went over to the blank wall

and began feeling cautiously about as if for a secret
spring hidden in the plaster.

"No one in the back room," said Kennedy rejoining me in the den itself with the prisoner. "He's out,
all right."

Before Craig was a mirror. As he looked into it, at
an angle, he could see a part of the decorations of the
wall behind him actually open out. For an instant the
evil face of Wu Fang appeared.

Without a word, Craig walked into the back room.
As he did so, Wu Fang, knife in hand, stealthily
opened the sliding panel its full length and noiselessly
entered the room behind me. With knife upraised for
instant action he moved closer and closer to me. He
had almost reached me and paused to gloat as he
poised the knife ready to strike, when I heard a shout
from Kennedy, and a scuffle.

Craig had leaped out from behind a screen near the
doorway to the back room where he had hidden to
lure Wu on. With a powerful grasp, he twisted the
knife from Wu's hand and it fell with a clatter on the
floor. I was at Wu myself an instant later. He was
a powerful fighter, but we managed to snap the hand-
cuffs on him finally, also.

"Walter," panted Kennedy straightening himself
out after the fracas, " I'll stay here with the prisoners.
Go get the police."

I hurried out and rushed down the street seeking an
officer.

Up in the den, Wu Fang, silent, stood with his back
to the wall, scowling sullenly. Close beside him hung
a sort of bell-cord, just out of reach. Kennedy, re-

volver in hand, was examining the writing-table to discover whatever evidence he could. Slowly, imperceptibly, inch by inch, Wu moved toward the bell-cord. He was reaching out with his manacled hands to seize it when Kennedy, alert, turned, saw him, and instantly shot. Wu literally crumpled up and dropped to the floor as Craig bounded over to him.

By this time I had found a policeman and he had summoned the wagon from the Elizabeth Street station, a few blocks away. As we drove up before the den, I leaped out and the police followed.

Imagine my surprise at seeing Wu stretched on the floor. Kennedy had tried to staunch the flow of blood from a wound on Wu's shoulder with a handkerchief and now was making a temporary bandage which he bound on him.

"How are you, sergeant?" nodded Kennedy. "Well, I guess you'll admit I made good this time."

The sergeant smiled, recalling a previous occasion when the slippery Wu had squirmed through our fingers.

Kennedy's restless eye fell on the bell-rope which had caused the trouble. Somehow, he seemed to have an irresistible desire to pull that rope. He gazed about the room.

"Walter, you and the sergeant take the prisoners into the next room," he said. "I want to see what this thing really is."

We moved Wu and his servant and stood in the doorway. Craig gave the rope a yank.

Instantly there was an explosion. A concealed shotgun in the wall fired, scattering shot all over the front

of Wu's table, just where we had been standing, knocking over and breaking vases, scattering papers and in
general wrecking everything before it.

" So, that's it," whistled Craig. " You fellows can
come back now. Two of you men I'm going to leave
here to watch the place and make other arrests if you
can. Come on."

With Kennedy I left the tenement while the sergeant
marched the prisoners out, and we drove off with them.
Quite a crowd had collected outside by the time we
came out. Among them, naturally, were many Chinamen, and we could not see two of them hiding behind
the rest on the outskirts, jabbering in low tones together and making hasty plans. As we clanged away
down the street they followed more slowly on foot.

Common humanity dictated that we take Wu first of
all to a hospital and get him fixed up and to a hospital
we went. Kennedy and I entered with our prisoners,
closely guarded by the police.

Craig handed Wu over to two young doctors and a
nurse. By this time Wu was very weak from loss of
blood. Still he had his iron nerve and that was carrying him through. The two young doctors and the
nurse had scarcely begun to take off Craig's rude bandage to replace it properly, when a noise outside told
us that a weeping and gesticulating delegation of
Chinese had arrived.

" Keep 'em back," called one of the doctors to an
attendant.

The attendant tried to drive them away, but nothing
could force them back more than an inch or two as,
in broken English, they sought to find out how Wu

was. Their importunity proved too much for only one attendant. Still gibbering and gesticulating, the crowd brushed past him as if he had been a mere reed. The attendant raged about until he lost his head. But it was no use. There was nothing for him to do but to follow them in.

Kennedy by this time had finished talking to the doctors and handing Wu over to them. They had taken him into a room in the dispensary. Just then the chattering crowd pushed in, some asking questions, others bewailing the fate of the great Wu Fang. They were so insistent that at last one of the doctors was forced to demand that the police drive them out. They started to push them back.

In the mêlée, one of their number managed to get away from the rest and reach the doorway to the emergency room. He was, as we found out later, dressed almost precisely like Wu, although he had on a somewhat different cap. In build and size as well as features he was a veritable Dromio.

The other Chinaman drew back behind the screen which hid the doorway to the emergency room and concealed himself.

Meanwhile, Kennedy and I were laughing at the truly ludicrous antics of the astounded Celestials, thunderstruck at the capture of the peerless leader, while the police forced them back.

" Well, good-bye," nodded Craig to the first doctor and nurse who had attended Wu Fang outside.

"Good-bye. We'll fix him up and take good care that he doesn't cheat the law," they said, with a nod to the sergeant.

.   .   .   .

In the emergency room, Wu was placed on an operating table and there was bound up properly, though
he was terribly weak now.

Back of the screen, however, the other Chinaman
was hiding, able to get an occasional glance at what was
going on.   There happened to be a table near him on
which were gauze, cotton and other things.   He
reached over and took the gauze and quickly made it
into a bandage, keeping one eye on the bandaging of
Wu.   Then he placed the bandage over his own shoulder and arm in the same way that he saw the doctors
doing with Wu.

They had finished with Wu and one of the doctors
moved over to the doorway to call the sergeant.   For
the moment the rest had left Wu alone, his eyes apparently half closed through weakness.   Each was busy
about his own especial task.

From behind the screen which was only a few feet
from the operating table, the secreted Chinaman
stepped out.   Quickly he placed his own hat on Wu
and took Wu's, then took Wu's place on the table while
Wu slipped behind the screen.

The doctor turned to the supposed Wu.   "Come
now," he ordered, handing him over to the police.
"Here he is at last."

The sergeant started to lead the prisoner out.   As he
did so, he looked sharply at him.   He could scarcely
believe his eyes.   There was something wrong.   All
Chinaman might look alike to some people but not to
him.

"That's not Wu Fang!" he exclaimed.

Instantly there was the greatest excitement. The doctors were astounded as all rushed into the emergency room again. One of them looked behind the screen. There was an open window.

" That's how he got away," he cried.

Meanwhile, several blocks from the hospital, Wu, still weak but more than ever nerved up, came out of his place of concealment, gazed up and down the street, and, seeing no one following, hurried away from the hospital as fast as his shaky legs would bear him.

.   .   .   .

Confident that at last our arch enemy was safely landed in the hands of the police, Kennedy and I had left the hospital and were hastening to Elaine with the news. We stopped at the laboratory only long enough to get the torpedo from the safe and at a toy store where Craig bought a fine little clockwork battleship.

We found Elaine and Aunt Josephine in the conservatory and quickly Kennedy related how we had captured Wu.

But, like all inventors, his pet was the torpedo and soon we were absorbed in his description of it. As he unwrapped it, Elaine drew back, timidly, from the fearful engine of destruction.

Kennedy smiled. " No, it isn't dangerous," he said reassuringly. " I've removed its charge and put in a percussion cap. Let me show you, on a small scale, how it works," he added, winding up the battleship and placing it in the fountain.

Next he placed the torpedo in the water at the other end of the tank. " Come over here," he said, indicating to us to follow him into the palms.

There he had placed the strange wireless apparatus which controlled the torpedo. He pressed a lever. We peered out through the fronds of the palms. That uncanny little cigar-shaped thing actually started to move over the surface of the water.

"Of course I could make it dive," explained Craig, " but I want you to see it work."

Around the tank it went, turned, cut a figure eight, as Kennedy manipulated the levers. Then it headed straight toward the battleship. It struck. There was a loud report, a spurt of water. One of the skeleton masts fell over. The battleship heeled over, and slowly sank, bow first.

"Wonderful!" exclaimed Elaine. "That was very realistic."

We brushed our way out through the thick palms, congratulating Kennedy on the perfect success of his demonstration.

So astonished were we that we did not hear the door-bell ring. Jennings answered it and admitted two men.

"Is Professor Kennedy here?" asked one. "We have been to his apartment and to the laboratory."

"I'll see," said Jennings discretely, taking the card of one of them and leaving them in the drawing-room.

"Two gentlemen to see you, Mr. Kennedy," Jennings interrupted our congratulations, handing Craig a card. "Shall I tell them you are here, sir?"

Craig glanced at the card. "I wonder what that can be?" he said, turning the card toward us.

It was engraved:

W. R. Barnes
U. S. Secret Service.

" Yes, I'll see them," he said, then to us, " Please excuse me? "

Elaine, Aunt Josephine and I strolled off in the palms toward the Fifth Avenue side, while Jennings went out toward the back of the house.

" Well, gentlemen," greeted Kennedy as he met the two detectives, " what can I do for you? "

The leader looked about, then leaned over and whispered, " We've just had word, Professor, that your model of the torpedo has been stolen from the Navy Department in Washington."

" Stolen? " repeated Kennedy, staring aghast.

" Yes. We fear that an agent of a foreign government has found a traitor in the department."

Rapidly Kennedy's mind pictured what might be done with the deadly weapon in the hands of an enemy.

" And," added the Secret Service man, " we have reason to believe that this foreign agent is using a Chinaman, Wu Fang."

"But Wu has been arrested," replied Craig. " I arrested him myself. The police have him now."

" Then you don't know of his escape? "

Kennedy could only stare as they told the story.

Suddenly, down the hall, came cries of, " Help! Help! "

.   .   .   .

While Craig was showing us the torpedo, the criminal machinery which Wu had set in motion at orders from the foreign agents was working rapidly.

Outside the Dodge house, a man had shadowed us. He waited until we went in, then slunk in himself by the back way and climbed through an open window into the cellar.

Quietly he made his way up through the cellar until finally he reached the library. Listening carefully he could hear us talking in the conservatory. Stealthily he moved out of the library.

We had left the conservatory when he entered, peering through the palms. On he stole till he came to the fountain. He looked about. There, bobbing up and down, was the model of the torpedo for which he had dared so much. He picked it up and looked at it, gloating.

The crook was about to move back toward the library, hugging the precious model close to himself when he heard Jennings coming. He started back to the conservatory. Jennings entered just in time to catch a fleeting glimpse of some one. His suspicions were roused and he followed.

The crook reached the conservatory and opened a glass window leading out into the little garden beside the house. He was about to step out when the sound of voices in the garden arrested him. Elaine, Aunt Josephine and I had gone out and Elaine was showing me a new rose which had just been sent her.

The crook fell back and dropped down behind the palms. Jennings looked about, but saw no one and stood there puzzled. Then the crook, fearing that he might be captured at any moment, looked about to see where he might hide the torpedo. There did not seem to be any place. Quickly he began to dig out the earth in one of the palm pots. He dropped the torpedo, wrapped still in the handkerchief, into the hole and covered it up.

Jennings was clearly puzzled. He had seen some one rush in, but the conservatory was apparently empty. He had just turned to go out when he saw a palm move. There was a face! He made a dive for it and in a moment both he and the crook were rolling over and over.

.   .   .   .

Kennedy and the Secret Service men were talking earnestly when they heard the cry for help and the scuffle. They rushed out and into the conservatory in time to see the crook, who had broken away, knock out Jennings. He sprang to his feet and darted away.

Kennedy's mind was working rapidly. Had the man been after the other model? The detectives went after him. But Craig went for the torpedo. As he looked in the tank, it was gone! He turned and followed the crook.

I was still in the garden with Elaine and Aunt Josephine when I heard sounds of a struggle and a moment later a man emerged through the window of the conservatory followed by two other men. I went for him, but he managed to elude me and dashed for the wall in the back of the garden. The Secret Service men fired at him but he kept on. A moment later Craig came through the window.

" Did any of you take the torpedo? " he asked.

" No," replied Elaine, " we left it just as you had it."

Kennedy seemed wild with anxiety. " Then both

8

models have been stolen!" he cried, dashing after the Secret Service men with me close behind.

The crook by this time had reached the top of the wall. Just as he was about to let himself down safely on the other side, a shot struck him. He pitched over and we ran forward.

But he had just enough of a start. In spite of the shock and the wound he managed to pick himself up and with the help of a confederate hobbled into a waiting car, which sped away just as we came over the wall.

We dropped to the ground just as another car approached. Craig commandeered it from its astonished driver, the Secret Service men and I piled in and we were off in a few seconds in hot pursuit.

.   .   .   .

Down at the terminal where trains came in from Washington, Wu, much better now, was waiting.

He had pulled a long coat over his Chinese clothes and wore a slouch hat. As he looked at the incoming passengers he spied the man he was waiting for, the young crook who had been waiting in the shrubbery outside the Navy Building when the torpedo model was thrown out.

The man had the model carefully wrapped up, under his arm. As his eye travelled over the crowd he recognized Wu but did not betray it. He walked by and, as he passed, hastily handed Wu the package containing the model. Wu slipped it under his coat. Then each went his way, in opposite directions.

.   .   .   .

It was a close race between the car bearing the two crooks and that which Kennedy had impressed into service, but we kept on up through the city and out across the country, into Connecticut.

Time and again they almost got away until it became a question of following tire tracks. Once we came to a cross-road and Kennedy stopped and leaped out. Deeply planted in the mud, he could see the tracks of the car ahead leading out by the left road. Close beside the tire tracks were the footprints of two men going up the right hand road toward the Sound.

" You follow the car and the driver," decided Craig, hastily indicating the road by which it had gone. " I'll follow the footprints."

The Secret Service men jumped back into the car and Kennedy and I went along the shore road following the two crooks.

Already the wounded crook, supported by his pal, had made his way down to the water and had come to a long wharf. There, near the land-end, they had a secret hiding-place into which they went. The other crook drew forth a smoke signal and began to prepare it.

Kennedy and I were able, now, to move faster than they. As we came in sight of the wharf, Kennedy paused.

" There they are, two of them," he indicated.

I could just make them out in their hiding-place. The fellow who had stolen the torpedo was by this time so weak from loss of blood that he could hardly hold his head up, while the other hurried to fix the smoke signal. He happened to glance up, and saw us.

" Come, Red, brace up," he muttered. " They're on our trail."

The wounded man was almost too weak to answer. " I—I can't," he gasped weakly, " You—go." Then, with a great effort, remembering the mission on which he had been sent, he whispered hoarsely, " I hid the second torpedo model in the Dodge house in the bottom of—" He tried hard to finish, but he was too weak. He fell back, dead.

His pal had waited as long as he dared to learn the secret. He jumped up and ran out just as we burst into the hiding-place.

Kennedy dropped down by the dead man and searched him, while I dashed after the other fellow. But I was not so well acquainted with the lay of the land as he and, before I knew it, he had darted into another of his numerous hiding-places. I hunted about, but I had lost the track.

When I returned, I found Kennedy writing a hasty note.

" I couldn't follow him, Craig," I confessed.

" Too bad," frowned Craig evidently greatly worried by what had happened, as he folded the note. " Walter," he added seriously, " I want you to go find the fellow." He handed me the note. " And if anything separates us to-day—give this note to Elaine."

I did not pay much attention to the tone he assumed, but often afterward I pondered over it and the serious and troubled look on his face. I was too chagrined at losing my man to think much of it then. I took the note and hurried out again after him.

Meanwhile, as nearly as I can now make out, Kennedy searched the dead man again. There was certainly no clue to his identity on him, nor had he the torpedo model. Craig looked about. Suddenly, he fell flat on his stomach.

There was Wu Fang himself, coming to the wharf, carrying the model of the torpedo which had been stolen in Washington and brought up to him by his emissary.

Kennedy, crouching down and taking advantage of every object that sheltered him, crawled cautiously into an angle. Unsuspecting, Wu came to the land-end of the wharf.

There he saw his lieutenant, dead—and the smoke signal still beside him, unlighted. He bent over in amazement and examined the man.

From his hiding-place Kennedy crept stealthily. He had scarcely got within reach of Wu when the alert Chinaman seemed to sense his presence. He rose quickly and swung around.

The two arch enemies gazed at each other a moment silently. Each knew it was the final, fatal encounter.

Slowly Wu drew a long knife and leaped at Kennedy who grappled with him. They struggled mercilessly.

In the struggle, Craig managed to tear the torpedo out of Wu's hands, just as they rolled over. It fell on a rock. Instantly an explosion tore a hole in the sand, scattering the gravel all about.

Relentlessly the combat raged. Out on the wharf itself they went, right up to the edge.

Then both went over into the water, locked in each other's vice-like grip.

Even in the water, they struggled, frantically.

.   .   .   .

My search for the escaped crook was unsuccessful.

Somehow, however, it led me across country to a road. As I approached, I heard a car and looked up. There were the Secret Service men. I called them and stepped out of the bushes. They stopped and jumped out of the car and I ran to them.

"Come back with me," I urged. "We found two of them. One is dead. Craig sent me to trace the other. I've lost the trail. Perhaps you can find it for me."

We crashed through the brush quickly. Suddenly I heard something that caused me to start. It sounded like an explosion.

"There's the place—over there," I pointed, pausing and indicating the direction of the wharf whence had come the explosion.

What was it? We did not stop a moment, but hurried in that direction.

We reached the shore where we saw marks of the explosion and of a fight. Out on the pier I ran breathlessly. I rushed to the very edge and gazed over, then climbed down the slippery piling and peered into the black water beneath.

A few bubbles seemed to ooze up from below. Was that all?

No, as I gazed down I saw that some dark object was there. Slowly Wu Fang's body floated to the surface and lay there, rocked by the waves. Deep in his breast stuck his own knife with its handle of the Sign of the Serpent!

I reached down and seized him, as I peered about for Kennedy.

There was nothing more there.

"Craig!" I called desperately, "Craig!"

There was no answer. The silence, the echo of the lapping water under the wharf was appalling, mocking.

I managed to call the Secret Service men and they got Wu Fang's body up on the wharf.

But I could not leave the spot.

Where was Craig? There was not a sign of him. I could not realize it, even when the men brought grappling irons and began to search the black water.

It was all a hideous dream. I saw and heard, in a daze.

.   .   .   .

It was not until late that night that I returned to the Dodge house.

I had delayed my return as long as I could, but I knew that I must see Elaine some time.

As I entered even Jennings must have seen that something was wrong. Elaine, who was sitting in the library with Aunt Josephine, rose as she saw me.

"Did you get them?" she asked eagerly.

I could not speak. She seemed to read the tragic look on my haggard face and stopped.

"Why," she gasped, clutching at the desk, "what is the matter?"

As gently as I could, I told her of the chase, of leaving Craig, of the explosion, of the marks of the struggle and of the finding of Wu Fang.

As I finished, I thought she would faint.

"And you—you went over everything about the wharf?"

"Everything. The men even dragged for the—"

I checked myself over the fateful word.

Elaine looked at me wildly. I thought that she would lose her reason. She did not cry. The shock was too great for that.

Suddenly I remembered the note. "Before I left him—the last time," I blurted out, " he wrote a note—to you."

I pulled the crumpled paper from my pocket and Elaine almost tore it from me—the last word from him—and read :

DEAREST :

I may not return until the case is settled and I have found the stolen torpedo. Matters involving millions of lives and billions of dollars hang on the plot back of it. No matter what happens, have no fear. Trust me.

Lovingly,

CRAIG.

She finished reading the note and slowly laid it down. Then she picked it up and read it again. Slowly she turned to me.

I think I have never seen so sublime a look of faith on any one's face before. If I had not seen and heard what I had, it might have shaken my own convictions.

"He told me to trust him and to have no fear," she said simply, gripping herself mentally and physically by main force, then with an air of defiance she looked at me. " I do not believe that he is dead!"

I tried to comfort her. I wanted to do so. But I could do nothing but shake my head sadly. My own heart was full to overflowing. An intimacy such as had been ours could not be broken except with a shock that tore my soul. I knew that the poor girl had not seen what I had seen. Yet I could not find it in my heart to contradict her.

She saw my look, read my mind.

" No," she cried, still defiant, " no—a thousand times, no! I tell you—he is not dead!"

CHAPTER VI

THE LOST TORPEDO

FROM the rocks of a promontory that jutted out not far from the wharf where Wu Fang's body was found and Kennedy had disappeared, opened up a beautiful panorama of a bay on one side and the Sound on the other.

It was a deserted bit of coast. But any one who had been standing near the promontory the next day might have seen a thin line as if the water, sparkling in the sunlight, had been cut by a huge knife. Gradually a thin steel rod seemed to rise from the water itself, still moving ahead, though slowly now as it pushed its way above the surface. After it came a round cylinder of steel, studded with bolts. It was the hatch of a submarine and the rod was the periscope.

As the submarine lay there at rest, the waves almost breaking over it, the hatch slowly opened and a hand appeared groping for a hold. Then appeared a face with a tangle of curly black hair and keen forceful eyes. After it the body of a man rose out of the hatch, a tall, slender, striking person. He reached down into the hold of the boat and drew forth a life preserver.

"All right," he called down in an accent slightly foreign, as he buckled on the belt. " I shall communicate with you as soon as I have something to report."

Then he deliberately plunged overboard and struck out for the shore. Hand over hand, he churned his way through the water toward the beach until at last his feet touched bottom and he waded out, shaking the water from himself like a huge animal.

The coming of the stranger had not been entirely unheralded. Along the shore road by which Kennedy and I had followed the crooks whom we thought had the torpedo, on that last chase, was waiting now a powerful limousine with its motor purring. A chauffeur was sitting at the wheel and inside, at the door, sat a man peering out along the road to the beach. Suddenly the man in the machine signalled to the driver.

"He comes," he cried eagerly. "Drive down the road, closer, and meet him."

The chauffeur shot his car ahead. As the swimmer strode shivering up the roadway, the car approached him. The assistant swung open the door and ran forward with a thick, warm coat and hat.

Neither the master nor the servant spoke as they met, but the man wrapped the coat about him, hurried into the car, the driver turned and quickly they sped toward the city.

Secret though the entrance of the stranger had been planned, however, it was not unobserved.

Along the beach, on a boulder, gazing thoughtfully out to sea and smoking an old briar pipe sat a bent fisherman clad in an oilskin coat and hat and heavy, ungainly boots. About his neck was a long woolen muffler which concealed the lower part of his face quite as effectually as his scraggly, grizzled whiskers.

Suddenly, he seemed to discover something that interested him, slowly rose, then turned and almost ran up the shore. Quickly he dropped behind a large rock and waited, peering out.

As the limousine bearing the stranger, on whom the fisherman had kept his eyes riveted, turned and drove away, the old salt rose from behind his rock, gazed after the car as if to fix every line of it in his memory and then he, too, quickly disappeared up the road.

The stranger's car had scarcely disappeared when the fisherman turned from the shore road into a clump of stunted trees and made his way to a hut. Not far away stood a small, unpretentious closed car, also with a driver.

" I shall be ready in a minute," the fisherman nodded almost running into the hut, as the driver moved his car up closer to the door.

The larger motor had disappeared far down the bend of the road when the fisherman reappeared. In an almost incredible time he had changed his oilskins and muffler for a dark coat and silk hat. He was no longer a fisherman, but a rather fussy-looking old gentleman, bewhiskered still, with eyes looking out keenly from a pair of gold-rimmed glasses.

" Follow that car—at any cost," he ordered simply as he let himself into the little motor, and the driver shot ahead down a bit of side road and out into the main shore road again, urging the car forward to overtake the one ahead.

Such was the entrance of the stranger—Marcius Del Mar—into America.

.   .   .   .

How I managed to pass the time during the first days after the strange disappearance of Kennedy, I don't know. It was all like a dream—the apartment empty, the laboratory empty, my own work on the *Star* uninteresting, Elaine broken-hearted, life itself a burden.

Hoping against hope the next day I decided to drop around at the Dodge house. As I entered the library unannounced, I saw that Elaine, with a faith for which I envied her, was sitting at a table, her back toward the door. She was gazing sadly at a photograph. Though I could not see it, I needed not to be told whose it was.

She did not hear me come in, so engrossed was she in her thoughts. Nor did she notice me at first as I stood just behind her. Finally I put my hand on her shoulder as if I had been an elder brother.

She looked up into my face. "Have you heard from him yet?" she asked anxiously.

I could only shake my head sadly. She sighed. Involuntarily she rose and together we moved toward the garden, the last place we had seen him about the house.

We had been pacing up and down the garden talking earnestly only a short time when a man made his way in from the Fifth Avenue gate.

"Is this Miss Dodge?" he asked.

"Yes," she replied eagerly.

Neither Elaine nor I knew him at the time, though I think she thought he might be the bearer of some message from Craig. As a matter of fact he was the emissary to whom the stenographer had thrown the torpedo model from the Navy Building in Washington.

His visit was only a part of a deep-laid scheme. Only a few minutes before, three crooks—among them our visitor—had stopped just below the house on a side street.   To him the others had given final instructions and a note, and he had gone on, leaving the two standing there.

"I have a note for you," he said, bowing and handing an envelope to Elaine, which she tore open and read.

WASHINGTON, D. C.

MISS ELAINE DODGE,
   Fifth Avenue, New York.
MY DEAR MISS DODGE,
   The bearer, Mr. Bailey, of the Secret Service, would like to question you regarding the disappearance of Mr. Kennedy and the model of his torpedo.
MORGAN BERTRAND,
   U. S. Secret Service.

Even as we were talking the other two crooks had already moved up and had made their way around back of the stone wall that cut off the Dodge garden back of the house.   There they stood, whispering eagerly and gazing furtively over the wall as their man talked to Elaine.

After a moment I stepped aside, while Elaine read the note, and as he asked her a few questions, I could not help feeling that the affair had a very suspicious look.   The more I thought of it, the less I liked it. Finally I could stand it no longer.

"I beg your pardon," I excused myself to the alleged Mr. Bailey, "but may I speak to Miss Dodge alone just a minute?"

He bowed, rather ungraciously I thought, and Elaine followed me aside while I told her my fears.

"I don't like the looks of it myself," she agreed. "Yes, I'll be very careful what I say."

While we were talking I could see out of the corner of my eye that the fellow was looking at us askance and frowning. But if I had had an X-ray eye, I might have seen his two companions on the other side of the wall, peering over as they had been before and showing every evidence of annoyance at my interference.

The man resumed his questioning of Elaine regarding the torpedo and she replied guardedly, as in fact she could not do otherwise.

Suddenly we heard shouts on the other side of the wall, as though some one were attacking some one else.

There seemed to be several of them, for a man quickly flung himself over the wall and ran to us.

"They're after us," he shouted to Bailey.

Instantly our visitor drew a gun and followed the newcomer as he ran to get out of the garden in the opposite direction.

Just then a tall, well-dressed, striking man came over the wall, accompanied by another dressed as a policeman, and rushed toward us.

.   .   .   .

The car bearing the mysterious stranger, Del Mar, kept on until it reached New York, then made its way through the city until it came to the Hotel La Coste.

Del Mar jumped out of the car, his wet clothes covered completely by the long coat. He registered

128 THE ROMANCE OF ELAINE

and rode up in the elevator to rooms which had already been engaged for him. In his suite a valet was already unpacking some trunks and laying out clothes when Del Mar and his assistant entered.

With an exclamation of satisfaction at his unostentatious entry into the city, Del Mar threw off his heavy coat. The valet hastened to assist him in removing the clothes still wet and wrinkled from his plunge into the sea.

Scarcely had Del Mar changed his clothes than he received two visitors. Strangely enough they were men dressed in the uniform of policemen.

"First of all we must convince them of our honesty," he said looking fixedly at the two men. "Orders have been given to the men employed by Wu Fang to be about in half an hour. We must pretend to arrest them on sight. You understand?"

"Yes, sir," they nodded.

"Very well, come on," Del Mar ordered taking up his hat and preceding them from the room.

Outside the La Coste, Del Mar and his two policemen entered the car which had driven Del Mar from the sea coast and were quickly whisked away, up-town, until they came near the Dodge house.

Del Mar leaped from the car followed by his two policemen. "There they are, already," he whispered, pointing up the avenue.

All three hastened up the avenue now where, beside a wall, they could see two men looking through intently as though very angry at something going on inside.

"Arrest them!" shouted Del Mar as his own men ran forward.

The fight was short and sharp, with every evidence of being genuine. One of the men managed to break away and jump the garden wall, with Del Mar and one of the policemen after him, while the other only reached the wall to be dragged down by the other policeman.

Elaine and I had been, as I have said, talking with the man named Bailey who posed as a Secret Service man, when the rumpus began. As the man came over the fence, warning Bailey, it was evident that neither of them had time to escape. With his club the policeman struck the newcomer of the two flat while the tall, athletic gentleman leaped upon Bailey and before we knew it had him disarmed. In a most clean-cut and professional way he snapped the bracelets on the man.

Elaine was astounded at the kaleidoscopic turn of affairs, too astounded even to make an outcry. As for me, it was all so sudden that I had no chance to take part in it. Besides I should not have known quite on which side to fight. So I did nothing.

But as it was over so quickly, I took a step forward to our latest arrival.

"Beg pardon, old man," I began, "but don't you think this is just a little raw? What's it all about?"

The newest comer eyed me for a moment, then with quiet dignity drew from his pocket and handed me his card which read simply:

M. Del Mar, Private Investigator.

As I looked up, I saw Del Mar's other policeman bringing in another manacled man.

9

"These are crooks—foreign agents," replied Del Mar pointing to the prisoners. "The government has employed me to run them down."

"What of this?" asked Elaine holding up the note from Bertrand.

"A fake, a forgery," reiterated Del Mar, looking at it a moment critically. Then to the men uniformed as police he ordered, "You can take them to jail. They're the fellows, all right."

As the prisoners were led off, Del Mar turned to Elaine. "Would you mind answering a few questions about these men?"

"Why—no," she hesitated. "But I think we'd better go into the house, after such a thing as this. It makes me feel nervous."

With Del Mar I followed Elaine in through the conservatory.

.   .   .   .

Del Mar had scarcely registered at the La Coste when the smaller car which had been waiting at the fisherman's hut drew up before the hotel entrance. From it alighted the fussy old gentleman who bore such a remarkable resemblance to the fisherman, hastily paid his driver and entered the hotel.

He went directly to the desk and with well-manicured finger, scarcely reminiscent of a fisherman, began tracing the names down the list until he stoppe' before one which read:

Marcius Del Mar and valet. Washington, D. C. Room 520.

With a quick glance about, he made a note of it,

and turned away, leaving the La Coste to take up quarters of his own in the Prince Henry down the street.

Not until Del Mar had left with his two policemen did the fussy old gentleman reappear in the La Coste. Then he rode up to Del Mar's room and rapped at the door.

" Is Mr. Del Mar in?" he inquired of the valet.

" No, sir," replied that functionary.

The little old man appeared to consider, standing a moment dandling his silk hat. Absent-mindedly he dropped it. As the valet stooped to pick it up, the old gentleman exhibited an agility and strength scarcely to be expected of his years. He seized the valet, while with one foot he kicked the door shut.

Before the surprised servant knew what was going on, his assailant had whipped from his pocket a handkerchief in which was concealed a thin tube of anesthetic. Then leaving the valet prone in a corner with the handkerchief over his face, he proceeded to make a systematic search of the rooms, opening all drawers, trunks and bags.

He turned pretty nearly everything upside down, then started on the desk. Suddenly he paused. There was a paper. He read it, then with an air of extreme elation shoved it into his pocket.

As he was going out he stopped beside the valet, removed the handkerchief from his face and bound him with a cord from the portieres. Then, still immaculate in spite of his encounter, he descended in the elevator, reentered a waiting car and drove off.

Quite evidently, however, he wanted to cover his tracks for he had not gone a half dozen blocks before he stopped, paid and tipped the driver generously, and disappeared into the theatre crowd.

Back again in the Prince Henry, whither the fussy little old man made his way as quickly as he could through a side street, he went quietly up to his room.

His door was now locked. He did not have to deny himself to visitors, for he had none. Still, his room was cluttered by a vast amount of paraphernalia and he was seated before a table deep in work.

First of all he tied a handkerchief over his nose and mouth. Then he took up a cartridge from the table and carefully extracted the bullet. Into the space occupied by the bullet he poured a white powder and added a wad of paper, like a blank cartridge, placing the cartridge in the chamber of a revolver and repeating the operation until he had it fully loaded. It was his own invention of an asphyxiating bullet.

Perhaps half an hour later, the old gentleman, his room cleaned up and his immaculate appearance restored, sauntered forth from the hotel down the street like a veritable Turveydrop, to show himself.

.   .   .   .

Elaine seemed quite impressed with our new friend, Del Mar, as we made our way to the library, though I am not sure but that it was a pose on her part. At any rate he seemed quite eager to help us.

"What do you suppose has become of Mr. Kennedy?" asked Elaine.

Del Mar looked at her earnestly. "I should be glad to search for him," he returned quickly. "He was the greatest man in our profession. But first I must execute the commission of the Secret Service. We must find his torpedo model before it falls into foreign hands."

We talked for a few moments, then Del Mar with a glance at his watch excused himself. We accompanied him to the door, for he was indeed a charming man. I felt that, if in fact he were assigned to the case, I ought to know him better.

"If you're going down-town," I ventured, "I might accompany you part of the way."

"Delighted," agreed Del Mar.

Elaine gave him her hand and he took it in such a deferential way that one could not help liking him. Elaine was much impressed.

As Del Mar and I walked down the avenue, he kept up a running fire of conversation until at last we came near the La Coste.

"Charmed to have met you, Mr. Jameson," he said, pausing. "We shall see a great deal of each other I hope."

I had not yet had time to say good-bye myself when a slight exclamation at my side startled me. Turning suddenly, I saw a very brisk, fussy old gentleman who had evidently been hurrying through the crowd. He had slipped on something on the sidewalk and lost his balance, falling near us.

We bent over and assisted him to his feet. As I took hold of his hand, I felt a peculiar pressure from him. He had placed something in my hand. My mind worked quickly. I checked my first impulse to speak and, more from curiosity than anything else, kept the thing he had passed to me surreptitiously.

"Thank you, gentlemen," he puffed, straightening

himself out. "One of the infirmities of age. Thank you, thank you."

In a moment he had bustled off quite comically.

Again Del Mar said good-bye and I did not urge him to stay. He had scarcely gone when I looked at the thing the old man had placed in my hand. It was a little folded piece of paper. I opened it slowly. Inside was printed in pencil, disguised:

"BE CAREFUL. WATCH HIM."

I read it in amazement. What did it mean?

.   .   .   .

At the La Coste, Del Mar was met by two of his men in the lobby and they rode up to his room.

Imagine their surprise when they opened the door and found the valet lying bound on the floor.

"Who the deuce did this?" demanded Del Mar as they loosened him.

The valet rose weakly to his feet. "A little old man with gray whiskers," he managed to gasp.

Del Mar looked at him in surprise. Instantly his active mind recalled the little old man who had fallen before us on the street.

Who—what was he?

"Come," he said quickly, beckoning his two companions who had come in with him.

Some time later, Del Mar's car stopped just below the Dodge house.

"You men go around back of the house and watch," ordered Del Mar.

As they disappeared he turned and went up the Dodge steps.

.   .   .   .

I walked back after my strange experience with the
fussy little old gentleman, feeling more than ever, now
that Craig was gone, that both Elaine and Aunt Josephine needed me.

As we sat talking in the library, Rusty, released from
the chain on which Jennings kept him, bounded with a
rush into the library.

"Good old fellow," encouraged Elaine, patting him.

Just then Jennings entered and a moment later was
followed by Del Mar, who bowed as we welcomed him.

"Do you know," he began, "I believe that the lost
torpedo model is somewhere in this house and I have
reason to anticipate another attempt of foreign agents
to find it. If you'll pardon me, I've taken the liberty of
surrounding the place with some men we can trust."

While Del Mar was speaking, Elaine picked up a
ribbon from the table and started to tie it about
Rusty's neck. As Del Mar proceeded she paused, still
holding the ribbon. Rusty, who hated ribbons, saw
his chance and quietly sidled out, seeking refuge in the
conservatory.

Alone in the conservatory, Rusty quickly forgot
about the ribbon and began nosing about the palms. At
last he came to the pot in which the torpedo model had
been buried in the soft earth by the thief the night it
had been stolen from the fountain.

Quickly Elaine recalled herself and, seeing the ribbon in her hand and Rusty gone, called him. There
was no answer, and she excused herself, for it was
against the rules for Rusty to wander about.

In his haste the thief had left just a corner of the

handkerchief sticking out of the dirt. What none of us had noticed, Rusty's keen eyes and nose discovered and his instinct told him to dig for it. In a moment he uncovered the torpedo and handkerchief and sniffed.

Just then he heard his mistress calling him. Rusty had been whipped for digging in the conservatory and now, with his tail between his legs, he seized the torpedo in his mouth and bolted for the door of the drawing-room, for he had heard voices in the library. As he did so he dropped the handkerchief and the little propeller, loosened by his teeth, fell off.

Elaine entered the conservatory, still calling. Rusty was not there. He had reached the stairs, scurrying up to the attic, still holding the torpedo model in his mouth. He pushed open the attic door and ran in. Rusty's last refuge in time of trouble was back of a number of trunks, among which were two of almost the same size and appearance. Behind one of them, he had hidden a miscellaneous collection of bones, pieces of biscuit and things dear to his heart. He dropped the torpedo among these treasures.

Del Mar, meanwhile, had followed Elaine through the hall and into the conservatory. As he entered he could see her stooping down to look through the palms for Rusty. She straightened up and went on out.

Del Mar followed. Beside the palm pot where Rusty had found the torpedo, he happened to see the old handkerchief soiled with dirt. Near-by lay the little propeller. He picked them up.

"She has found it!" he exclaimed in wonder, following Elaine.

By this time Rusty had responded to Elaine's calls and came tearing down-stairs again.

" Naughty Rusty," chided Elaine, tying the ribbon on him.

" So—you have found him at last? " remarked Del Mar looking quickly at Elaine to see if she would get a double meaning.

" Yes. He's had a fine time running away," she replied.

Del Mar was scarcely able to conceal his suspicion of her. Was she a clever actress, hiding her discovery, he wondered?

.   .   .   .

Outside, on the lawn, Del Mar's men had been looking about, but had discovered nothing. They paused a moment to speak.

" Look out! " whispered one of them. " There's some one coming."

They dropped down in the shadow. There in the light of the street lamps was the fussy old gentleman coming across the lawn. He stole up to the door of the conservatory and looked through. Del Mar's men crawled a few feet closer. The little old man entered the conservatory and looked about again stealthily. The two men followed him in noiselessly and watched as he bent over the palm pot from which the dog had dug up the torpedo. He looked at the hole curiously. Just then he heard sounds behind him and sprang to his feet.

" Hands up! " ordered one of the men covering him with a gun.

The little old man threw up his hands, raising his cane still in his right hand. The man with the gun took a step closer. As he did so, the little old man brought down his cane with a quick blow and knocked the gun out of his hand. The second man seized the cane. The old man jerked the cane back and was standing there with a thin tough steel rapier. It was a sword-cane. Del Mar's man held the sheath.

As the man attacked with the sheath, the little old man parried, sent it flying from his grasp, and wounded him. The wounded man sank down, while the little old man ran off through the palms, followed by the other of Del Mar's men.

Around the hall, he ran, and back into the conservatory where he picked up a heavy chair and threw it through the glass, dropping himself behind a convenient hiding-place near-by. Del Mar's man, close after him, mistaking the crash of glass for the escape of the man he was pursuing, went on through the broken exit. Then the little old man doubled on his tracks and made for the front of the house.

.   .   .   .

With Aunt Josephine I had remained in the library.

"What's that?" I exclaimed at the first sounds. "A fight?"

Together we rushed for the conservatory.

The fight followed so quickly by the crash of glass also alarmed Elaine and Del Mar in the hallway and they hurried toward the library, which we had just left, by another door.

As they entered, they saw a little old gentleman rushing in from the conservatory and locking the door behind him. He whirled about, and he and Del Mar recognized each other at once. They drew guns together, but the little old man fired first.

His bullet struck the wall back of Del Mar and a cloud of vapor was instantly formed, enveloping Del Mar and even Elaine. Del Mar fell, overcome, while Elaine sank more slowly. The little old man ran forward.

In the conservatory, Aunt Josephine and I heard the shooting, just as one of Del Mar's men ran in again. With him we ran back toward the library.

By this time the whole house was aroused. Jennings and Marie were hurrying down-stairs, crying for help and making their way to the library also.

In the library, the little old man bent over Del Mar and Elaine. But it was only a moment later that he heard the whole house aroused. Quickly he shut and locked the folding-doors to the drawing-room, as, with Del Mar's man, I was beating at the rear library door.

"I'll go around," I suggested, hurrying off, while Del Mar's man tried to beat in the door.

Inside the little old man who had been listening saw that there was no means of escape. He pulled off his coat and vest and turned them inside out. On the inside he had prepared an exact copy of Jennings' livery.

It was only a matter of seconds before he had completed his change. For a moment he paused and looked at the two prostrate figures before him. Then he took a rose from a vase on the table and placed it in Elaine's hand.

Finally, with his whiskers and wig off he moved to the rear door where Del Mar's man was beating and opened it.

"Look," he cried pointing in an agitated way at
Del Mar and Elaine. " What shall we do?"

Del Mar's man, who had never seen Jennings, ran
to his master and the little old man, in his new disguise,
slipped quietly into the hall and out the front door,
where he had a taxicab waiting for him, down the
street.

A moment later I burst open the other library door
and Aunt Josephine followed me in, just as Jennings
himself and Marie entered from the drawing-room.

It was only a moment before we had Del Mar, who
was most in need of care, on the sofa and Elaine, already regaining consciousness, lay back in a deep easy
chair.

As Del Mar moved, I turned again to Elaine who
was now nearly recovered.

"How do you feel?" I asked anxiously.

Her throat was parched by the asphyxiating fumes,
but she smiled brightly, though weakly.

"Wh-where did I get that?" she managed to gasp
finally, catching sight of the rose in her hand. "Did
you put it there?"

I shook my head and she gazed at the rose, wondering.

Whoever the little man was, he was gone.

I longed for Craig.

CHAPTER VII

So confident was Elaine that Kennedy was still **alive** that she would not admit to herself what to the **rest** of us seemed obvious.

She even refused to accept Aunt Josephine's hints and decided to give a masquerade ball which she **had** planned as the last event of the season before she closed the Dodge town house and opened her country house **on** the shore of Connecticut.

It was shortly after the strange appearance of **the** fussy old gentleman that I dropped in one afternoon to find Elaine addressing invitations, while **Aunt** Josephine helped her. As we chatted, I picked up one from the pile and mechanically contemplated the **ad**dress:

" M. Del Mar, Hotel La Coste, New York City."

" I don't like that fellow," I remarked, shaking my head dubiously.

" Oh, you're—jealous, Walter," laughed Elaine, taking the envelope away from me and piling it again with the others.

Thus it was that in the morning's mail, Del **Mar**, along with the rest of us, received a neatly **engraved** little invitation:

141

Miss Elaine Dodge
requests the pleasure
of your presence at the
masquerade ball to be
given at her residence
on Friday evening
June 1st.

"Good!" he exclaimed, reaching for the telephone,
"I'll go."

.   .   .   .

In a restaurant in the white light district two of
those who had been engaged in the preliminary plot to
steal Kennedy's wireless torpedo model, the young
woman stenographer who had betrayed her trust and
the man to whom she had passed the model out of the
window in Washington, were seated at a table.

So secret had been the relations of all those in the
plot that one group did not know the other and the
strangest methods of communication had been adopted.

The man removed a cover from a dish. Underneath,
perhaps without even the waiter's knowledge, was a
note.

"Here are the orders at last," he whispered to the
girl, unfolding and reading the note. "Look. The
model of the torpedo is somewhere in her house. Go
to-night to the ball as a masquerader and search for it."

"Oh, splendid!" exclaimed the girl. "I'm crazy
for a little society after this grind. Pay the check and
let's get out and choose our costumes."

The man paid the check and they left hurriedly.
Half an hour later they were at a costumer's shop

choosing their disguises, both careful to get the fullest masks that would not excite suspicion.

.   .   .   .

It was the night of the masquerade.

During the afternoon Elaine had been thinking more than ever of Kennedy. It all seemed unreal to her. More than once she stopped to look at his photograph. Several times she checked herself on the point of tears.

"No," she said to herself with a sort of grim determination. "No—he *is* alive. He will come back to me—he *will*."

And yet she had a feeling of terrific loneliness which even her most powerful efforts could not throw off. She was determined to go through with the ball, now that she had started it, but she was really glad when it came time to dress, for even that took her mind from her brooding.

As Marie finished helping her put on a very effective and conspicuous costume, Aunt Josephine entered her dressing-room.

"Are you ready, my dear?" she asked, adjusting the mask which she carried so that no one would recognize her as Martha Washington.

"In just a minute, Auntie," answered Elaine, trying hard to put out of her mind how Craig would have liked her dress.

Somewhat earlier, in my own apartment, I had been arraying myself as Boum-Boum and modestly admiring the imitation I made of a circus clown as I did a couple of comedy steps before the mirror.

But I was not really so light-hearted. I could not

help thinking of what this night might have been if Kennedy had been alive. Indeed, I was glad to take up my white mask, throw a long coat over my outlandish costume and hurry off in my waiting car in order to forget everything that reminded me of him in the apartment.

Already a continuous stream of guests was trickling in through the canopy from the curb to the Dodge door, carriages and automobiles arriving and leaving amid great gaping from the crowd on the sidewalk.

As I entered the ballroom it was really a brilliant and picturesque assemblage. Of course I recognized Elaine in spite of her mask, almost immediately.

Characteristically, she was talking to the one most striking figure on the floor, a tall man in red—a veritable Mephistopheles. As the music started, Elaine and his Satanic Majesty laughingly fox-trotted off but were not lost to me in the throng.

I soon found myself talking to a young lady in a spotted domino. She seemed to have a peculiar fascination for me, yet she did not monopolize all my attention. As we trotted past the door, I could see down the hall. Jennings was still admitting late arrivals, and I caught a glimpse of one costumed as a gray friar, his cowl over his head and his eyes masked.

Chatting, we had circled about to the conservatory. A number of couples were there and, through the palms, I saw Elaine and Mephisto laughingly make their way.

As my spotted domino partner and I swung around again, I happened to catch another glimpse of the gray friar. He was not dancing, but walking, or rather stalking, about the edge of the room, gazing about as if searching for some one.

In the conservatory, Elaine and Mephisto had seated themselves in the breeze of an open window, somewhat in the shadow.

" You are Miss Dodge," he said earnestly.

" You knew me? " she laughed. " And you? "

He raised his mask, disclosing the handsome face and fascinating eyes of Del Mar.

" I hope you don't think I'm here in character," he laughed easily, as she started a bit.

" I—I—well, I didn't think it was you," she blurted out.

" Ah—then there is some one else you care more to dance with? "

" No—no one—no."

" I may hope, then? "

He had moved closer and almost touched her hand. The pointed hood of the gray friar in the palms showed that at last he saw what he sought.

" No—no. Please—excuse me," she murmured rising and hurrying back to the ballroom.

A subtle smile spread over the gray friar's masked face.

Of course I had known Elaine. Whether she knew me at once I don't know or whether it was an accident, but she approached me as I paused in the dance a moment with my domino girl.

" From the—sublime—to the ridiculous," she cried excitedly.

My partner gave her a sharp glance. " You will excuse me? " she said, and, as I bowed, almost ran off

10

to the conservatory, leaving Elaine to dance off with me.

.   .   .   .

Del Mar, quite surprised at the sudden flight of Elaine from his side, followed more slowly through the palms.

As he did so he passed a Mexican attired in brilliant native costume. At a sign from Del Mar he paused and received a small package which Del Mar slipped to him, then passed on as though nothing had happened. The keen eyes of the gray friar, however, had caught the little action and he quietly slipped out after the Mexican bolero.

Just then the domino girl hurried into the conservatory. " What's doing? " she asked eagerly.

" Keep close to me," whispered Del Mar, as she nodded and they left the conservatory, not apparently together.

Up-stairs, away from the gayety of the ballroom, the bolero made his way until he came to Elaine's room, dimly lighted. With a quick glance about, he entered cautiously, closed the door, and approached a closet which he opened. There was a safe built into the wall.

As he stooped over, the man unwrapped the package Del Mar had handed him and took out a curious little instrument. Inside was a dry battery and a most peculiar instrument, something like a little flat telephone transmitter, yet attached by wires to ear-pieces that fitted over the head after the manner of those of a wireless detector.

He adjusted the head-piece and held the flat instru-

ment against the safe, close to the combination which
he began to turn slowly. It was a burglar's microphone, used for picking combination locks. As the
combination turned, a slight sound was made when
the proper number came opposite the working point.
Imperceptible ordinarily to even the most sensitive ear,
to an ear trained it was comparatively easy to recognize the fall of the tumblers over this microphone.

As he worked, the door behind him opened softly
and the gray friar entered, closing it and moving noiselessly over back of the shelter of a big mahogany
high-boy, around which he could watch.

At last the safe was opened. Rapidly the man went
through its contents. "Confound it!" he muttered.
"She didn't put it here—anyhow."

The bolero started to close the safe when he heard
a noise in the room and looked cautiously back of him.
Del Mar himself, followed by the domino girl, entered.

"I've opened it," whispered the emissary stepping
out of the closet and meeting them, "but I can't find
the——"

"Hands up—all of you!"

They turned in time to see the gray friar's gun
yawning at them. Most politely he lined them up.
Still holding his gun ready, he lifted up the mask of
the domino girl.

"So—it's you," he grunted.

He was about to lift the mask of the Mexican, when
the bolero leaped at him. Del Mar piled in. But
sounds down-stairs alarmed them and the emissary,
released, fled quickly with the girl. The gray friar,

however, kept his hold on Mephistopheles, as if he had been wrestling with a veritable devil.

.   .   .   .

Down in the hall, I had again met my domino girl, a few minutes after I had resigned Elaine to another of her numerous admirers.

"I thought you deserted me," I said, somewhat piqued.

"You deserted me," she parried, nervously. "However, I'll forgive you if you'll get me an ice."

I hastened to do so. But no sooner had I gone than Del Mar stalked through the hall and went up-stairs. My domino girl was watching for him, and followed.

When I returned with the ice, I looked about, but she was gone. It was scarcely a moment later, however, that I saw her hurry down-stairs, accompanied by the Mexican bolero. I stepped forward to speak to her, but she almost ran past me without a word.

"A nut," I remarked under my breath, pushing back my mask.

I started to eat the ice myself, when, a moment later, Elaine passed through the hall with a Spanish cavalier.

"Oh, Walter, here you are," she laughed. "I've been looking all over for you. Thank you very much, sire," she bowed with mock civility to the cavalier. "It was only one dance, you know. Please let me talk to Boum-Boum."

The cavalier bowed reluctantly and left us.

"What are you doing here alone?" she asked, taking off her own mask. "How warm it is."

Before I could reply, I heard some one coming down-stairs back of me, but not in time to turn.

"Elaine's dressing-table," a voice whispered in my ear.

I turned suddenly. It was the gray friar. Before I could even reach out to grasp his robe, he was gone.

"Another nut!" I exclaimed involuntarily.

"Why, what did he say?" asked Elaine.

"Something about your dressing-table."

"My dressing-table?" she repeated.

We ran quickly up the steps. Elaine's room showed every evidence of having been the scene of a struggle, as she went over to the table. There she picked up a rose and under it a piece of paper on which were some words printed with pencil roughly.

"Look," she cried, as I read with her:

> Do honest assistants search safes?
> Let no one see this but Jameson.

"What does it mean?" I asked.

"My safe!" she cried moving to a closet. As she opened the door, imagine our surprise at seeing Del Mar lying on the floor, bound and gagged before the open safe. "Get my scissors on the dresser," cried Elaine.

I did so, hastily cutting the cords that bound Del Mar.

"What does it all mean?" asked Elaine as he rose and stretched himself.

Still clutching his throat, as if it hurt, Del Mar choked, "I found a man, a foreign agent, searching the safe. But he overcame me and escaped."

"Oh—then that is what the—"

Elaine checked herself. She had been about to hand the note to Del Mar when an idea seemed to come to her. Instead, she crumpled it up and thrust it into her bosom.

On the street the bolero and the domino girl were hurrying away as fast as they could.

Meanwhile, the gray friar had overcome Del Mar, had bound and gagged him, and trust him into the closet. Then he wrote the note and laid it, with a rose from a vase, on Elaine's dressing-table before he, too, followed.

More than ever I was at a loss to make it out.

.   .   .   .

It was the day after the masquerade ball that a taxicab drove up to the Dodge house and a very trim but not over-dressed young lady was announced as " Miss Bertholdi."

" Miss Dodge? " she inquired as Jennings held open the portieres and she entered the library where Elaine and Aunt Josephine were.

If Elaine had only known, it was the domino girl of the night before who handed her a note and sat down, looking about so demurely, while Elaine read:

MY DEAR MISS DODGE,

The bearer, Miss Bertholdi, is an operative of mine. I would appreciate it if you would employ her in some capacity in your house, as I have reason to believe that certain foreign agents will soon make another attempt to find Kennedy's lost torpedo model.

Sincerely,

M. DEL MAR.

Elaine looked up from reading the note. Miss Bertholdi was good to look at, and Elaine liked pretty girls about her.

" Jennings," she ordered, " call Marie."

To the butler and her maid, Elaine gave the most careful instructions regarding Miss Bertholdi. " She can help you finish the packing, first," she concluded.

The girl thanked her and went out with Jennings and Marie, asking Jennings to pay her taxicab driver with money she gave him, which he did, bringing her grip into the house.

Later in the day, Elaine had both Marie and Bertholdi carrying armsful of her dresses from the closets in her room up to the attic where the last of her trunks were being packed. On one of the many trips, Bertholdi came alone into the attic, her arms full as usual. Before her were two trunks, very much alike, open and nearly packed. She laid her armful of clothes on a chair near-by and pulled one of the trunks forward. On the floor lay the trays of both trunks already packed. Bertholdi began packing her burden in one trunk which was marked in big white letters, " E. Dodge."

Down in Elaine's room at the time Jennings entered. " The expressman for the trunks is here, Miss Elaine," he announced.

" Is he? I wonder whether they are all ready," Elaine replied hurrying out of the room. " Tell him to wait."

In the attic, Bertholdi was still at work, keeping her eyes open to execute the mission on which Del Mar had sent her.

Rusty, forgotten in the excitement by Jennings, had roamed at will through the house and seemed quite interested.   For this was the trunk behind which he had his cache of treasures.

As Bertholdi started to move behind the trunk, Rusty could stand it no longer. He darted ahead of her into his hiding-place.   Among the dog biscuit and bones was the torpedo model which he had dug up from the palm pot in the conservatory.   He seized it in his mouth and turned to carry it off.

There, in his path, was his enemy, the new girl. Quick as a flash, she saw what it was Rusty had, and grabbed at it.

" Get out! " she ordered, looking at her prize in triumph and turning it over and over in her hands.

At that moment she heard Elaine on the stairs. What should she do? She must hide it. She looked about.   There was the tray, packed and lying on the floor near the trunk marked, " E. Dodge." She thrust it hastily into the tray pulling a garment over it.

" Nearly through? " panted Elaine.

" Yes, Miss Dodge."

" Then please tell the expressman to come up."

Bertholdi hesitated, chagrined.   Yet there was nothing to do but obey.   She looked at the trunk by the tray to fix it in her mind, then went down-stairs.

As she left the room, Elaine lifted the tray into the trunk and tried to close the lid. But the tray was too high. She looked puzzled. On the floor was another tray almost identical.

" The wrong trunk," she smiled to herself, lifting the tray out and putting the other one in, while she placed the first tray with the torpedo concealed in the other, unmarked, trunk where it belonged. Then she closed the first trunk.

A moment later the expressman entered, with Bertholdi.

" You may take that one," indicated Elaine.

" Miss Dodge, here's something else to go in," said Bertholdi in desperation, picking up a dress.

" Never mind. Put it in the other trunk."

Bertholdi was baffled, but she managed to control herself. She must get word to Del Mar about that trunk marked " E. Dodge."

.   .   .   .

Late that afternoon, before a cheap restaurant might have been seen our old friend who had posed as Bailey and as the Mexican. He entered the restaurant and made his way to the first of a row of booths on one side.

" Hello," he nodded to a girl in the booth.

Bertholdi nodded back and he took his seat. She had begged an hour or two off on some pretext.

Outside the restaurant, a heavily-bearded man had been standing looking intently at nothing in particular when Bertholdi entered. As Bailey came along, he followed and took the next booth, his hat pulled over his eyes. In a moment he was listening, his ear close up to the partition.

" Well, what luck? " asked Bailey. " Did you get a clue? "

" I had the torpedo model in my hands," she replied, excitedly telling the story. " It is in a trunk marked ' E. Dodge.' "

All this and more the bearded stranger drank in eagerly.

A moment later Bailey and Bertholdi left the booth and went out of the restaurant followed cautiously by the stranger.   On the street the two emissaries of Del Mar stopped a moment to talk.

"All right, I'll telephone him," she said as they parted in opposite directions.

The stranger took an instant to make up his mind, then followed the girl.   She continued down the street until she came to a store with telephone booths.   The bearded stranger followed still, into the next booth but did not call a number.   He had his ear to the wall.

He could hear her call Del Mar, and although he could not hear Del Mar's answers, she repeated enough for him to catch the drift.   Finally, she came out, and the stranger, instead of following her further, took the other direction hurriedly.

.   .   .   .

Del Mar himself received the news with keen excitement.   Quickly he gave instructions and prepared to leave his rooms.

A short time later his car pulled up before the La Coste and, in a long duster and cap, Del Mar jumped in, and was off.

Scarcely had his car swung up the avenue when, from an alleyway down the street from the hotel, the chug-chug of a motor-cycle sounded.   A bearded man, his face further hidden by a pair of goggles, ran out with his machine, climbed on and followed.

On out into the country Del Mar's car sped.   At every turn the motor-cycle dropped back a bit, observed the turn, then crept up and took it, too. So they went for some time.

.   .   .   .

On the level of the Grand Central where the trains left for the Connecticut shore where Elaine's summer home was located, Bailey was now edging his way through the late crowd down the platform. He paused before the baggage-car just as one of the baggage motor trucks rolled up loaded high with trunks and bags. He stepped back as the men loaded the luggage on the car, watching carefully.

As they tossed on one trunk marked " E. Dodge," he turned with a subtle look and walked away. Finally he squirmed around to the other platform. No one was looking and he mounted the rear of the baggage-car and opened the door. There was the baggageman sitting by the side door, his back to Bailey. Bailey closed the door softly and squeezed behind a pile of trunks and bags.

.   .   .   .

Finally Del Mar reached a spot on the railroad where there were both a curve and a grade ahead. He stopped his car and got out.

Down the road the bearded and goggled motor-cyclist stopped just in time to avoid observation. To make sure, he drew a pocket field-glass and leveled it ahead.

" Wait here," ordered Del Mar. " I'll call when I want you."

Back on the road the bearded cyclist could see Del Mar move down the track though he could not hear the directions. It was not necessary, however. He

dragged his machine into the bushes, hid it, and hurried down the road on foot.

Del Mar's chauffeur was waiting idly at the wheel
when suddenly the cold nose of a revolver was stuck
under his chin.

" Not a word—and hands up—or I'll let the moonlight through you," growled out a harsh voice.

Nevertheless, the chauffeur managed to lurch out of
the car and the bearded stranger, whose revolver it
was, found that he would have to shoot. Del Mar was
not far enough away to risk it.

The chauffeur flung himself on him and they struggled fiercely, rolling over and over in the dust of the
road.

But the bearded stranger had a grip of steel and
managed to get his fingers about the chauffeur's throat
as an added insurance against a cry for help.

He choked him literally into insensibility. Then,
with a strength that he did not seem to possess, he
picked up the limp, blue-faced body and carried it off
the road and around the car.

.   .   .   .

In the baggage-car, the baggageman was smoking a
surreptitious pipe of powerful tobacco between stations
and contemplating the scenery thoughtfully through
the open door.

As the engine slowed up to take a curve and a grade,
Bailey who had now and then taken a peep out of a
little grated window above him, crept out from his
hiding-place. Already he had slipped a dark silk mask
over his face.

As he made his way among the trunks and boxes,

the train lurched and the baggageman who had his back to Bailey heard him catch himself. He turned and leaped to his feet. Bailey closed with him instantly.

Over and over they rolled. Bailey had already drawn his revolver before he left his hiding-place. A shot, however, would have been fatal to his part in the plans and was only a last resort for it would have brought the trainmen.

Finally Bailey rolled his man over and getting his right arm free, dealt the baggageman a fierce blow with the butt of the gun.

The train was now pulling slowly up the grade. More time had been spent in overcoming the baggageman than he expected and Bailey had to work quickly. He dragged the trunk marked "E. Dodge" from the pile to the door and glanced out.

.   .   .   .

Just around the curve in the railroad, Del Mar was waiting, straining his eyes down the track.

There was the train, puffing up the grade. As it approached he rose and waved his arms. It was the signal and he waited anxiously. Had his plans been carried out?

The train passed. From the baggage-car came a trunk catapulted out by a strong arm. It hurtled through the air and landed with its own and the train's momentum.

Over it rolled in the bushes, then stopped—unbroken, for Elaine had had it designed to resist even the most violent baggage-smasher.

Del Mar ran to it. As the tail light of the train disappeared he turned around in the direction from which he had come, placed his two hands to his mouth and shouted.

.   .   .   .

From the side of the road by Del Mar's car the bearded motor-cyclist had just emerged, buttoning the chauffeur's clothes and adjusting his goggles to his own face.

As he approached the car, he heard a shout. Quickly he tore off the black beard which had been his disguise and tossed it into the grass. Then he drew the coat high up about his neck.

" All right!" he shouted back, starting along the road.

Together he and Del Mar managed to scramble up the embankment to the road and, one at each handle of the trunk, they carried it back to the car, piling it in the back.

The improvised chauffeur started to take his place at the wheel and Del Mar had his foot on the running-board to get beside him, when the now unbearded stranger suddenly swung about and struck Del Mar full in the face. It sent him reeling back into the dust.

The engine of the car had been running and before Del Mar could recover consciousness, the stranger had shot the car ahead, leaving Del Mar prone in the roadway.

.   .   .   .

The train, with Bailey on it, had not gained much speed, yet it was a perilous undertaking to leap. Still, it was more so now to remain. The baggageman stirred. It was now a case of murder or a getaway.

Bailey jumped.

Scratched and bruised and shaken, he scrambled to his feet in the briars along the track. He staggered up to the road, pulled himself together, then hurried back as fast as his barked shins would let him.

He came to the spot which he recognized as that where he had thrown off the trunk. He saw the trampled and broken bushes and made for the road.

He had not gone far when he saw, far down, Del Mar suddenly attacked and thrown down, apparently by his own chauffeur. Bailey ran forward, but it was too late. The car was gone.

As he came up to Del Mar lying outstretched in the road, Del Mar was just recovering consciousness.

"What was the matter?" he asked. "Was he a traitor?"

He caught sight of the real chauffeur on the ground, stripped.

Del Mar was furious. "No," he swore, "it was that confounded gray friar again, I think. And he has the trunk, too!"

.   .   .   .

Speeding up the road the former masquerader and motor-cyclist stopped at last.

Eagerly he leaped out of Del Mar's car and dragged the trunk over the side regardless of the enamel.

It was the work of only a moment for him to break the lock with a pocket jimmy.

One after another he pulled out and shook the clothes

until frocks and gowns and lingerie lay strewn all about.

But there was not a thing in the trunk that even remotely resembled the torpedo model.

The stranger scowled.

Where was it?

CHAPTER VIII

THE VANISHING MAN

DEL MAR had evidently, by this time, come to the conclusion that Elaine was the storm centre of the peculiar train of events that followed the disappearance of Kennedy and his wireless torpedo.

At any rate, as soon as he learned that Elaine was going to her country home for the summer, he took a bungalow some distance from Dodge Hall. In fact, it was more than a bungalow, for it was a pretentious place surrounded by a wide lawn and beautiful shade trees.

There, on the day that Elaine decided to motor in from the city, Del Mar arrived with his valet.

Evidently he lost no time in getting to work on his own affairs, whatever they might be. Inside his study, which was the largest room in the house, a combination of both library and laboratory, he gave an order or two to his valet, then immediately sat down to his new desk. He opened a drawer and took out a long hollow cylinder, closed at each end by air-tight caps, on one of which was a hook.

Quickly he wrote a note and read it over: " Install submarine bell in place of these clumsy tubes. Am having harbor and bridges mined as per instructions from Government. D."

He unscrewed the cap at one end of the tube, inserted the note and closed it. Then he pushed a button on his desk. A panel in the wall opened and one of the men who had played policeman once for him stepped out and saluted.

"Here's a message to send below," said Del Mar briefly.

The man bowed and went back through the panel, closing it.

Del Mar cleaned up his desk and then went out to look his new quarters over, to see whether everything had been prepared according to his instructions.

From the concealed entrance to a cave on a hillside, Del Mar's man who had gone through the panel in the bungalow appeared a few minutes later and hurried down to the shore. It was a rocky coast with stretches of cliffs and now and then a ravine and bit of sandy beach. Gingerly he climbed down the rocks to the water.

He took from his pocket the metal tube which Del Mar had given him and to the hook on one end attached a weight of lead. A moment he looked about cautiously. Then he threw the tube into the water and it sank quickly. He did not wait, but hurried back into the cave entrance.

  • • • ◦ ◦ • • • •

Elaine, Aunt Josephine and I motored down to Dodge Hall from the city. Elaine's country house was on a fine estate near the Long Island Sound and after the long run we were glad to pull up before the big house and get out of the car. As we approached the door, I happened to look down the road.

"Well, that's the country, all right," I exclaimed, pointing down the road. "Look."

Lumbering along was a huge heavy hay rack on top of which perched a farmer chewing a straw. Following along after him was a dog of a peculiar shepherd breed which I did not recognize. Atop of the hay the old fellow had piled a trunk and a basket.

To our surprise the hay rack stopped before the house. "Miss Dodge?" drawled the farmer nasally.

"Why, what do you suppose he can want?" asked Elaine moving out toward the wagon while we followed. "Yes?"

"Here's a trunk, Miss Dodge, with your name on it," he went on dragging it down. "I found it down by the railroad track."

It was the trunk marked "E. Dodge" which had been thrown off the train, taken by Del Mar and rifled by the motor-cyclist.

"How do you suppose it ever got here?" cried Elaine in wonder.

"Must have fallen off the train," I suggested. "You might have collected the insurance under this new baggage law!"

"Jennings," called Elaine. "Get Patrick and carry the trunk in."

Together the butler and the gardener dragged it off.

"Thank you," said Elaine, endeavoring to pay the farmer.

"No, no, Miss," he demurred as he clucked to his horses.

We waved to the old fellow. As he started to drive away, he reached down into the basket and drew out

some yellow harvest apples. One at a time he tossed
them to us as he lumbered off.

"Truly rural," remarked a voice behind us.

It was Del Mar, all togged up and carrying a magazine in his hand.

We chatted a moment, then Elaine started to go into
the house with Aunt Josephine. With Del Mar I
followed.

As she went Elaine took a bite of the apple. To
her surprise it separated neatly into two hollow halves.
She looked inside. There was a note. Carefully she
unfolded it and read. Like the others, it was not
written but printed in pencil:

> Be careful to unpack all your trunks your-
> self. Destroy this note.—A Friend.

What did these mysterious warnings mean, she
asked herself in amazement. Somehow so far they
had worked out all right. She tore up the note and
threw the pieces away.

Del Mar and I stopped for a moment to talk. I
did not notice that he was not listening to me, but was
surreptitiously watching Elaine.

Elaine went into the house and we followed. Del
Mar, however, dropped just a bit behind and, as he
came to the place where Elaine had thrown the pieces
of paper, dropped his magazine. He stooped to pick
it up and gathered the pieces, then rejoined us.

"I hope you'll excuse me," said Elaine brightly.
"We've just arrived and I haven't a thing unpacked."

Del Mar bowed and Elaine left us. Aunt Josephine

followed shortly. Del Mar and I sat down at a table. As he talked he placed the magazine in his lap beneath the table, on his knees. I could not see, but he was in reality secretly putting together the torn note which the farmer had thrown to Elaine.

Finally he managed to fit all the pieces. A glance down was enough. But his face betrayed nothing. Still under the table, he swept the pieces into his pocket and rose.

"I'll drop in when you are more settled," he excused himself, strolling leisurely out again.

.   .   .   .

Up in the bedroom Elaine's maid, Marie, had been unpacking.

"Well, what do you know about that?" she exclaimed as Jennings and Patrick came dragging in the banged-up trunk.

"Very queer," remarked Jennings, detailing the little he had seen, while Patrick left.

The entrance of Elaine put an end to the interesting gossip and Marie started to open the trunk.

"No, Marie," said Elaine. "I'll unpack them myself. You can put the things away later. You and Jennings may go."

Quickly she took the things out of the battered trunk. Then she started on the other trunk which was like it but not marked. She threw out a couple of garments, then paused, startled.

There was the lost torpedo—where Bertholdi had stuck it in her haste! Elaine picked it up and looked at it in wonder as it recalled all those last days before

Kennedy was lost. For the moment she did not know quite what to make of it. What should she do?

Finally she decided to lock it up in the bureau drawer and tell me. Not only did she lock the drawer but, as she left her room, she took the key of the door from the lock inside and locked it outside.

.   .   .   .

Del Mar did not go far from the house, however. He scarcely reached the edge of the grounds where he was sure he was not observed when he placed his fingers to his lips and whistled. An instant later two of his men appeared from behind a hedge.

"You must get into her room," he ordered. "That torpedo is in her luggage somewhere, after all."

They bowed and disappeared again into the shrubbery while Del Mar turned and retraced his steps to the house.

In the rear of the house the two emissaries of Del Mar stole out of the shelter of some bushes and stood for a moment looking. Elaine's windows were high above them, too high to reach. There seemed to be no way to get to them and there was no ladder in sight.

"We'll have to use the Dutch house-man's method," decided one.

Together they went around the house toward the laundry. It was only a few minutes later that they returned. No one was about. Quickly one of them took off his coat. Around his waist he had wound a coil of rope. Deftly he began to climb a tree whose upper branches fell over the roof. Cat-like he made his way out along a branch and managed to reach the roof. He made his way along the ridge pole to a

chimney which was directly back of and in line with
Elaine's windows.   Then he uncoiled the rope and
made one end fast to the chimney.   Letting the other
end fall free down the roof, he carefully lowered himself over the edge.   Thus it was not difficult to get
into Elaine's room by stepping on the window-sill and
going through the open window.

The man began a rapid search of the room, turning
up and pawing everything that Elaine had unpacked.
Then he began on the little writing-desk, the dresser
and the bureau drawers.   A subtle smile flashed over
his face as he came to one drawer that was locked.
He pulled a sectional jimmy from his coat and forced
it open.

There lay the precious torpedo.

The man clutched at it with a look of exultation.
Without another glance at the room he rushed to the
window, seized the rope and pulled himself to the roof,
going as he had come.

.   .   .   .

It did not take me long to unpack the few things I
had brought and I was soon back again in the living-
room, where Aunt Josephine joined me in a few minutes.

Just as Elaine came hurriedly down the stairway
and started toward me, Del Mar entered from the
porch.   She stopped.   Del Mar watched her closely.
Had she found anything?   He was sure of it.

Her hesitation was only for a moment, however.
"Walter," she said, "may I speak to you a moment?
Excuse us, please?"

Aunt Josephine went out toward the back of the

house to see how the servants were getting on, while I followed Elaine up-stairs. Del Mar with a bow seated himself and opened his magazine. No sooner had we gone, however, than he laid it down and cautiously followed us.

Elaine was evidently very much excited as she entered her dainty little room and closed the door. "Walter," she cried, "I've found the torpedo!"

We looked about at the general disorder. "Why," she exclaimed nervously, "some one has been here—and I locked the door, too."

She almost ran over to her bureau drawer. It had been jimmied open in the few minutes while she was down-stairs. The torpedo was gone. We looked at each other, aghast.

Behind us, however, we did not see the keen and watchful eyes of Del Mar, opening the door and peering in. As he saw us, he closed the door softly, went down-stairs and out of the house.

.   .   .   .

Perhaps half a mile down the road, the farmer abandoned his hay rack and now, followed by his peculiar dog, walked back. He stopped at a point in the road where he could see the Dodge house in the distance, sat on the rail fence and lighted a blackened corn-cob pipe.

There he sat for some time apparently engrossed in his own thoughts about the weather, the dog lying at his feet. Now and then he looked fixedly toward Dodge Hall.

Suddenly his vagrant attention seemed to be riveted on the house. He drew a field-glass from his pocket

and levelled it. Sure enough, there was a man coming
out of a window, pulling himself up to the roof by a
rope and going across the roof tree. He lowered the
glasses quickly and climbed off the fence with a hith-
erto unwonted energy.

"Come, Searchlight," he called to the dog, as together they moved off quickly in the direction he had
been looking.

Del Mar's men were coming through the hedge that
surrounded the Dodge estate just as the farmer and
his dog stepped out in front of them from behind a
thicket.

"Just a minute," he called. "I want to speak to
you."

He enforced his words with a vicious looking gun.
It was two to one and they closed with him. Before
he could shoot, they had knocked the gun out of his
hand. Then they tried to break away and run.

But the farmer seized one of them and held him.
Meanwhile the dog developed traits all his own. He
ran in and out between the legs of the other man until
he threw him. There he stood, over him. The man
attempted to rise. Again the dog threw him and kept
him down. He was a trained Belgian sheep hound, a
splendid police dog.

"Confound the brute," growled the man, reaching
for his gun.

As he drew it, the dog seized his wrist and with a
cry the man dropped the gun. That, too, was part of
the dog's training.

While the farmer and the other man struggled on
the ground, the torpedo worked its way half **from**

the man's pocket. The farmer seized it. The man
fell back, limp, and the farmer, with the torpedo in
one hand, grasped at the gun on the ground and
straightened up.

He had no sooner risen than the man was at him
again. His unconsciousness had been merely feigned.
The struggle was renewed.

At that point, the hedge down the road parted and
Del Mar stepped out. A glance was enough to tell
him what was going on. He drew his gun and ran
swiftly toward the combatants.

As Del Mar approached, his man succeeded in
knocking the torpedo from the farmer's hand. There
it lay, several feet away. There seemed to be no
chance for either man to get it.

Quickly the farmer bent his wrist, aiming the gun
deliberately at the precious torpedo. As fast as he
could he pulled the trigger. Five of the six shots penetrated the little model.

So surprised was his antagonist that the farmer
was able to knock him out with the butt of his gun.
He broke away and fled, whistling on a police whistle
for the dog just as Del Mar ran up. A couple of shots
from Del Mar flew wild as the farmer and his dog disappeared.

Del Mar stopped and picked up the model. It had
been shot into an unrecognizable mass of scrap. In a
fury, Del Mar dashed it on the ground, cursing his
men as he did so.

.   .   .   .

The strange disappearance of the torpedo model
from Elaine's room worried both of us. Doubtless if

Kennedy had been there he would have known just what to do. But we could not decide.

"Really," considered Elaine, "I think we had better take Mr. Del Mar into our confidence."

"Still, we've had a great many warnings," I objected.

"I know that," she persisted, "but they have all come from very unreliable sources."

"Very well," I agreed finally, "then let's drive over to his bungalow."

Elaine ordered her little runabout and a few moments later we climbed into it and Elaine shot the car away.

As we rode along, the country seemed so quiet that no one would ever have suspected that foreign agents lurked all about. But it was just under such a cover that the nefarious bridge and harbor-mining work ordered by Del Mar's superiors was going ahead quietly.

As our car climbed a hill on the other side of which, in the valley, was a bridge, we could not see one of Del Mar's men in hiding at the top. He saw us, however, and immediately wigwagged with his handkerchief to several others down at the bridge where they were attaching a pair of wires to the planking.

"Some one coming," muttered one who was evidently a lookout.

The men stopped work immediately and hid in the brush. Our car passed over the bridge and we saw nothing wrong. But no sooner had we gone than the men crept out and resumed work which had progressed to the point where they were ready to carry the wires of an electric connection through the grass, concealing them as they went.

In the study of his bungalow, all this time, Del Mar was striding angrily up and down, while his men waited in silence.

Finally he paused and turned to one of them. " See that the coast is clear and kept clear," he ordered. " I want to go down."

The man saluted and went out through the panel. A moment later Del Mar gave some orders to the other man who also saluted and left the house by the front door, just as our car pulled up.

Del Mar, the moment the man was gone, put on his hat and moved toward the panel in the wall. He was about to enter when he heard some one coming down the hall to the study and stepped back, closing the panel. It was the butler announcing us.

We had entered Del Mar's bungalow and now were conducted to his library, There Elaine told him the whole story, much to his apparent surprise, for Del Mar was a wonderful actor.

" You see," he said as she finished telling of the finding and the losing of the torpedo, " just what I had feared would happen has happened. Doubtless the foreign agents have the deadly weapon, now. However, I'll not quit. Perhaps we may run them down yet."

He reassured us and we thanked him as we said good-bye. Outside, Elaine and I got into the car again and a moment later spun off, making a little detour first through the country before hitting the shore road back again to Dodge Hall.

.   .   .   .

On the rocky shore of the promontory, several men were engaged in sinking a peculiar heavy disk which they submerged about ten or twelve feet. It seemed to be held by a cable and to it wires were attached, apparently so that when a key was pressed a circuit was closed.

It was an " oscillator ", a new system for the employment of sound for submarine signalling, using water instead of air as a medium to transmit sound waves. It was composed of a ring magnet, a copper tube lying in an air-gap in a magnetic field and a stationary central armature. The tube was attached to a steel diaphragm. Really it was a submarine bell which could be used for telegraphing or telephoning both ways through water.

The men finished executing the directions of Del Mar and left, carefully concealing the land connections and key of the bell, while we were still at Del Mar's.

We had no sooner left, however, than one of the men who had been engaged in installing the submarine bell entered the library.

" Well? " demanded Del Mar.

" The bell is installed, sir," he said. " It will be working soon."

" Good," nodded Del Mar.

He went to a drawer and from it took a peculiar looking helmet to which was attached a sort of harness fitting over the shoulders and carrying a tank of oxygen. The head-piece was a most weird contrivance, with what looked like a huge glass eye in front. It was in reality a submarine life-saving apparatus.

Del Mar put it on, all except the helmet which he carried with him, and then, with his assistant, went out through the panel in the wall. Through the underground passage the two groped their way, lighted by an electric torch, until at last they came to the entrance hidden in the underbrush, near the shore.

Del Mar went over to the concealed station from which the submarine bell was sounded and pressed the key as a signal. Then he adjusted the submarine helmet to his head and deliberately waded out into the water, further and further, up to his head, then deeper still.

As he disappeared into the water, his emissary turned and went back toward the shore road.

.   .   .   .

The ride around through the country and back to the shore road from Del Mar's was pleasant. In fact it was always pleasant to be with Elaine, especially in a car.

We were spinning along at a fast clip when we came to a rocky part of the coast. As we made a turn a sharp breeze took off my hat and whirled it far off the road and among the rocks of the shore. Elaine shut down the engine, with a laugh at me, and we left the car by the road while we climbed down the rocks after the hat.

It had been carried into the water, close to shore and, still laughing, we clambered over the rocks. Elaine insisted on getting it herself and in fact did get it. She was just about to hand it to me, when something bobbed up in the water just in front of us. She reached for it and fished it out. It was a cylinder with air-tight caps on both ends, in one of which was a hook.

" What do you suppose it is? " she asked, looking it over as we made our way up the rocks again to the car. " Where did it come from? "

We did not see a man standing by our car, but he saw us. It was Del Mar's man who had paused on his way to watch us. As we approached he hid on the other side of the road.

By this time we had reached the car and opened the cylinder. Inside was a note which read:

" Chief arrived safely. Keep watch."

" What does it mean? " repeated Elaine, mystified.

Neither of us could guess and I doubt whether we would have understood any better if we had seen a sinister face peering at us from behind a rock near-by, although doubtless the man knew what was in the tube and what it meant.

We climbed into the car and started again. As we disappeared, the man came from behind the rocks and ran quickly up to the top of the hill. There, from the bushes, he pulled out a peculiar instrument composed of a strange series of lenses and mirrors set up on a tripod.

Eagerly he placed the tripod, adjusting the lenses and mirrors in the sunlight. Then he began working them, and it was apparent that he was flashing light beams, using a Morse code. It was a heliograph.

Down the shore on the top of the next hill sat the man who had already given the signal with the hand-

kerchief to those in the valley who were working on
the mining of the bridge. As he sat there, his eye
caught the flash of the heliograph signal. He sprang
up and watched intently. Rapidly he jotted down the
message that was being flashed in the sunlight:

> Dodge girl has message from below.
> Coming in car. Blow first bridge she
> crosses.

Down the valley the lookout made his way as fast as
he could. As he approached the two men who had
been mining the bridge, he whistled sharply. They
answered and hurried to meet him.

"Just got a heliograph," he panted. "The Dodge
girl must have picked up one of the messages that
came from below. She's coming over the hill now in
a car. We've got to blow up the bridge as she
crosses."

The men were hurrying now toward the bridge
which they had mined. Not a moment was to be lost,
for already they could see us coming over the crest of
the hill.

In a few seconds they reached the hidden plunger
firing-box which had been arranged to explode the
charge under the bridge. There they crouched in the
brush ready to press the plunger the moment our car
touched the planking.

One of the men crept out a little nearer the road.
"They're coming!" he called back, dropping down
again. "Get ready!"

.   .   .   .

Del Mar's emissaries had not reckoned, however, that any one else might be about to whom the heliograph was an open book.

But, further over on the hill, hiding among the trees, the old farmer and his dog were sitting quietly. The old man was sweeping the Sound with his glasses, as if he expected to see something any moment.

To his surprise, however, he caught a flash of the heliograph from the land. Quickly he turned and jotted down the signals. As he did so, he seemed greatly excited, for the message read:

> Dodge girl has message from below. Coming in car. Blow first bridge she crosses.

Quickly he turned his glasses down the road. There he could see our car rapidly approaching. He put up his glasses and hurried down the hill toward the bridge. Then he broke into a run, the dog scouting ahead.

We were going along the road nicely now, coasting down the hill. As we approached the bridge, Elaine slowed up a bit, to cross, for the planking was loose.

Just then the farmer who had been running down the hill saw us.

"Stop!" he shouted.

But we did not hear. He ran after us, but such a chase was hopeless. He stopped, in despair.

With a gesture of vexation he took a step or two mechanically off the road.

Elaine and I were coming fast to the bridge now.

In their hiding-place, Del Mar's men were watching

12

breathlessly. The leader was just about to press the plunger when all of a sudden a branch in the thicket beside him crackled. There stood the farmer and his dog!

Instantly the farmer seemed to take in the situation. With a cry he threw himself at the man who had the plunger. Another man leaped at the farmer. The dog settled him. The others piled in and a terrific struggle followed. It was all so rapid that, to all, seconds seemed like hours.

We were just starting to cross the bridge.

One of the men broke away and crawled toward the plunger box.

Our car was now in the middle of the bridge.

Over and over rolled the men, the dog doing his best to help his master. The man who had broken away reached toward the plunger.

With a shout he pushed it down.

.   .   .   .

Our car had just cleared the bridge when we were startled by a terrific roar behind us. It was as though a thousand tires had blown out at once. Elaine shut off the engine automatically and we looked back.

The whole bridge had been blown up. A second before we had been in the middle of it.

As the explosion came, the men who had been struggling in the thicket, paused, startled, and stared out. At that instant the old farmer saw his chance. It was all over and he bolted, calling the dog.

Along the road to the bridge he ran, two of the men after him.

"Come back," growled the leader. "Let him go. Do you want us all to get caught?"

As the farmer ran up to the bridge, he saw it in ruins. But down the road he could see Elaine and myself, sitting in the car, staring back at the peril which we had so narrowly escaped. His face lighted up in as great joy as a few moments before it had showed despair.

"What can that have been?" asked Elaine, starting to get out of the car. "What caused it?"

"I don't know," I returned, taking her arm firmly. "But enough has happened to-day. If it was intended for us, we'd better not stop. Some one might take a shot at us. Come. We have the car. We can get out before any one does anything more. Let's do it. Things are going on about us of which we know nothing. The safest thing is to get away."

Elaine looked at the bridge in ruins and shuddered. It was the closest we could have been to death and have escaped. Then she turned to the wheel quickly and the little car fairly jumped ahead.

"Oh, if Craig were only here," she murmured. "He would know what to do."

As we disappeared over the crest of the next hill, safe, the old farmer and his dog looked hard at us.

The silence after the explosion was ominous.

He glanced about. No one was pursuing him. That seemed ominous, too. But if they did pursue he was prepared to elude them. They must never recognize the old farmer.

As he turned, he deliberately pulled off his beard, then plunged again into the woods and was lost.

CHAPTER IX

THE SUBMARINE HARBOR

IT was not long after the almost miraculous escape of Elaine and myself from the blowing up of the bridge on the shore road that Del Mar returned from his mysterious mission which had, apparently, taken him actually down to the bottom of the sea.

The panel in the wall of his library opened and in the still dripping submarine suit, holding under his arm the weird helmet, Del Mar entered. No sooner had he begun to remove his wet diving-suit than the man who had signalled with the heliograph that we had found Del Mar's message from "below," whatever that might mean, entered the house and was announced by the valet.

"Let him come in immediately," ordered Del Mar, placing his suit in a closet. Then to the man, as he entered, he said, "Well, what's new?"

"Quite a bit," returned the man, frowning still over Elaine's accidental discovery of the under-water communication. "The Dodge girl happened to pick up one of the tubes with a message just after you went down. I tried to get her by blowing up the bridge, but it didn't work, somehow."

"We'll have to silence her," remarked Del Mar

180

angrily with a sinister frown. "You stay here and wait for orders."

A moment later he made his way down to a private dock on his grounds and jumped aboard a trim little speed boat moored there. He started the motor and off the boat feathered in a cloud of spray.

It was only a moment by water before he reached the Dodge dock. There he tied his boat and hurried up the dock.

. . . .

Elaine and I arrived home without any further experiences after our hairbreadth escape from the explosion at the bridge.

We were in doubt at first, however, just what to do about the mysterious message which we had picked up in the harbor.

"Really, Walter," remarked Elaine, after we had considered the matter for some time, "I think we ought to send that message to the government at Washington."

Already she had seated herself at her desk and began to write, while I examined the metal tube and the note again.

"There," she said at length, handing me the note she had written. "How does that sound?"

I read it while she addressed the envelope. "Very good," I replied, handing it back.

She folded it and shoved it into the envelope on which she had written:

Chief,
    Secret Service,
        Washington, D. C.

I was studying the address, wondering whether this was just the thing to do, when Elaine decided the matter by energetically ringing the bell for Jennings.

" Post that, Jennings, please," she directed.

The butler bowed just as the door-bell rang. He turned to go.

" Just a minute," I interrupted. " I think perhaps I'd better mail it myself, after all."

He handed me the letter and went out.

" Yes, Walter," agreed Elaine, " that would be better.   Register it, too."

" How do you do? " greeted a suave voice.

It was Del Mar. As he passed me to speak to Elaine, apparently by accident, he knocked the letter from my hand.

" I beg your pardon," he apoligized, quickly stooping and picking it up.

Though he managed to read the address, he maintained his composure and handed the letter back to me. I started to go out, when Elaine called to me.

" Excuse me just a moment, Mr. Del Mar? " she queried, accompanying me out on the porch.

Already a saddle horse had been brought around for me.

" Perhaps you'd better put a special delivery stamp on it, too, Walter," she added, walking along with me. " And be very careful."

" I will," I promised, as I rode off.

Del Mar, alone, seized the opportunity to go over quietly to the telephone. It was the work of only a moment to call up his bungalow where the emissary who had placed the submarine bell was waiting for orders. Quickly Del Mar whispered his instructions which the man took, and hung up the receiver.

"I hope you'll pardon me," said Elaine, entering just as Del Mar left the telephone. "Mr. Jameson was going into town and I had a number of little things I wanted him to do. Won't you sit down?"

They chatted for a few moments, but Del Mar did not stay very long. He excused himself shortly and Elaine bade him good-bye at the door as he walked off, apparently, down the road I had taken.

.   .   .   .

Del Mar's emissary hurried from the bungalow and almost ran down the road until he came to a spot where two men were hiding.

"Jameson is coming with a letter which the Dodge girl has written to the Secret Service," he cried pointing excitedly up the road. "You've got to get it, see?"

I was cantering along nicely down the road by the shore, when suddenly, from behind some rocks and bushes, three men leaped out at me. One of them seized the horse's bridle, while the other two quickly dragged me out of the saddle.

It was very unexpected, but I had time enough to draw my gun and fire once. I hit one of the men, too, in the arm, and he staggered back, the blood spurting all over the road.

But before I could fire at the others, they knocked the gun from my hand. Frightened, the horse turned and bolted, riderless.

Together, they dragged me off the road and into the thicket where I was tied and gagged and laid on the ground while one of them bound up the wounded arm of the man I had hit. It was not long before one of them began searching me.

"Aha!" he growled, pulling the letter from my pocket and looking at it with satisfaction. "Here it is."

He tore the letter open, throwing the envelope on the ground, and read it.

"There, confound you," he muttered. "The government 'll never get that. Come on, men. Bring him this way."

He shoved the letter into his pocket and led the way through the underbrush, while the others half-dragged, half-pushed me along. We had not gone very far before one of the three men, who appeared to be the leader, paused.

"Take him to the hang-out," he ordered gruffly. "I'll have to report to the Chief."

He disappeared down toward the shore of the harbor while the others prodded me along.

·   ·   ·   ·   ·   ·   ·   ·

Down near the Dodge dock, along the shore, walked a man wearing a broad-brimmed hat and a plain suit of duck. His prim collar and tie comported well with his smoked glasses. Instinctively one would have called him "Professor", though whether naturalist, geologist, or plain "bugologist", one would have had difficulty in determining.

He seemed, as a matter-of-fact, to be a naturalist, for he was engrossed in picking up specimens. But he was not so much engrossed as to fail to hear the approach of footsteps down the gravel walk from Dodge

Hall to the dock. He looked up in time to see Del Mar coming, and quietly slipped into the shrubbery up on the shore.

On the dock, Del Mar stood for some minutes, waiting. Finally, along the shore came another figure. It was the emissary to whom Del Mar had telephoned and who had searched me. The naturalist drew back into his hiding-place, peering out keenly.

" Well? " demanded Del Mar. " What luck? "

" We've got him," returned the man with brief satisfaction. " Here's the letter she was sending to the Secret Service."

Del Mar seized the note which the man handed to him and read it eagerly. " Good," he exclaimed. " That would have put an end to the whole operations about here. Come on. Get into the boat."

For some reason best known to himself, the naturalist seemed to have lost all interest in his specimens and to have a sudden curiosity about Del Mar's affairs. As the motor-boat sped off, he came slowly and cautiously out of his hiding-place and gazed fixedly at Del Mar.

No sooner had Del Mar's boat got a little distance out into the harbor than the naturalist hurried down the Dodge dock. There was tied Elaine's own fast little runabout. He jumped into it and started the engine, following quickly in Del Mar's wake.

" Look," called the emissary to Del Mar, spying the Dodge boat with the naturalist in it, skimming rapidly after them.

Del Mar strained his eyes back through his glass at the pursuing boat. But the naturalist, in spite of his smoked glasses, seemed not to have impaired his eye-sight by his studies. He caught the glint of the sun on the lens at Del Mar's eye and dropped down into the bottom of his own boat where he was at least safe from scrutiny, if his boat were not.

Del Mar lowered his glass. "That's the Dodge boat," he said thoughtfully. "I don't like the looks of that fellow. Give her more speed."

.   .   .   .

Del Mar had not been gone long before Elaine decided to take a ride herself. She ordered her horse around from the stables while she donned her neat little riding-habit. A few minutes later, as the groom held the horse, she mounted and rode away, choosing the road by which I had gone, expecting to meet me on the return from town.

She was galloping along at a good clip when suddenly her horse shied at something.

"Whoa, Buster," pacified Elaine.

But it was of no use. Buster still reared up.

"Why, what is the matter?" she asked. "What do you see?"

She looked down at the ground. There was a spot of blood in the dust. Buster was one of those horses to whom the sight of blood is terrifying.

Elaine pulled up beside the road. There was a revolver lying in the grass. She dismounted and picked it up. No sooner had she looked at it than she discovered the initials "W. J." carved on the butt.

"Walter Jameson!" she exclaimed, realizing suddenly that it was mine. "It's been fired, too!"

Her eye fell again on the blood spots. "Blood and

—footprints—into the brush!" she gasped in horror, following the trail. "What could have happened to Walter?"

With the revolver, Elaine followed where the bushes were trampled down until she came to the place where I had been bound. There she spied some pieces of paper lying on the ground and picked them up.

She put them together. They were pieces of the envelope of the letter which we had decided to send to Washington.

"Which way did they take him?" she asked, looking all about but discovering no trail.

She was plainly at a loss what course to pursue.

"What would Craig do?" she asked herself.

Finding no answer, she stood thinking a moment, slowly tearing the envelope to pieces. If she were to do anything at all, it must be done quickly. Suddenly an idea seemed to occur to her. She threw the pieces of paper into the air and let them blow away. It was unscientific detection, perhaps, but the wind actually took them and carried them in the direction in which the men had forced me to walk.

"That's it!" cried Elaine to herself. "I'll follow that direction."

.   .   .   .

Meanwhile, the men had hurried me off along a trail that led to the foot of a cliff. Then the trail wound up the cliff. We climbed it until we reached the top.

There in the rock was a rude stairway. I drew back. But one man drew a gun and the other preceded me down. Along the steep stone steps cut out in the face of the rock, they forced me.

Below, in a rift in the very wall of the cliff, was a cave in which already were two more of Del Mar's men, talking in low tones, in the dim light.

As we made our way down the breakneck stairway, the foremost of my captors stepped on a large flat rock. As he did so, it gave way slightly under his foot.

A light in the cave flashed up. Under the rock was a secret electric connection which operated a lamp.

"Some one coming," muttered the two men, on guard instantly.

It was a somewhat precarious footing as we descended and for the moment I was more concerned for my safety from a fall than anything else. Once my foot did slip and a shower of pebbles and small pieces of rock started down the face of the cliff.

As we passed down, the man behind me, still keeping me covered, raised the flat stone on the top step. Carefully, he reset the connection of the alarm rock, a series of metal points that bent under the weight of a person and made a contact which signalled down in the cavern the approach of any one who did not know the secret.

As he did so, the light in the cavern went out. "It's all right," said one of the men down there, with a look of relief.

We now went down the perilous stairway until we came to the cave.

"I've got a prisoner—orders of the Chief," growled one of my captors, thrusting me in roughly.

They forced me into a corner where they tied me again, hand and foot. Then they began debating in low, sinister tones, what was to be done with me next.

Once in a while I could catch a word. Fear made my senses hypersensitive.

They were arguing whether they should make away with me now or later!

Finally the leader rose. " It's three to one," I heard him mutter. " He dies now."

He turned and took a menacing step toward me.

" Hands up! "

It was a shrill, firm voice that rang out at the mouth of the cave as a figure cut off what little light there was.

.   .   .   .

Elaine passed along, hunting for the trail. Suddenly a shower of pebbles came falling down from a cliff above her. Some of them hit her and she looked up quickly.

There she could see me being led along by my captors. She hid in the brush and watched. During all the operations of the descent of the rock stairway and the resetting of the alarm, she continued to watch, straining her eyes to see what they were doing.

As we entered the cave, she stepped out from her concealment and looked sharply up at us, as we disappeared. Then she climbed the path up the cliff until she came to the flight of stone steps leading downward again.

Already she had seen the man behind me doing something with the stone that formed the top step. She stooped down and examined the stone. Carefully she raised it and looked underneath before stepping on it. There she could see the electric connection. She set the stone aside and looked again down the dangerous stairway.

It made her shudder. " I must get him," she murmured to herself. " Yes, I must. Even now it may
be too late."

With a supreme effort of determination she got herself together, drew my gun which she had picked up,
and started down the cliff, stepping noiselessly.

At last Elaine came to the cave. She stood just
aside from the door, gun in hand, and listened, aghast.

Inside she could hear voices of four men, and they
were arguing whether they should kill me or not. It
was four against one woman, but she did not falter.
' They had just decided to make away with me immediately and the leader had turned toward me with
the threat still on his lips. It was now or never. Reso-
lutely she took a step forward and into the cave.

" Hands up ! " she demanded, firmly.

The thing was so unexpected in the security of their
secret hiding-place protected by the rock alarm that,
before they knew it, Elaine had them all lined up
against the wall.

Keeping them carefully covered, she moved over
toward me. She picked up a knife that lay near-by
and started to cut the ropes which held me.

As she did so, one of the men, with an oath, leaped
forward to rush her. But Elaine was not to be caught
off her guard. Instantly she fired. The man staggered
back, and fell.

That cooled the ardor of the other three considerably, especially now as I was free, too. While she held
them up still, with their hands in the air, I went through
their pockets, taking out their weapons.

Then, still keeping them covered, we backed out of

the cave.   Backward we made our way up the dangerous flight of steps again with guns levelled at the cave
entrance, Elaine going up first.

Once a head stuck itself out of the cave entrance.   I
fired instantly and it jerked itself back in again just in
time.   That was the only trouble we had, apparently.

Cautiously and slowly we made our way toward the
top of the cliff.

．　　．　　．　　．　　．　　．　　．　　．　　．

One look backward from his motor-boat was enough
for Del Mar.   He must evade that inquisitive naturalist.   He turned to his man.

" Get out that apparatus," he ordered.

The man opened a locker and brought out the curious
submarine rescue helmet and suit.   Del Mar took them
up and began to put the suit on, stooping down in the
shelter of the boat so that his actions could not be seen
by the naturalist in the pursuing boat.

The naturalist was all this time peering ahead keenly
at Del Mar's boat, trying to make it out.   He bent over
and adjusted the engine to get up more speed and the
boat shot ahead faster.

By this time, Del Mar had put on the submarine apparatus, all except the helmet, and was crouching low in
the boat.   Hastily, he rolled a piece of canvas into the
semblance of a body, put his coat and hat on it and set
it on the seat which he had occupied before.

Just then Del Mar's boat ran around the promontory
where Wu Fang had met the submarine that had
brought Del Mar into the country and landed him so
strangely.

The boat slowed down under shelter of the rocks

and Del Mar added a pair of heavy lead-soled shoes to his outfit in order to weight himself down. Finally he put on the helmet, let himself over the side of the boat, and disappeared into the water.

His aide started the motor and the boat shot ahead again, with the dummy still occupying Del Mar's seat. As the boat swung out and made a wide sweeping curve away from the point at which Del Mar had gone overboard, the naturalist in the Dodge boat came around the promontory and saw it, changing his course accordingly, and gaining somewhat.

.   .   .   .

Del Mar sank, upright and rapidly, down in the shallow water to the bottom. Once having his feet on something approaching firm ground, he gazed about through the window-like eye of the helmet until he got his bearings. Then he began to walk heavily along the bottom of the harbor, over sand and rocks.

It was a strange walk that he took, half stumbling, slowly and cumbersomely groping his way like a queer under-water animal.

If any one could have seen him, he would have noted that Del Mar was going toward the base of a huge rocky cliff that jutted far out into the harbor, where the water was deep, a dangerous point, avoided by craft of all kinds. Far over his head the waves beat on the rocks angrily. But down there, concealed beneath the surface of the harbor, was a sort of huge arch of stone, through which a comparatively rapid current ran as the tide ebbed and flowed.

Del Mar let himself be carried along with the current which was now running in and thus with comparative ease made his way, still groping, through the arch. Once under it and a few feet beyond, he deliberately kicked off the leaden-soled shoes and, thus lightened, rose rapidly to the surface of the water.

As he bobbed up, a strange sight met his eyes—not strange however, to Del Mar. Above, the rocks formed a huge dome over the water which the tides forced in and out through the secret entrance through which he came. No other entrance, apparently, except that from the waters of the harbor led to this peculiar den.

Lying quietly moored to the rocky piers lay three submarine boats. Further back, on a ledge of rocks, blasted out, stood a little building, a sort of office or headquarters. Near-by was a shed where were kept gas and oil, supplies and ammunition, in fact everything that a submarine might need.

This was the reason for Del Mar's presence in the neighborhood. It was the secret submarine harbor of the foreign agents who were operating in America!

Already a sentry, pacing up and down, had seen the bubbles in the water that indicated that some one had come through the archway and was down "below," as Del Mar and his men called it.

Gazing down the sentry saw the queer helmeted figure float up from the bottom of the pool. He reached out and helped the figure clamber up out of the water to the ledge on which he stood. Del Mar saluted, and the sentry returned the secret salute, helping him remove the dripping helmet and suit.

A moment later, in the queer little submarine office, Del Mar had evidently planned to take up the nefarious secret work on which he was engaged. Several men

13

of a naval and military bearing were seated about a
table, already, studying maps and plans and documents
of all descriptions. They did not seem to belong to any
nation in particular. In fact their uniforms, if such
they might be called, were of a character to disguise
their nationality. But ɩhat they were hostile to the
country under which they literally had their hidden
retreat, of that there could be no doubt.

How high Del Mar stood in their counsels could have
been seen at a glance from the instant deference exhibited at the mere mention of his name by the sentry
who entered with the submarine suit while Del Mar
got himself together after his remarkable trip.

The men at the council table rose and saluted as Del
Mar himself entered. He returned the salute and
quietly made his way to the head of the table where he
took a seat, naturally.

"This is the area in which we must work first of
all," he began, drawing toward him a book and opening
it. "And we must strike quickly, for if they heed the
advice in this book, it may be too late for us to take
advantage of their foolish unpreparedness."

It was a book entitled "Defenseless America",
written by a great American inventor, Hudson Maxim.

Del Mar turned the pages until he came to and
pointed out a map. The others gathered about him,
leaning forward eagerly as he talked to them.

There, on the map, with a radius of some one hundred and seventy miles, was drawn a big segment of a
circle, with Peekskill, New York, as a centre.

"That is the heart of America," said Del Mar,
earnestly. "It embraces New York, Boston, Phila-

delphia. But that is not the point. Here are the great majority of the gun and armor factories, the powder and cartridge works, together with the principal coal fields of Pennsylvania."

He brought his fist down decisively on the table. "If we hold this section," he declared, "we practically hold America!"

Eagerly the other emissaries listened as Del Mar laid before them the detailed facts which he was collecting, the greater mission than the mere capture of Kennedy's wireless torpedo which had brought him into the country. Detail after detail of their plans they discussed as they worked out the gigantic scheme.

It was a war council of a secret advance guard of the enemies of America!

.   .   .   .

Meanwhile, Del Mar's man in his boat, cutting a wide circle and avoiding the Dodge boat carrying the naturalist, made his way across the harbor until he came to the shore.

There he landed and proceeded up the beach to the foot of a rocky cliff, where he turned and followed a trail up it to the top. It was the same path already travelled by my captors with me and later followed by Elaine.

As he came stealthily out from under cover, Del Mar's man gazed down the stairway. He drew back at what he saw. Slowly he pulled a gun from his pocket, watching down the steps with tense interest. There he could see Elaine and myself wearily climbing toward the top, our backs toward him, as we covered the men in the cave.

So surprised was he at what he saw that he forgot that his boat below had been followed by the mysterious naturalist, who, the moment Del Mar's man had landed, put on the last burst of speed and ran the Dodge boat close to the spot where the aide had left Del Mar's.

A glance into the boat sufficed to tell the naturalist that the figure in it was only a dummy. He did not pause, but followed the trail up the hill, until he was close after the emissary ahead, going more slowly.

Only a few feet further along the cliff, the naturalist paused, too, keeping well under cover, for the man was now just ahead of him. He looked fixedly at him and saw him gaze down the cliff. Then he saw him slowly draw a gun.

Who could be below? Quickly the naturalist's mind seemed to work. He crouched down, as if ready to spring.

The emissary slowly raised his revolver and took careful aim at the backs of Elaine and myself, as we came up the steps.

But before he could pull the trigger, the naturalist, more like one of the wild animals which he studied than like a human being, sprang from his concealment in the bushes and pounced on the man from behind, seizing him firmly.

Over and over they rolled, struggling almost to the brink of the precipice.

.   .   .   .

Elaine and I had got almost to the top of the flight of steps, when suddendy we heard a shout above us and sounds of a terrific struggle. We turned, to see two

men, neither of whom we knew, fighting. One seemed
to be a professor of natural history from his dress and
general appearance. The other had a sinister nonde-
script look.

Nearer and nearer the edge of the cliff they rolled.
We crouched closer to the rocky wall, gazing up at the
death grapple of the two. Who they were we did not
know but that one was fighting for and the other
against us we could readily see.

The more vicious of the two seemed to be forcing
the naturalist slowly back, when, with a superhuman
effort, the naturalist braced himself. His foot was
actually on a small ledge of rock directly at the edge of
the cliff.

He swung around quickly and struck the other man.
The vicious looking man pitched headlong over the
cliff.

We shrank back closer to the rock as the man hurtled
through the air only a few feet from us. Down below,
we could hear him land with a sickening thud.

Far over the edge Elaine leaned in a sort of fascination at the awful sight. For a moment, I thought the
very imp of the perverse had got possession of her and
that she herself would fall over. She brushed her hand
unsteadily over her eyes and staggered. I caught her
just in time.

It was only an instant before the brave girl recovered
control of herself. Then, together, we started again to
climb up.

As we did so the naturalist looked down and caught
sight of us approaching. Hastily he hid in the bushes.

We reached the top of the stairway and gazed about

for the victor in the contest.   To our surprise he was gone.

"Come," I urged.   "We had better get away, quickly."

As Elaine and I disappeared, the naturalist slowly emerged again from the bushes and looked after us. Then he gave a hasty glance over the edge of the cliff at the man, twisted and motionless, far below.

If we had looked back we might have seen the naturalist shake his head in a manner strangely reminiscent as he turned and gazed again after us.

CHAPTER X

THE CONSPIRATORS

" You remember Lieutenant Woodward, the inventor of trodite? " I asked Elaine one day after I had been out for a ride through the country.

" Very well indeed," she nodded with a look of wistfulness as the mention of his name recalled Kennedy. " Why? "

" He's stationed at Fort Dale, not very far from here, at the entrance of the Sound," I answered.

" Then let's have him over at my garden party tonight," she exclaimed, sitting down and writing.

DEAR LIEUTENANT,

I have just learned that you are stationed at Fort Dale and would like to have you meet some of my friends at a little garden party I am holding tonight.

Sincerely,
ELAINE DODGE.

Thus it was that a few hours afterward, in the officers' quarters at the Fort, an orderly entered with the mail and handed a letter to Lieutenant Woodward.

199

He opened it and read the invitation with pleasure. He had scarcely finished reading and was hastening to write a reply when the orderly entered again and saluted.

"A Professor Arnold to see you, Lieutenant," he announced.

"Professor Arnold?" repeated Woodward. "I don't know any Professor Arnold. Well, show him in, anyhow."

The orderly ushered in a well-dressed man with a dark, heavy beard and large horn spectacles. Woodward eyed him curiously and a bit suspiciously, as the stranger seated himself and made a few remarks.

The moment the orderly left the room, however, the professor lowered his voice to a whisper. Woodward listened in amazement, looked at him more closely, then laughed and shook hands cordially.

The professor leaned over again. Whatever it was that he said, it made a great impression on the Lieutenant.

"You know this fellow Del Mar?" asked Professor Arnold finally.

"No," replied Woodward.

"Well, he's hanging around Miss Dodge all the time," went on Arnold. "There's something queer about his presence here at this time."

"I've an invitation to a garden party at her house to-night," remarked Woodward.

"Accept," urged the professor, "and tell her you are bringing a friend."

Woodward resumed writing and when he had finished handed the note to the stranger, who read:

Dear Miss Dodge,

I shall be charmed to be with you to-night and with your permission will bring my friend, Professor Arnold.

Truly yours,
EDWARD WOODWARD.

' "Good," nodded the professor, handing the note back.

Woodward summoned an orderly. "See that that is delivered at Dodge Hall to Miss Dodge herself as soon as possible," he directed, as the orderly took the note and saluted.

Elaine, Aunt Josephine and I were in the garden when Lieut. Woodward's orderly rode up and delivered the letter.

Elaine opened it and read. "That's all right," she thanked the orderly. "Oh, Walter, he's coming to the garden party, and is going to bring a friend of his, a Professor Arnold."

We chatted a few moments about the party.

"Oh," exclaimed Elaine suddenly, "I have an idea."

"What is it?" we asked, smiling at her enthusiasm.

"We'll have a fortune teller," she cried. "Aunt Josephine, you shall play the part."

"All right, if you really want me," consented Aunt Josephine smiling indulgently as we urged her.

.   .   .   .

Down in the submarine harbor that afternoon, Del Mar and his men were seated about the conference table.

"I've traced out the course and the landing points

of the great Atlantic cable," he said. "We must cut it."

Del Mar turned to one of the men. "Take these plans to the captain of the steamer and tell him to get ready," he went on. "Find out and send me word when the cutting can be done best."

The man saluted and went out.

Leaving the submarine harbor in the usual manner, he made his way to a dock on the shore around the promontory and near the village. Tied to it was a small tramp steamer. The man walked down the dock and climbed aboard the boat. There several rough looking sailors were lolling and standing about. The emissary selected the captain, a more than ordinarily tough looking individual.

"Mr. Del Mar sends you the location of the Atlantic cable and the place where he thinks it best to pick it up and cut it," he said.

The captain nodded. "I understand," he replied. "I'll send him word later when it can be done best."

A few minutes after dispatching his messenger, Del Mar left the submarine harbor himself and entered his bungalow by way of the secret entrance. There he went immediately to his desk and picked up the mail that had accumulated in his absence. One letter he read:

DEAR MR. DEL MAR,

We shall be pleased to see you at a little garden party we are holding to-night.

Sincerely,

ELAINE DODGE.

As he finished reading, he pushed the letter carelessly aside as though he had no time for such frivolity. Then an idea seemed to occur to him. He picked it up again and read it over.

"I'll go," he said to himself, simply.

.   .   .   .

That night Dodge Hall was a blaze of lights and life, overflowing to the wide verandas and the garden. Guests in evening clothes were arriving from all parts of the summer colony and were being received by Elaine. Already some of them were dancing on the veranda.

Among the late arrivals were Woodward and his friend, Professor Arnold.

"I'm so glad to know that you are stationed at Fort Dale," greeted Elaine. "I hope it will be for all summer."

"I can't say how long it will be, but I shall make every effort to make it all summer," he replied gallantly. "Let me present my friend, Professor Arnold."

The professor bowed low and unprofessorially over Elaine's hand and a moment later followed Woodward out into the next room as the other guests arrived to be greeted by Elaine. For a moment, however, she looked after him curiously. Once she started to follow as though to speak to him. Just then, however, Del Mar entered.

"Good evening," he interrupted, suavely.

He stood for a moment with Elaine and talked.

One doorway in the house was draped and a tent had been erected in the room. Over the door was a sign which read: " The past and the future are an open book to Ancient Anna." There Aunt Josephine held forth in a most effective disguise as a fortune teller.

Aunt Josephine had always had a curious desire to play the old hag in amateur dramatics and now she had gratified her desire to the utmost. Probably none of the guests knew that Ancient Anna was in reality Elaine's guardian.

Elaine being otherwise occupied, I had selected one of the prettiest of the girls and we were strolling through the house, seeking a quiet spot for a chat.

" Why don't you have your fortune told by Ancient Anna? " laughed my companion as we approached the tent.

" Do you tell a good fortune reasonably? " I joked, entering.

" Only the true fortunes, young man," returned Ancient Anna severely, starting in to read my palm. " You are very much in love," she went on, " but the lady is not in this tent."

Very much embarrassed, I pulled my hand away.

" How shocking! " mocked my companion, making believe to be very much annoyed. " I don't think I'll have my fortune told," she decided as we left the room.

We sauntered along to the veranda where another friend claimed my companion for a dance which she had promised. As I strolled on alone, Del Mar and Elaine were already finishing a dance. He left her a moment later and I hurried over, glad of the opportunity to see her at last.

Del Mar made his way alone among the guests and passed Aunt Josephine disguised as the old hag seated before her tent. Just then a waiter came through with a tray of ices. As he passed, Del Mar stopped him, reached out and took an ice.

Under the ice, as he had known, was a note. He took the note surreptitiously, turned and presented the ice to Ancient Anna with a bow.

"Thank you, kind sir," she curtsied, taking it.

Del Mar stepped aside and glanced at the little slip of paper. Then he crumpled it up and threw it aside, walking away.

No sooner had he gone than Aunt Josephine reached out and picked up the paper. She straightened it and looked at it. There was nothing on the paper but a crude drawing of a sunrise on the ocean.

"What's that?" asked Aunt Josephine, in surprise.

Just then Elaine and Lieutenant Woodward came in and stopped before the tent. Aunt Josephine motioned to Elaine to come in and Elaine followed. Lieutenant Woodward started after her.

"No, no, young man," laughed Ancient Anna, shaking her forefinger at him, "I don't want you. It's the pretty young lady I want."

Woodward stood outside, though he did not know quite what it was all about. While he was standing there, Professor Arnold came up. He had not exactly made a hit with the guests. At least, he seemed to make little effort to do so. He and Woodward walked away, talking earnestly.

In the tent Aunt Josephine handed Elaine the piece of paper she had picked up.

"What does it mean?" asked Elaine, studying the curious drawing in surprise.

"I'm sure I don't know," confessed Aunt Josephine.

"Nor I."

Meanwhile Lieutenant Woodward and his friend had moved to a corner of the veranda and stood looking intently into the moonlight. There was Del Mar deep in conversation with a man who had slipped out, at a quiet signal, from his hiding-place in the shrubbery.

"That fellow is up to something, mark my words," muttered Arnold under his breath. "I'd like to make an arrest, but I've got to have some proof."

They continued watching Del Mar but, so far at least, he did nothing that would have furnished them any evidence of anything.

So the party went on, most merrily until, long after the guests had left, Elaine sat in her dressing-gown up in her room, about to retire.

Her maid had left her and she picked up the slip of paper from her dresser, looking at it thoughtfully.

"What can a crude drawing of a sunrise on the sea mean?" she asked herself.

For a long time she studied the paper, thinking it over. At last an idea came to her.

"I'll bet I have it," she exclaimed to herself. "Something is going to happen on the water at sunrise."

She took a pretty little alarm clock from the table, set it, and placed it near her bed.

. . . .

Returning from the party to his library, Del Mar entered. Except for the moonlight streaming in through the windows the room was dark. He turned on the lights and crossed to the panel in the wall. As he touched a button the panel opened. Del Mar switched off the lights and went through the panel, closing it.

Outside, at the other end of the passageway, was one of his men, waiting in the shadows as Del Mar came up. For a moment they talked. " I'll be there, at sunrise," agreed Del Mar, as the man left and he reentered the secret passage.

While he was conferring, at the library window appeared a face. It was Professor Arnold's. Cautiously he opened the window and listened. Then he entered.

First he went over to the door and set a chair under the knob. Next he drew an electric pocket bull's-eye and flashed it about the room. He glanced about and finally went over to Del Mar's desk where he examined a batch of letters, his back to the secret panel.

Arnold was running rapidly through the papers on the desk, as he flashed his electric bull's-eye on them, when the panel in the wall opened slowly and Del Mar stepped into the room noiselessly. To his surprise he saw a round spot of light from an electric flashlight focussed on his desk. Some one was there! He drew a gun.

Arnold started suddenly. He heard the cocking of a revolver. But he did not look around. He merely thought an instant, quicker than lightning, then pulled out a spool of black thread with one hand, while with the other he switched off the light, and dived down on his stomach on the floor in the shadow.

"Who's that?" demanded Del Mar. "Confound it! I should have fired at sight."

The room was so dark now that it was impossible to see Arnold. Del Mar gazed intently. Suddenly Arnold's electric torch glowed forth in a spot across the room.

Del Mar blazed at it, firing every chamber of his revolver, then switched on the lights.

No one was in the room. But the door was open. Del Mar gazed about, vexed, then ran to the open door.

For a second or two he peered out in rage, finally turning back into the empty room. On the mantle-piece lay the torch of the intruder. It was one in which the connection is made by a ring falling on a piece of metal. The ring had been left up by Arnold. Connection had been made as he was leaving the room by pulling the thread which he had fastened to the ring. Del Mar followed the thread as it led around the room to the doorway.

"Curse him!" swore Del Mar, smashing down the innocent torch on the floor in fury, as he rushed to the desk and saw his papers all disturbed.

Outside, Arnold had made good his escape. He paused in the moonlight and listened. No one was pursuing. He drew out two or three of the letters which he had taken from Del Mar's desk, and hastily ran through them.

"Not a thing in them," he exclaimed, tearing them up in disgust and hurrying away.

.   .   .   .

At the first break of dawn the little alarm clock awakened Elaine. She started up and rubbed her eyes at the suddenness of the awakening, then quickly reached out and stopped the bell so that it would not disturb others in the house. She jumped out of bed hurriedly and dressed.

Armed with a spy glass, Elaine let herself out of the house quietly. Directly to the shore she went, walking along the beach. Suddenly she paused. There were three men. Before she could level her glass at them, however, they disappeared.

"That's strange," she said to herself, looking through the glass. "There's a steamer at the dock that seems to be getting ready for something. I wonder what it can be doing so early."

She moved along in the direction of the dock. At the dock the disreputable steamer to which Del Mar had dispatched his emissary was still tied, the sailors now working under the gruff orders of the rough captain. About a capstan were wound the turns of a long wire rope at the end of which was a three-pronged drag-hook.

"You see," the captain was explaining, "we'll lower this hook and drag it along the bottom. When it catches anything we'll just pull it up. I have the location of the cable. It ought to be easy to grapple."

Already, on the shore, at an old deserted shack of a fisherman, two of Del Mar's men had been waiting since before sun-up, having come in a dirty, dingy fishing smack anchored offshore.

"Is everything ready?" asked Del Mar, coming up.

14

"Everything, sir," returned the two, following him along the shore.

"Who's that?" cautioned one of the men, looking ahead.

They hid hastily, for there was Elaine. She had seen the three and was about to level her glass in their direction as they hid. Finally she turned and discovered the steamer. As she moved toward it, Del Mar and the others came out from behind a rock and stole after her.

Elaine wandered on until she came to the dock. No one paid any attention to her, apparently, and she made her way along the dock and even aboard the boat without being observed.

No sooner had she got on the boat, however, than Del Mar and his men appeared on the dock and also boarded the steamer.

The captain was still explaining to the men just how the drag-hook worked when Elaine came up quietly on the deck. She stood spellbound as she heard him outline the details of the plot. Scarcely knowing what she did, she crouched back of a deck-house and listened.

Behind her, Del Mar and his men came along, cat-like. A glance was sufficient to tell them that she had overheard what the captain was saying.

"Confound that girl!" ground out Del Mar. "Will she always cross my path? We'll get her this time!"

The men scattered as he directed them. Sneaking up quietly, they made a sudden rush and seized her. As she struggled and screamed, they dragged her off, thrusting her into the captain's cabin and locking the door.

"Cast off!" ordered Del Mar.

A few moments later, out in the harbor, Del Mar was busy directing the dragging for the Atlantic cable at a spot where it was known to run. They let the drag-hook down over the side and pulled it along slowly on the bottom.

In the cabin, Elaine beat on the door and shouted in vain for help.

. . . .

I had decided to do some early morning fishing the day after the party, and knowing that Elaine and the others were usually late risers, I said nothing about it, determined to try my luck alone.

So it happened that only a few minutes after Elaine let herself out quitely, I did the same, carrying my fishing-tackle. I made my way toward the shore, undecided whether to fish from a dock or boat. Finally I determined to do some casting from the shore.

I had cast once or twice before I was aware that I was not alone in the immediate neighborhood. Some distance away I saw a little steamer at a wharf. A couple of men ran along the deck, apparently cautioning the captain against something.

Then I saw them run to one side and drag out a girl, screaming and struggling as they hurried her below. I could scarcely believe my eyes. It was Elaine!

Only a second I looked. They were certainly too many for me. I dropped my rod and line and ran toward the dock, however. As I came down it, I saw that I was too late. The little steamer had cast off and

was now some distance from the dock. I looked about
for a motor-boat in desperation—anything to follow
them in. But there was nothing, absolutely nothing,
not even a rowboat.

I ran back along the dock as I had come and struck
out down the shore.

.   .   .   .

Out at the parade grounds at Fort Dale, in spite of
the early hour, there was some activity, for the army
is composed of early risers.

Lieutenent Woodward and Professor Arnold left
the house in which the Lieutenant was quartered,
where he had invited Arnold to spend the night. Already an orderly had brought around two horses.
They mounted for an early morning ride through the
country.

Off they clattered, naturally bending their course
toward the shore. They came soon to a point in the
road where it emerged from the hills and gave them a
panoramic view of the harbor and sound.

"Wait a minute," called the professor.

Woodward reined up and they gazed off over the
water.

"What's that—an oyster boat?" asked Woodward,
looking in the direction Arnold indicated.

"I don't think so, so early," replied Arnold, pulling
out his pocket glass and looking carefully.

Through it he could see that something like a hook
was being cast over the steamer's side and drawn back
again.

"They're dragging for something," he remarked
as they brought up an object dark and covered with

seagrowth, then threw it overboard as though it was not what they wanted. "By George—the Atlantic cable lands here—they're going to cut it!"

Woodward took the glasses himself and looked in in surprise. "That's right," he cried, his surprise changed to alarm in an instant. "Here, take the glass again and watch. I must get back to the Fort."

He swung his horse about and galloped off, leaving Arnold sitting in the saddle gazing at the strange boat through his glass.

By the time Woodward reached the parade ground again, a field-gun and its company were at drill. He dashed furiously across the field.

"What's the trouble?" demanded the officer in charge of the gun.

Woodward blurted out what he had just seen. "We must stop it—at any cost," he added, breathlessly.

The officer turned to the company. A moment later the order to follow Woodward rang out, the horses were wheeled about, and off the party galloped. On they went, along the road which Woodward and Arnold had already traversed.

Arnold was still gazing, impatiently now, through the glass. He could see the fore-deck of the ship where Del Mar, muffled up, and his men had succeeded in dragging the cable to the proper position on the deck. They laid it down and Del Mar was directing the preparations for cutting it. Arnold lowered his glass and looked about helplessly.

Just then Lieutenant Woodward dashed up with the officer and company and the field-gun. They wheeled it about and began pointing it and finding the range.

Would they never get it? Arnold was almost beside himself. One of Del Mar's men seized an axe and was about to deliver the fatal blow. He swung it and for a moment held it poised over his head.

Suddenly a low, deep rumble of a reverberation echoed and reechoed from the hills over the water. The field-gun had bellowed defiance.

A solid shot crashed through the cabin, smashing the door. Astounded, the men jumped back. As they did so, in their fear, the cable, released, slipped back over the rail in a great splash of safety into the water and sank.

"The deuce take you—you fools," swore Del Mar, springing forward in rage, and looking furiously toward the shore.

Two of the men had been hit by splinters. It was impossible to drag again. Besides, again the gun crew loaded and fired.

The first shot had dismantled the doorway of the cabin. Elaine crouched fearfully in the furthest corner, not knowing what to expect next. Suddenly another shot tore through just beside the door, smashing the woodwork terrificaily. She shrank back further, in fright.

Anything was better than this hidden terror. Nerved up, she ran through the broken door.

Arnold was gazing through his glass at the effect of the shots. He could now see Del Mar and the others leaping into a swift little motor-boat alongside the steamer which they had been using to help them in dragging for the cable.

Just then he saw Elaine run, screaming, out from the cabin and leap overboard.

" Stop ! " shouted Arnold in a fever of excitement, lowering his glass. " There's a girl—by Jove—it's Miss Dodge ! "

" Impossible ! " exclaimed Woodward.

" I tell you, it is," reiterated Arnold, thrusting the glass into the Lieutenant's hand.

The motor-boat had started when Del Mar saw Elaine in the water. " Look," he growled, pointing, " There's the Dodge girl."

Elaine was swimming frantically away from the boat. " Get her," he ordered, shielding his face so that she could not see it.

They turned the boat and headed toward her. She struck out harder than ever for the shore. On came the motor-boat.

Arnold and Woodward looked at each other in despair. What could they do?

.   .   .   .

Somehow, by a sort of instinct, I suppose, I made my way as quickly as I could along the shore toward Fort Dale, thinking perhaps of Lieutenant Woodward.

As I came upon the part of the grounds of the Fort that sloped down to the beach, I saw a group of young officers standing about a peculiar affair on the shore in the shallow water—half bird, half boat.

As I came closer, I recognized it as a Thomas hydroaeroplane.

It suggested an idea and I hurried, shouting.

One of the men, seated in it, was evidently explaining its working to the others.

"Wait," he said, as he saw me running down the shore, waving and shouting at them. "Let's see what this fellow wants."

It was, as I soon learned, the famous Captain Burnside, of the United States Aerial Corps. Breathless, I told him what I had seen and that we were all friends of Woodward's.

Burnside thought a moment, and quickly made up his mind.

"Come—quick—jump up here with me," he called. Then to the other men, "I'll be back soon. Wait here. Let her go!"

I had jumped up and they spun the propeller. The hydroaeroplane feathered along the water, throwing a cloud of white spray, then slowly rose in the air.

The sensation of flying was delightful, as the fresh morning wind cut our faces. We seemed to be hardly moving. It was the earth or rather the water that rushed past under us. But I forgot all about my sensations in my anxiety for Elaine.

As we rose we could see over the curve in the shore.

"Look!" I exclaimed, straining my eyes. "She's overboard. There's a motor-boat after her. Faster—over that way!"

"Yes, yes," shouted Burnside above the roar of the engine which almost made conversation impossible.

He shifted the planes a bit and crowded on more speed.

The men in the boat saw us. One figure, tall, muffled, had a familiar look, but I could not place it and in the excitement of the chase had no chance to try. But I could see that he saw us and was angry.

Apparently the man gave orders to turn, for the boat swung around just as we swooped down and ran along the water.

Elaine was exhausted. Would we be in time?

We planed along the water, while the motor-boat sped off with its baffled passengers. Finally we stopped, in a cloud of spray.

Together, Burnside and I reached down and caught Elaine, not a moment too soon, dragging her into the boat of the hydroaeroplane.

If we had not had all we could do, we might have heard a shout of encouragement and relief from the hill where Woodward and Arnold and the rest were watching anxiously.

I threw my coat about her, as the brave girl heroically clung to us, half conscious.

"Oh—Walter," she murmured, "you were just in time."

"I wish I could have been sooner," I apologized.

"They—they didn't cut the cable—did they?" she asked, as we rose from the water again, bearing her now to safety. "I did my best."

CHAPTER XI

THE WIRELESS DETECTIVE

DEL MAR made his way cautiously along the bank of a little river at the mouth of which he left the boat after escaping from the little steamer.

Quite evidently he was worried by the failure to cut the great Atlantic cable and he was eager to see whether any leak had occurred in the organization which, as secret foreign agent, he had so carefully built up in America.

As he skirted the shore of the river, he came to a falls. Here he moved even more cautiously than before, looking about to make certain that no one had followed him.

It was a beautiful sheet of water that tumbled with a roar over the ledge of rock, then raced away swiftly to the sea in a cloud of spray.

Assured that he was alone, he approached a crevice in the rocks, near the falls. With another hasty look about, he reached in and pulled a lever.

Instantly a most marvellous change took place, incredible almost beyond belief. The volume of water that came over the falls actually and rapidly decreased until it almost stopped, dripping slowly in a thin veil. There was the entrance of a cave—literally hidden behind the falls!

Del Mar walked in. Inside was the entrance to another, inner cave, higher up in the sheer stone of the
wall that the waters had eroded. From the floor to
this entrance led a ladder. Del Mar climbed it, then
stopped just inside the entrance to the inner cave. For
a moment he paused. Then he pressed another lever.
Almost immediately the thin trickle of water grew
until at last the roaring falls completely covered the
cave entrance. It was a clever concealment, contrived
by damming the river above and arranging a new outlet controlled by flood-gates.

There Del Mar stood, in the inner cave. A man
sat at a table, a curious gear fastened over his head and
covering his ears. Before him was a huge apparatus
from which flared a big bluish-green spark, snapping
and crackling above the thunder of the waves. From
the apparatus ran wires apparently up through cables
that penetrated the rocky roof of the cavern and the
river above.

It was Del Mar's secret wireless station, close to the
hidden submarine harbor which had been established
beneath the innocent rocks of the promontory up the
coast. Far overhead, on the cliff over the falls, were
the antennæ of the wireless.

" How is she working? " asked Del Mar.

" Pretty well," answered the man.

" No interference? " queried Del Mar, adjusting the
apparatus.

The man shook his head in the negative.

" We must get a quenched spark apparatus," went
on Del Mar, pleased that nothing was wrong here.
" This rotary gap affair is out of date. By the way, I

want you to be ready to send a message, to be relayed across to our people. I've got to consult the board below in the harbor, first, however. I'll send a messenger to you."

"Very well, sir," returned the man, saluting as Del Mar went out.

.   .   .   .

Out at Fort Dale, Lieutenant Woodward was still entertaining his new friend, Professor Arnold, and had introduced him to Colonel Swift, the commanding officer at the Fort.

They were discussing the strange events of the early morning, when an orderly entered, saluted Colonel Swift and handed him a telegram. The Colonel tore it open and read it, his face growing grave. Then he handed it to Woodward, who read:

WASHINGTON, D. C.
Radio station using illegal wave length in your vicinity. Investigate and report.
BRANDON,
Radio Bureau.

Professor Arnold shook his head slowly, as he handed the telegram back. "There's a wireless apparatus of my own on my yacht," he remarked slowly. "I have an instrument there which I think can help you greatly. Let's see what we can do."

"All right," nodded Colonel Swift to Woodward. "Try."

The two went out and a few minutes later, on the

shore, jumped into Arnold's fast little motor-boat and sped out across the water until they swung around alongside the trim yacht which Arnold was using.

It was a compact and comfortable little craft with lines that indicated both gracefulness and speed. On one of the masts, as they approached, Woodward noticed the wireless aerial. They climbed up the ladder over the side and made their way directly to the wireless room, where Arnold sat down and at once began to adjust the apparatus.

Woodward seemed keenly interested in inspecting the plant which was of a curious type and not exactly like any that he had seen before.

"Wireless apparatus," explained Arnold, still at work, "as you know, is divided into three parts, the source of power, the making and sending of wireless waves, including the key, spark, condenser and tuning coil, and the receiving apparatus—head telephones, antennæ, ground and detector. This is a very compact system with facilities for a quick change from one wave length to another. It has a spark gap, quenched type, break system relay—operator can hear any interference while transmitting—transformation by a single throw of a six-point switch which tunes the oscillating and open circuits to resonance."

Woodward watched him keenly, following his explanation carefully, as Arnold concluded.

"You might call it a radio detective," he added.

. . . .

Even the startling experience of the morning when she was carried off and finally jumped from the little tramp steamer that had attempted to cut the cable did

not dampen Elaine's ardor.   She missed the guiding
hand of Kennedy, yet felt impelled to follow up and
investigate the strange things that had been happening
in the neighborhood of her summer home since his disappearance.

I succeeded in getting her safely home after Burnside and I rescued her in the hydroaeroplane, but no
sooner had she changed her clothes for dry ones than
she disappeared herself.   At least I could not find her,
though, later, I found that she had stolen away to town
and there had purchased a complete outfit of men's
clothes from a second hand dealer.

Cautiously, with the large bundle under her arm, she
returned to Dodge Hall and almost sneaked into her
own home and up-stairs to her room.   She locked the
door and hastily unwrapped the bundle taking out a
tattered suit and the other things, holding them up and
laughing gleefully as she took off her own pretty
clothes and donned these hideous garments.

Quickly she completed her change of costume and
outward character.   As she surveyed herself in the
dainty mirror of her dressing-table she laughed again
at the incongruity of her pretty boudoir and the rough
men's clothes she was wearing.   Deftly she arranged
her hair so that her hat would cover it.   She picked a
black mustache from the table and stuck it on her soft
upper lip.   It tickled and she made a wry face over it.
Then she hunted up a cigarette from the bundle which
she had brought in, lighted it and stuck it in the corner
of her mouth, letting it droop jauntily.   It made her
cough tremendously and she threw it away.

Finally she went to the door and down-stairs.   No

one was about. She opened the door and gazed around. All was quiet. It was a new rôle for her, but, with a bold front, she went out and passed down to the gate of the grounds, pulling her hat down over her eyes and assuming a tough swagger.

Only a few minutes before, down in the submarine harbor, the officers of the board of foreign agents had been grouped about Del Mar, who had entered and taken his place at their head, very angry over the failure to cut the cable. As they concluded their hasty conference, he wrote a message on a slip of paper.

"Take this to our wireless station," he ordered, handing it to one of the men.

The man took it, rose, and went to a wardrobe from which he extracted one of the submarine suits. With the message in his hand, he went out of the room, buckling on the suit.

A few minutes later the messenger in the submarine suit bobbed up out of the water, near the promontory, and climbed slowly over the rocks toward a crevice, where he began to take off the diving outfit.

Having finished, he hid the suit among the rocks and then went along to the little river, carefully skirting its banks into the ravine in which were the falls and the wireless cave.

In her disguise, Elaine had made her way by a sort of instinct along the shore to the rocky promontory where we had discovered the message in the tin tube in the water.

Something, she knew not what, was going on about there, and she reasoned that it was not all over yet. She was right. As she looked about keenly she did see something, and she hid among the rocks. It was a man, all dripping, in an outlandish helmet and suit.

She saw him slink into a crevice and take off the suit, then, as he moved toward the river ravine, she stole up after him.

Suddenly she stopped stark still, surprised, and stared.

The man had actually gone up to the very waterfall. He had pressed what looked like a lever and the water over the falls seemed to stop. Then he walked directly through into a cave.

In the greatest wonder, Elaine crept along toward the falls. Inside the cave Del Mar's emissary started to climb a ladder to an inner cave. As he reached the top, he glanced out and saw Elaine by the entrance. With an oath he jumped into the inner entrance. His hand reached eagerly for a lever in the rocks and as he found and held it, he peered out carefully.

Elaine cautiously came from behind a rock where she had hidden herself and seeing no one apparently watching, now, advanced until she stood directly under the trickle of water which had once been the falls. She gazed into the cave, curiously uncertain whether she dared to go in alone or not.

The emissary jerked fiercely at the lever as he saw Elaine.

Above the falls a dam had been built and by a system of levers the gates could be operated so that the water could be thrown over the falls or diverted away, at will. As the man pressed the lever, the flood gates worked quickly.

Elaine stood gazing eagerly into the blackness of

the cave. Just then a great volume of water from above crashed down on her, with almost crushing weight.

How she lived through it she never knew. But, fortunately, she had not gone quite far enough to get the full force of the water. Still, the terrific flood easily overcame her.

She was swept, screaming, down the stream.

.   .   .   .

Rather alarmed at the strange disappearance of Elaine after I brought her home, I had started out along the road to the shore to look for her, thinking that she might perhaps have returned there.

As I walked along a young tough—at least at the time I thought it was a young tough, so good was the disguise she had assumed and so well did she carry it off—slouched past me.

What such a character could be doing in the neighborhood I could not see. But he was so noticeably tough that I turned and looked. He kept his eyes averted as if afraid of being recognized.

"Great Cæsar," I muttered to myself, "that's a roughneck. This place is sure getting to be a hang-out for gunmen."

I shrugged my shoulders and continued my walk. It was no business of mine. Finding no trace of Elaine, I returned to the house. Aunt Josephine was in the library, alone.

"Where's Elaine?" I asked anxiously.

"I don't know," she replied. "I don't think she's at home."

"Well, I can't find her anywhere," I frowned wan-
15

dering out at a loss what to do, and thrusting my
hands deep in my pockets as an aid to thought.

Somehow, I felt, I didn't seem to get on well as a
detective without Kennedy. Yet, so far, a kind providence seemed to have watched over us. Was it because we were children—or—I rejected that alter-
native.

Walking along leisurely I made my way down to the
shore. At a bridge that crossed a rather turbulent
stream as it tumbled its way toward the sea, I paused
and looked at the water reflectively.

Suddenly my vagrant interest was aroused. Up the
stream I saw some one struggling in the water and
shouting for help as the current carried her along,
screaming.

It was Elaine. The hat and mustache of her disguise were gone and her beautiful Titian hair was
spread out on the water as it carried her now this way,
now that, while she struck out with all her strength to
keep afloat. I did not stop to think how or why she
was there. I swung over the bridge rail, stripping off
my coat, ready to dive. On she came with the swift
current to the bridge. As she approached I dived. It
was not a minute too soon. In her struggles she had
become thoroughly exhausted. She was a good swimmer but the fight with nature was unequal.

I reached her in a second or so and took her hand.
Half pulling, half shoving her, I struck out for the
shore. We managed to make it together where the
current was not quite so strong and climbed safely up
a rock.

Elaine sank down, choking and gasping, not unconscious but pretty much all in and exhausted. I looked at her in amazement. She was the tough character I had just seen.

"Why, where in the world did you get those togs?" I queried.

"Never mind my clothes, Walter," she gasped. "Take me home for some dry ones. I have a clue."

She rose, determined to shake off the effects of her recent plunge and went toward the house. As I helped her she related breathlessly what she has just seen.

Meanwhile, back of that wall of water, the wireless operator in the cave was sending the messages which Del Mar's emissary dictated to him, one after another.

.   .   .   .

With the high resistance receiving apparatus over his head, Arnold was listening to the wireless signals that came over his "radio detective" on the yacht, moving the slider back and forth on a sort of tuning coil, as he listened. Woodward stood close beside him.

"As you know," Arnold remarked, "by the use of an aerial, messages may be easily received from any number of stations. Laws, rules, and regulations may be adopted by the government to shut out interlopers and to plug busybody ears, but the greater part of whatever is transmitted by the Hertzian waves can be snatched down by this wireless detective of mine. Here I can sit in my wireless room with this ear-phone clamped over my head drinking in news, plucking the secrets of others from the sky—in other words, this is eavesdropping by a wireless wire-tapper."

"Are you getting anything now?" asked Woodward.

Arnold nodded, as he seized a pencil and started to write. The lieutenant bent forward in tense interest. Finally Arnold read what he had written and with a peculiar, quiet smile handed it over.

Woodward read. It was a senseless jumble of dots and dashes of the Morse code but, although he was familiar with the code, he could make nothing out of it.

"It's the Morse code all right," he said, handing it back with a puzzled look, "but it doesn't make any sense."

Arnold smiled again, took the paper, and without a word wrote on it some more. Then he handed it back to Woodward. "An old trick," he said. "Reverse the dots and dashes and see what you get."

Woodward looked at it, as Arnold had reversed it and his face lighted up.

"Harbor successfully mined," he quoted in surprise.

"I'll show you another thing about this radio detective of mine," went on Arnold energetically. "It's not only a wave length measurer, but by a process of my own I can determine approximately the distance between the sending and the receiving points of a message."

He attached another, smaller machine to the wireless detector. In the face was a moving finger which swung over a dial marked off in miles from one upward. As Arnold adjusted the new detector, the hand began to move slowly. Woodward looked eagerly. It did not move far, but came to rest above the figure "2."

"Not so very far away, you see, Lieutenant," remarked Arnold, pointing at the dial face.

He seized his glass and hurried to the deck, levelling it at the shore, leaning far over the rail in his eagerness. As he swept the shore, he stopped suddenly. There was a house-roof among the trees with a wireless aerial fastened to the chimney, but not quite concealed by the dense foliage.

"Look," he cried to Woodward, with an exclamation of satisfaction, handing over the glass.

Woodward looked. "A secret wireless station, all right," he agreed, lowering the glass after a long look.

"We'd better get over there right away," planned Arnold, leading the way to the ladder over the side of the yacht and calling to the sailor who had managed the little motor-boat to follow him.

Quickly they skimmed across to the shore. "I think we'd better send to the Fort for some men," considered Arnold as they landed. "We may need reinforcements before we get through."

Woodward nodded and Arnold hastily wrote a note on a rather large scrap of paper which he happened to have in his pocket.

"Take this to Colonel Swift at Fort Dale," he directed the sailor. "And hurry!"

The sailor loped off, half on a run, as Arnold and Woodward left down the shore, proceeding carefully.

. . . .

At top speed, Arnold's sailor made his way to Fort Dale and was directed by the sentry to Colonel Swift who was standing before the headquarters with several officers.

"A message from Lieutenant Woodward and Professor Arnold," he announced, approaching the commanding officer and handing him the note. Colonel Swift tore it open and read:

> Have located radio aerial in the woods along shore. Please send squad of men with bearer.—ARNOLD.

"You just left them?" queried the Colonel.

"Yes sir," replied the sailor. "We came ashore in his boat. I don't know exactly where they went but I know the direction and we can catch up with them easily if we hurry, sir."

The colonel handed the note quickly to a cavalry officer beside him who read it, saluted at the orders that followed, turned and strode off, hastily stuffing the paper in his belt, as the sailor went, too.

Meanwhile, Del Mar's valet was leaving the bungalow and walking down the road on an errand for his master. Up the road he heard the clatter of hoofs. He stepped back off the road and from his covert he could see a squad of cavalry headed by the captain and a sailor cantering past.

The captain turned in the saddle to speak to the sailor, who rode like a horse marine, and as he did so, the turning of his body loosened a paper which he had stuffed quickly into his belt. It fell to the ground. In their hurry the troop, close behind, rode over it. But it did not escape the quick eye of Del Mar's valet.

They had scarcely disappeared around a bend in the road when he stepped out and pounced on the paper,

reading it eagerly. Every line of his face showed
fear as he turned and ran back to the bungalow.

"See what I found," he cried breathlessly bursting
in on Del Mar who was seated at his desk, having returned from the harbor.

Del Mar read it with a scowl of fury. Then he
seized his hat, and a short hunter's axe, and disappeared through the panel into the subterranean passage which took him by the shortest cut through the
very hill to the shore.

.   .   .   .

Slowly Arnold and Woodward made their way along
the shore, carefully searching for the spot where they
had seen the house with the aerial. At last they came
to a place where they could see the deserted house, far
up on the side of a ravine above a river and a waterfalls. They dived into the thick underbrush for cover
and went up the hill.

Some distance off from the house, they parted the
bushes and gazed off across an open space at the ramshackle building. As they looked they could see a
man hurry across from the opposite direction and
into the house.

"As I live, I think that's Del Mar," muttered
Arnold.

Woodward nodded, doubtfully, though.

In the house, Del Mar hurried to a wall where he
found and pressed a concealed spring. A small cabinet in the plaster opened and he took out a little telephone which he rang and through which he spoke
hastily. "Pull in the wires," he shouted. "We're
discovered, I think."

Down in the wireless station in the cave, the operator at his instrument heard the signal of the telephone and quickly answered it. " All right, sir," he returned with a look of great excitement and anxiety. " Cut the wires and I'll pull them in."

Putting back the telephone, Del Mar ran to the window and looked out between the broken slats of the closed blinds. " Confound them!" he muttered angrily.

He could see Arnold and Woodward cautiously approaching. A moment later he stepped back and pulled a silk mask over his upper face, leaving only his eyes visible. Then he seized his hunter's axe and dashed up the stairs. Through the scuttle of the roof he came, making his way over to the chimney to which the wireless antennæ were fastened.

Hastily he cut the wires which ran through the roof from the aerial. As he did so he saw them disappear through the roof. Below, in the cave, down in the ravine back of the falls, the operator was hastily hauling in the wire Del Mar had cut.

Viciously next, Del Mar fell upon the wooden aerial itself, chopping it right and left with powerful blows. He broke it off and threw it over the roof.

Below, Arnold and Woodward, taking advantage of every tree and shrub for concealment, had almost reached the house when the broken aerial fell with a bang almost on them. In surprise they dropped back of a tree and looked up. But from their position they could see nothing. Together they drew their guns and advanced more cautiously at the house.

Del Mar made his way back quickly over the roof,

back through the scuttle and down the stairs again. Should he go out? He looked out of the window. Then he went to the door. An instant he paused thinking and listening, his axe raised, ready for a blow.

Arnold and Woodward, by this time, had reached the door which swung open on its rusty hinges. Woodward was about to go in when he felt a hand on his arm.

"Wait," cautioned Arnold. He took off his hat and jammed it on the end of a stick. Slowly he shoved the door open, then thrust the hat and stick just a fraction of a foot forward.

Del Mar, waiting, alert, saw the door open and a hat. He struck at it hard with the axe and merely the hat and stick fell to the floor.

"Now, come on," shouted Arnold to Woodward.

In the other hand, Del Mar held a chair. As Woodward dashed in with Arnold beside him, Del Mar shied the chair at their feet. Woodward fell over it in a heap and as he did so the delay was all that Del Mar had hoped to gain. Without a second's hesitation he dived through an open window, just as Arnold ran forward, avoiding Woodward and the chair. It was spectacular, but it worked. Arnold fired, but even that was not quick enough. He turned and with Woodward who had picked himself up in spite of his barked shins and they ran back through the door by which they had entered.

Recovering himself, Del Mar dashed for the woods just as Arnold and Woodward ran around the side of the house, still blazing away after him, as they followed, rapidly gaining.

.   .   .   .

Elaine changed her clothes quickly. Meanwhile she
had ordered horses for both of us and a groom brought
them around from the stables. It took me only a short
time to jump into some dry things and I waited impatiently.

She was ready very soon, however, and we mounted
and cantered off, again in the direction of the shore
where she had seen the remarkable waterfall, of which
she had told me.

We had not gone far when we heard sounds, as if
an army were bearing down on us. "What's that?"
I asked.

Elaine turned and looked. It was a squad of cavalry.

"Why, it's Lieutenant Woodward's friend, Captain
Price," she exclaimed, waving to the captain at the
head of the squad.

A moment later Captain Price pulled up and bowed.
Quickly we told him of what Elaine had just discovered.

"That's strange," he said. "This man—" indicating the sailor—"has just told me that Lieutenant
Woodward and Professor Arnold are investigating a
wireless outfit over near there. Perhaps there's some
connection."

"May we join you?" she asked.

"By all means," he returned. "I was about to suggest it myself."

We fell in behind with the rest and were off again.

Under the direction of the sailor we came at last to

the ravine where we looked about searchingly for some trace of Arnold and Woodward.

" What's that noise? " exclaimed one of the cavalry-men.

We could hear shots, above us.

" They may need us," cried Elaine, impatiently.

It was impossible to ride up the sheer height above.

" Dismount," ordered Captain Price.

His men jumped down and we followed him. Elaine struggled up, now helped by me, now helping me.

Further down the hill from the deserted house which we could see above us at the top was an underground passage which had been built to divert part of the water above the falls for power. Through it the water surged and over this boiling stream ran a board walk, the length of the tunnel.

Into this tunnel we could see that a masked man had made his way. As he did so, he turned for just a moment and fired a volley of shots.

Elaine screamed. There were Arnold and Woodward, his targets, coming on boldly, as yet unhit. They rushed in after him, in spite of his running fire, returning his shots and darting toward the tunnel entrance through which he still blazed back at them.

From our end of the ravine, we could see precisely what was going on. " Come—the other end of the tunnel," shouted Price, who had evidently been over the ground and knew it.

We made our way quickly to it and it seemed as if we had our man trapped, like a rat in a hole.

In the tunnel the man was firing back at his pursuers as he ran along the board walk for our end. He looked

up just in time as he approached us. There he could
see Price and his cavalry waiting, cutting off retreat.
We were too many for him. He turned and took a
step back. There were Arnold and Woodward with
levelled guns peering in as though they could not see
very clearly. In a moment their eyes would become accustomed as his to the darkness. What should he do?
There was not a second to waste. He looked down at
the planks beneath him and the black water slipping
past on its way to the power station. It was a desperate chance. But it was all that was left. He dropped
down and let himself without even a splash into the
water.

Arnold and Woodward took a step into the darkness, scarcely knowing what to expect, their eyes a bit
better accustomed to the dusk. But if they had been
there an hour, in all probability they could not have
seen what was at their very feet.

Del Mar had sunk and was swimming under water
in the swift black current sweeping under them. As
they entered, he passed out, nerved up to desperation.

Down the stream, just before it took its final plunge
to the power wheel, Del Mar managed by a superhuman effort to reach out and grasp a wooden support
of the flooring again and pull himself out of the stream.
Smiling grimly to himself, he hurried up the bank.

"Some one's coming," whispered Price. Get
ready."

We levelled our guns. I was about to fire.

"Look out! Don't shoot!" warned a voice sharply.
It was Elaine. Her keen eyes and quick perception

had recognized Arnold, leading Woodward. We lowered our guns.

"Did you see a man, masked, come out here?" cried Woodward.

"No—he must have gone your way," we called.

"No, he couldn't."

Arnold was eagerly questioning the captain as Elaine and I approached. "Dropped into the water—risked almost certain death," he muttered, half turning and seeing us.

"I want to congratulate you on your nerve for going in there," began Elaine, advancing toward the professor.

Apparently he neither heard nor saw us, for he turned as soon as he had finished with Price and went into the cave as though he were too busy to pay any attention to anything else.

Elaine looked up at me, in blank astonishment.

"What an impolite man," she murmured, gazing at the figure all stooped over as it disappeared in the darkness of the tunnel.

CHAPTER XII

THE DEATH CLOUD

OFF a lonely wharf in a deserted part of the coast some miles from the promontory which afforded Del Mar his secret submarine harbor, a ship was riding at anchor.

On the wharf a group of men, husky lascars, were straining their eyes at the mysterious craft.

" Here she comes," muttered one of the men, " at last."

From the ship a large yawl had put out. As she approached the wharf it could be seen that she was loaded to the gunwales with cases and boxes. She drew up close to the wharf and the men fell to unloading her, lifting up the boxes as though they were weighted with feathers instead of metal and explosives.

Down the shore, at the same time, behind a huge rock, crouched a rough looking tramp. His interest in the yawl and its cargo was even keener than that of the lascars.

" Supplies," he muttered, moving back cautiously and up the bluff. " I wonder where they are taking them ? "

Marcus Del Mar had chosen an old and ruined hotel not far from the shore as his storehouse and arsenal.

Already he was there, pacing up and down the rotted veranda which shook under his weight.

"Come, hurry up," he called impatiently as the first of the men carrying a huge box on his back made his appearance up the hill.

One after another they trooped in and Del Mar led them to the hotel, unlocking the door.

Inside, the old hostelry was quite as ramshackle as outside. What had once been the dining-room now held nothing but a long, rickety table and several chairs.

"Put them there," ordered Del Mar, directing the disposal of the cases. "Then you can begin work. I shall be back soon."

He went out and as he did so, two men seized guns from a corner near-by and followed him. On the veranda he paused and turned to the men.

"If any one approaches the house—any one, you understand—make him a prisoner and send for me," he ordered. "If he resists, shoot."

"Yes, sir," they replied, moving over and stationing themselves one at each angle of the narrow paths that ran before the old house.

Del Mar turned and plunged deliberately into the bushes, as if for a cross country walk, unobserved.

Meanwhile, by another path up the bluff, the tramp had made his way parallel to the line taken by the men. He paused at the top of the bluff where some bushes overhung and parted them.

"Their headquarters," he remarked to himself, under his breath.

.   .   .   .

Elaine, Aunt Josephine and I were on the lawn that

forenoon when a groom in resplendent livery came up to us.

"Miss Elaine Dodge?" he bowed.

Elaine took the note he offered and he departed with another bow.

"Oh, isn't that delightful," she cried with pleasure, handing the note to me.

I read it: "The Wilkeshire Country Club will be honored if Miss Dodge and her friends will join the paper chase this afternoon. L. H. Brown, Secretary."

"I suppose a preparation for the fox or drag hunting season?" I queried.

"Yes," she replied. "Will you go?"

"I don't ride very well," I answered, "but I'll go."

"Oh, and here's Mr. Del Mar," she added, turning. "You'll join us at the Wilkeshire hunt in a paper chase this afternoon, surely, Mr. Del Mar?"

"Charmed, I'm sure," he agreed gracefully.

For several minutes we chatted, planning, then he withdrew. "I shall meet you on the way to the Club," he promised.

It was not long before Elaine was ready, and from the stable a groom led three of the best trained cross-country horses in the neighborhood, for old Taylor Dodge, Elaine's father, had been passionately fond of hunting, as had been both Elaine and Aunt Josephine.

We met on the porch and a few minutes later mounted and cantered away. On the road Del Mar joined us and we galloped along to the Hunt Club, careful, however, to save the horses as much as possible for the dash over the fields.

.   .   .   .

For some time the uncouth tramp continued gazing fixedly out of the bushes at the deserted hotel.

Suddenly, he heard a noise and dropped flat on the ground, looking keenly about. Through the trees he could see one of Del Mar's men stationed on sentry duty. He was leaning against a tree, on the alert.

The tramp rose cautiously and moved off in another direction to that in which he had been making his way, endeavoring to flank the sentry. Further along, however, another of Del Mar's men was standing in the same attentive manner near a path that led from the woods.

As the tramp approached, the sentry heard a crackle of the brush and stepped forward. Before the tramp knew it, he was covered by a rifle from the sentry in an unexpected quarter.

Any one but the sentry, with half an eye, might have seen that the fear he showed was cleverly feigned. He threw his hands above his head even before he was ordered and in general was the most tractable captive imaginable. The sentry blew a whistle, whereat the other sentry ran in.

"What shall we do with him," asked the captor.

"Master's orders to take any one to the rendezvous," responded the other firmly, "and lock him up."

Together they forced the tramp to march double quick toward the old hotel. One sentry dropped back at the door and the other drove the tramp before him into the hotel, avoiding the big room on the side where the men were at work and forcing him up-stairs to the attic which had once been the servant's quarters.

There was no window in the room and it was empty.
16

The only light came in through a skylight in the roof.

The sentry thrust the tramp into this room and tried a door leading to the next room. It was locked. At the point of his gun the sentry frisked the tramp for weapons, but found none. As he did so the tramp trembled mightily. But no sooner had the sentry gone than the tramp smiled quietly to himself. He tried both doors. They were locked. Then he looked at the skylight and meditated.

Down below, although he did not know it, in the bare dining-room which had been arranged into a sort of chemical laboratory, Del Mar's men were engaged in manufacturing gas bombs much like those used in the war in Europe. Before them was a formidable array of bottles and retorts. The containers for the bombs were large and very brittle globes of hard rubber. As the men made the gas and forced it under tremendous pressure into tubes, they protected themselves by wearing goggles for the eyes and large masks of cloth and saturated cotton over their mouths and noses.

Satisfied with the safety of his captive, the sentry made his way down-stairs and out again to report to Del Mar.

At the bungalow, Del Mar's valet was setting the library in order when he heard a signal in the secret passage. He pressed the button on the desk and opened the panel. From it the sentry entered.

"Where is Mr. Del Mar?" he asked hurriedly, looking around. "We've been followed to the headquarters by a tramp whom I've captured, and I don't know what to do with him."

"He is not here," answered the valet. "He has gone to the Country Club."

"Confound it," returned the sentry, vexed at the enforced waste of time. "Do you think you can reach him?"

"If I hurry, I may," nodded the valet.

"Then do so," directed the sentry.

He moved back into the panel and disappeared while the valet closed it. A moment later he, too, picked up his hat and hurried out.

.   .   .   .

At the Wilkeshire Club a large number of hunters had arrived for the imitation meet. Elaine, Aunt Josephine, Del Mar and myself rode up and were greeted by them as the Master of Fox Hounds assembled us. Off a bit, a splendid pack of hounds was held by the huntsman while they debated whether to hold a paper chase or to try a drag hunt.

"You start your cross-country riding early," commented Del Mar.

"Yes," answered Elaine. "You see we can hardly wait until autumn and the weather is so fine and cool, we feel that we ought to get into trim during the summer. So we have paper chases and drag hunts as soon as we can, mainly to please the younger set."

The chase was just about to start, when the valet came up. Del Mar caught his eye and excused himself to us. What he said, we could not hear, but Del Mar frowned, nodded and dismissed him.

Just then the horn sounded and we went off, dashing across the road into a field in full chase after the hounds, taking the fences and settling down to a good half hour's run over the most beautiful country I have ever seen.

The hounds had struck the trail, which of course, as was finally decided, was nothing but that laid by an anise-seed bag dragged over the ground. It was none the less, in fact perhaps more interesting for that.

The huntsman winded his horn and mirthful shouts of " Gone away! " sounded in imitation of a real hunt. The blast of the horn once heard is never forgotten, thrilling the blood and urging one on.

The M. F. H. seemed to be everywhere at once, restraining those who were too eager and saving the hounds often from being ridden down by those new to the hunt who pressed them.

Elaine was one of the foremost. Her hunter was one carefully trained, and she knew all the tricks of the game.

Somehow, I got separated, at first, from the rest and followed, until finally I caught up, and then kept behind one of the best riders.

Del Mar also got separated, but, as I afterward learned, by intention, for he deliberately rode out of the course at the first opportunity he had and let Elaine and the rest of us pass without seeing him.

Elaine's blood was up, but somehow, in spite of herself, she went astray, for the hounds had distanced the fleetest riders and she, in an attempt at a short cut over the country which she thought she knew so well, went a mile or so out of the way.

She pulled up in a ravine and looked about. Intently she listened. There was no sign of the hunt. She was hot and tired and thirsty and, at a loss just how to join the field again, she took this chance to dismount and drink from a clear stream fed by mountain springs.

As she did so, floating over the peaceful woodland air came the faint strains of the huntsman's horn, far, far off. She looked about, straining her eyes and ears to catch the direction of sound. Just then her horse caught the winding of the horn. His ears went erect and without waiting he instantly galloped off, leaving her. Elaine called and ran after him, but it was too late. She stopped and looked dejectedly as he disappeared. Then she made her way up the side of the ravine, slowly.

On she climbed until, to her surprise, she came to the ruins of an old hotel. She remembered, as a child, when it had been famous as a health resort, but it was all changed now—a wreck. She looked at it a moment, then, as she had nothing better to do, approached it.

She advanced toward a window of the dining-room and looked in.

.   .   .   .

Del Mar waited only until the last straggler had passed. Then he dashed off as fast as his horse would carry him straight toward the deserted hotel which served him as headquarters for the supplies he was accumulating. As he rode up, one of his sentries appeared, as if from nowhere, and, seeing who it was, saluted.

"Here, take care of this horse," ordered Del Mar, dismounting and turning the animal over to the man,

who led him to the rear of the building as Del Mar
entered the front door, after giving a secret signal.

There were his men in goggles and masks at the
work, which his knock had interrupted.

"Give me a mask before I enter the room," he ordered of the man who had answered his signal.

The man handed the mask and goggles to him, as
well as a coat, which he put on quickly. Then he entered the room and looked at the rapid progress of the
work.

"Where's the prisoner?" asked Del Mar a moment
later, satisfied at the progress of his men.

"In the attic room," one of his lieutenants indicated.

"I'd like to take a look at him," added Del Mar, just
about to turn and leave the room.

As he did so, he happened to glance at one of the
windows. There, peering through the broken shutters,
was a face—a girl's face—Elaine!

"Just what I wanted guarded against," he cried angrily, pointing at the window. "Now—get her!"

The men had sprung up at his alarm. They could
all see her and with one accord dashed for the door.
Elaine sprang back and they ran as they saw that she
was warned. In genuine fear now she too ran from
the window. But it was too late.

For just then the sentry who had taken Del Mar's
horse came from behind the building cutting off her
retreat. He seized her just as the other men ran out.
Elaine stared. She could make nothing of them. Even
Del Mar, in his goggles and breathing mask was unrecognizable.

"Take her inside," he ordered disguising his voice.

Then to the sentry he added, " Get on guard again and don't let any one through."

Elaine was hustled into the big deserted hallway of the hotel, just as the tramp had been.

" You may go back to work," Del Mar signed to the other men, who went on, leaving one short but athletic looking fellow with Del Mar and Elaine.

" Lock her up, Shorty," ordered Del Mar, " and bring the other prisoner to me down here."

None too gently the man forced Elaine up-stairs ahead of him.

.   .   .   .

In the attic, the tramp, pacing up and down, heard footsteps approach on the stairs and enter the next room.

Quickly he ran to the doorway and peered through the keyhole. There he could see Elaine and the small man enter. He locked the door to the hall, then quickly took a step toward the door into the tramp's room.

There was just time enough for the tramp to see his approach. He ran swiftly and softly over to the further corner and dropped down as if sound asleep. The key turned in the lock and the small man entered, careful to lock the door to Elaine's room. He moved over to where the tramp was feigning sleep.

" Get up," he growled, kicking him.

The tramp sat up, yawning and rubbing his eyes. " Come now, be reasonable," demanded the man. " Follow me."

He started toward the door into the hall. He never reached it. Scarcely was his hand on the knob when the tramp seized him and dragged him to the floor.

One hand on the man's throat and his knees on his chest, the tramp tore off the breathing mask and goggles. Already he had the man trussed up and gagged.

Quickly the tramp undressed the man and left him in his underclothes, still struggling to get loose, as he took Shorty's clothes, including the strange head-gear, and unlocked the door into the next room with the key he also took from him.

.   .   .   .

Elaine was pacing anxiously up and down the little room into which she had been thrown, greatly frightened.

Suddenly the door through which her captor had left opened hurriedly again. A most disreputable looking tramp entered and locked the door again. Elaine started back in fear.

He motioned to her to be quiet. "You'll never get out alive," he whispered, speaking rapidly and thickly, as though to disguise his voice. "Here—take these clothes. Do just as I say. Put them on. Put on the mask and goggles. Cover up your hair. It is your only chance."

He laid the clothes down and went out into the hallway. Outside he listened carefully at the head of the stairs and looked about expecting momentarily to be discovered.

Elaine understood only that suddenly a friend in need had appeared. She changed her clothes quickly, finding fortunately that they fitted her pretty well. By pulling the hat over her hair and the goggles over her eyes and tying on the breathing mask, she made a very presentable man.

Cautiously she pushed open the door into the hallway. There was the tramp. " What shall I do? " she asked.

" Don't talk," he whispered close to her ear. " Go out—and if you meet any one, just salute and walk past."

" Yes—yes, I understand," she nodded back, " and—thank you."

He gave her no time to say more, even if it had been safe, but turned and locked the door of her room.

Trying to keep the old stairway from creaking and betraying her, she went down. She managed to reach the lower hallway without seeing anybody or being discovered. Quietly she went to the door and out. She had not gone far when she met an armed man, the sentry, who had been concealed in the shrubbery.

" Who goes there? " he challenged.

Elaine did not betray herself by speaking, but merely saluted and passed on as fast as she could without exciting further suspicion. Nonplused, the man turned and watched her curiously as she moved away down the path.

" Where's *he* going? " the sentry muttered, still staring.

Elaine in her eagerness was not looking as carefully where she was going as she was thinking about getting away in safety. Suddenly an overhanging branch of a tree caught her hat and before she knew it pulled it off her head. There was no concealing her golden hair now.

" Stop! " shouted the sentry.

Elaine did not pause, but dived into the bushes on the side of the path, just as the man fired and ran forward, still shouting for her to halt. She ran as fast as she could, pulling off the goggles and mask and looking back now and then in terror at her pursuer who was rapidly gaining on her.

Before she could catch herself she missed her footing and slipped over the edge of a gorge. Down she went, with a rush. It was unfortunate, dangerous, but, after all, it was the only thing that saved her, at least for the time. Half falling, half sliding, scratching herself and tearing her clothes, she descended.

The sentry checked himself just in time at the top of the gorge and leaned as far over the edge as he dared. He raised his gun again and fired. But Elaine's course was so hidden by the trees and so zigzag that he missed again. A moment he hesitated, then started and climbed down after her as fast as he could.

At the bottom of the hill she picked herself up and dashed again into the woods, the sentry still after her and gaining again.

At the same time, we who were still in the chase had circled about the country until we were very near where we started. Following the dogs over a rail fence, I drew up suddenly, hearing a scream.

There was Elaine, on foot, running as if her life depended on it. I needed no second glance. Behind her was a man with a rifle, almost overtaking her.

As luck would have it, the momentum of my horse carried me right at them. Careful to avoid Elaine, I rode square at the man, striking at him viciously with my riding crop before he knew what had struck him.

The fellow dropped, stunned. I leaped from my horse and ran to her, just as the rest of the hunt came up.

Eagerly questioning us, they gathered about.

.   .   .   .

Having waited until he was sure that Elaine had got away safely, the old tramp slowly and carefully followed down the stairs of the ruined hotel.

As he went down, he heard a shot from the woods. Could it be one of the sentries? He looked about keenly, hesitating just what to do.

In an instant, down below, he heard the scurry of footsteps from the improvised laboratory and shouts. He turned and stealthily ran up-stairs, just as the door opened.

The tramp had not been the only one who had been alarmed by the shot of the sentry.

Del Mar was talking again to the men when it rang out. "What's that?" he exclaimed. "Another intruder?"

The men stared at him blankly, while Del Mar dashed for the door, followed by them all. In the hall he issued his orders quickly.

"Here, you fellows," he called dividing the men, "get outside and see what is doing. You other men follow me. I want you to see if everything's all right up above."

Meanwhile the tramp had gained the upper hallway and dashed past the room which he occupied. Outside, in the hall, Del Mar and his men rushed up to the door of the room in which Elaine had been thrown. It was locked and they broke in. She was gone!

On into the next room they dashed, bearing down this door also. There was Shorty, trussed up in his underclothes. They hastened to release him.

"Where are they—where's the tramp?" demanded Del Mar angrily.

"I think I heard some one on the roof," replied Shorty weakly.

He was right. The tramp had managed to get through a scuttle on the roof. Then he climbed down to the edge and began to let himself hand over hand down the lightning rod.

Reaching the ground safely, he scurried about to the back of the building. There, tied, was the horse which Del Mar had ridden to the hunt. He untied it, mounted and dashed off down the path through the woods, taking the shortest cut in the direction of Fort Dale.

Dusty and flecked with foam, the tramp and his mount, a strange combination, were instantly challenged by the sentry at the Fort.

"I must see Lieutenant Woodward immediately," urged the tramp.

A heated argument followed until finally a corporal of the guards was called and led off the tramp toward the headquarters.

It was only a few minutes before Woodward was convinced of the identity of the tramp with his friend, Professor Arnold. At the head of a squad of cavalry, Woodward and the tramp dashed off.

Already on the *qui vive*, Elaine heard the sound of hoof-beats long before the rest of us crowded around her. For the moment we all stood ready to repel an attack from any quarter.

But it was not meant for us. It was Woodward at the head of a score or so of cavalrymen. With him rode a tramp on a horse which was strangely familiar to me.

"Oh," cried Elaine, "there's the man who saved me!"

As they passed, the tramp paused a moment and looked at us sharply. Although he carefully avoided Elaine's eyes, I fancied that only when he saw that she was safe was he satisfied to gallop off and rejoin the cavalry.

.   .   .   .

Around the old hotel, in every direction, Del Mar's men were searching for the tramp and Elaine, while in the hotel another search was in progress.

"Have you discovered anything?" asked Del Mar, entering.

"No, sir," they reported.

"Confound it!" swore Del Mar, going up-stairs again.

Here also were men searching. "Find anything?" he asked briefly.

"No luck," returned one.

Del Mar went on up to the top floor and out through the open scuttle to the roof. "That's how he got away, all right," he muttered to himself, then looking up he exclaimed under his breath, as his eye caught something far off, "The deuce—what's that?"

Leaning down to the scuttle, he called, "Jenkins— my field-glasses—quick!"

One of his men handed them to him and he adjusted them, gazing off intently. There he could see what looked like a squad of cavalry galloping along headed by an officer and a rough looking individual.

"Come—we must get ready for an attack!" he shouted diving down the scuttle again.

In the laboratory dining-room, his men, recalled, hastily took his orders. Each of them seized one of the huge black rubber newly completed gas bombs and ran out, making for a grove near-by.

Quickly as Del Mar had acted, it was not done so fast but that the troop of cavalry as they pulled up on the top of a hill and followed the directing finger of the tramp could see men running to the cover of the grove.

"Forward!" shouted Woodward.

As if all were one machine, the men and horses shot ahead, until they came to the grove about the old hotel. There they dismounted and spread out in a semi-circular order, advancing on the grove. As they did so, shots rang out from behind the trees. Del Mar's men, from the shelter were firing at them. But it seemed hopeless for the fugitives.

"Ready!" ordered Del Mar as the cavalrymen advanced, relentless.

Each of his men picked up one of the big black gas bombs and held it high up over his head.

"Come on!" urged Woodward.

His men broke into a charge on the grove.

"Throw them!" ordered Del Mar.

As far as he could hurl it, each of the men sent one of the black globes hurtling through the air. They fell almost simultaneously, a long line of them, each breaking into a thousand bits. Instantly dense, greenish-yellow fumes seemed to pour forth, enveloping everything. The wind which Del Mar had carefully noted when he chose the position in the grove, was blowing from his men toward the only position from which an attack could be made successfully.

Against Woodward's men as they charged, it seemed as if a tremendous, slow-moving wall of vapor were advancing from the trees. It was only a moment before it completely wrapped them in its stifling, choking, suffocating embrace. Some fell, overcome. Others tried to run, clutching frantically at their throats and rubbing their eyes.

" Get back—quick—till it rolls over," choked Woodward.

Those who were able to do so, picked up their stupefied comrades and retreated, as best they could, stumbling blindly back from the fearful death cloud of chlorine.

Meantime, under cover of this weird defence, Del Mar and his men, their own faces covered and unrecognizable in their breathing masks and goggles, dashed to one side, with a shout and disappeared walking and running behind and even through the safety of their impregnable gas barrier.

More slowly we of the hunt had followed Woodward's cavalry until, some distance off, we stood, witnessing and wondering at the attack. To our utter amazement we saw them carrying off their wounded and stupefied men. We hurried forward and gathered about, offering whatever assistance we could to resuscitate them.

As Elaine and I helped, we saw the unkempt figure of the tramp borne in and laid down. He was not completely overcome, having had presence of mind to tie a handkerchief over his nose and mouth.

Elaine hurried toward him with an exclamation of sympathy.   Just recovering full consciousness, he heard her.

With the greatest difficulty, he seemed to summon some reserve force not yet used. He struggled to his feet and staggered off, as though he would escape us.

" What a strange old codger," mused Elaine, looking from me at the retreating figure. " He saved my life—yet he won't even let me thank him—or help him! "

CHAPTER XIII

THE SEARCHLIGHT GUN

" I DON'T understand it," remarked Elaine one day as, with Aunt Josephine and myself, she was discussing the strange events that had occurred since the disappearance of Kennedy, " but, somehow, it is as if a strange Providence seems to be watching over us."

" Nor do I," I agreed. " It does seem that, although we do not see it, a mysterious power for good is about us. It's uncanny."

" A package for you, Miss Dodge," announced Marie, coming in with a small parcel which had been delivered by a messenger who did not wait for an answer.

Elaine took it, looked at it, turned it over, and then looked at the written address again.

" It's not the handwriting of any one which I recognize," she mused. " Now, I suppose I ought to be suspicious of it. Yet, I'm going to open it."

She did so. Inside, the paper wrapping covered a pasteboard box. She opened that. There lay a revolver, which she picked up and turned over. It was a curious looking weapon.

" I never knew so much about firearms as I have learned in the past few weeks," remarked Elaine.

" But what do you suppose this is—and who sent it to me—and why?"

She held the gun up. From the barrel stuck out a little rolled-up piece of paper. " See," she cried, reading and handing the paper to me, " there it is again— that mysterious power."

Aunt Josephine and I read the note:

DEAR MISS DODGE:

This weapon shoots exactly into the center of the light disc. Keep it by you.—A FRIEND.

"Let me see it," I asked, taking the gun. Sure enough, along the barrel was a peculiar tube. " A searchlight gun," I exclaimed, puzzled, though still my suspicions were not entirely at rest. " Suppose it's sighted wrong," I could not help considering. " It might be a plant to save some one from being shot."

"That's easily settled," returned Elaine. " Let's try it."

"Oh, mercy no,—not here," remonstrated Aunt Josephine.

"Why not—down cellar?" persisted Elaine. " It can't hurt anything there."

"I think it would be a good plan," I agreed, " just to make sure that it is all right."

Accordingly we three went down cellar. There, Elaine found the light switch and turned it. Eagerly I hunted about for a mark. There, in some rubbish that had not yet been carted away, was a small china plate. I set it up on a small shelf across the room and took the gun. But Elaine playfully wrenched it from my hand.

" No," she insisted, " it was sent to me. Let me try it first."

Reluctantly I consented.

" Switch off the light, Walter, please," she directed, standing a few paces from the plate.

I did so. In the darkness Elaine pointed the gun and pulled a little ratchet. Instantly a spot of light showed on the wall. She moved the revolver and the spot of light moved with it. As it rested on a little decorative figure in the center of the plate, she pulled the trigger. The gun exploded with a report, deafening, in the confined cellar.

I switched on the light and we ran forward. There was the plate—smashed into a hundred bits. The bullet had struck exactly in the centre of the little bull's-eye of light.

" Splendid," cried Elaine enthusiastically, as we looked at each other in surprise.

Though none of us guessed it, half an hour before, in the seclusion of his yacht, Woodward's friend, Professor Arnold, had been standing with the long barrelled gun in his hand, adjusting the tube which ran beneath the barrel.

In one hand he held the gun; in the other was a piece of paper. As he brought the paper before the muzzle and pressed a ratchet by gripping the revolver handle, a distinct light appeared on the paper, thrown out from the tube under the barrel.

Having adjusted the tube and sighted it, Arnold wrote a hasty note on another piece of paper and inserted it into the barrel of the gun, with the end sticking out just a bit. Then he wrapped the whole thing up in a box, rang a bell, and handed the package to a servant with explicit instructions as to its delivery to the right person and only to that person.

   .   .   .   .

Down in the submarine harbor, Del Mar was in conference with his board of strategy and advice, laying the plan for the attack on America.

"Ever since we have been at work," he remarked, "Elaine Dodge has been busy hindering and frustrating us. That girl must go!"

Before him, on the table, he placed a square package. "It must stop," he added ominously, tapping the package.

"But how?" asked one of the men. "We've done our best."

"This is a bomb," replied Del Mar, continuing to tap the package. "When our man—let me see, X had better do it,—arrives, have him look in the secret cavern by the landing-place. There I will leave it. I want him to put it in her house to-night."

He handed the bomb to one of his men who took it gingerly. Then with a few more words of admonition, he took up his diving helmet and left the hadquarters, followed by the man.

Several minutes later, Del Mar, alone, emerged from the water just outside the submarine harbor and took off his helmet.

He made his way over the rocks, carrying the bomb, until he came to a little fissure in the rocks, like a cavern. There he hid the bomb carefully. Still carrying the helmet, he hurried along until he came to the cave entrance that led to the secret passage to the panel in his bungalow library. Up through the secret passage he went, reaching the panel and opening it by a spring.

In the library Del Mar changed his wet clothes and hid them, then set to work on an accumulation of papers on his desk.

.   .   .   .

That afternoon, Elaine decided to go for a little ride through the country in her runabout.

As she started to leave her room, dressed for the trip, it was as though a premonition of danger came to her. She paused, then turned back and took from the drawer the searchlight gun which had been sent to her. She slipped it into the pocket of her skirt and went out.

Off she drove at a fast clip, thoroughly enjoying the ride until, near a bend in the road, as it swept down toward the shore, she stopped and got out, attracted by some wild flowers. They grew in such profusion that it seemed no time before she had a bunch of them. On she wandered, down to the rocks, watching the restless waters of the Sound. Finally she found herself walking alone along the shore, one arm full of flowers, while with her free hand she amused herself by skimming flat stones over the water.

As she turned to pick up one, her eye caught something in the rocks and she stared at it. There in a crevice, as though it had been hidden, was a strange square package. She reached down and picked it up. What could it be?

While she was examining it, back of her, another of those strange be-helmeted figures came up out of the water. It watched her for an instant, then sank back into the water again.

Elaine, holding the package in her hand, walked up the shore, oblivious to the strange eye that had been fixed on er.

"I must show this to Lieutenant Woodward," she said to herself.

In the car she placed the package, then jumped in herself carefully and started off.

A moment after she had gone, the diver reappeared, looking about cautiously. This time the coast was clear and he came all the way out, taking off his helmet and placed it in the secret hiding-place which Del Mar and his men used. Then, with another glance, now of anger, in the direction of Elaine, he hurried up the shore.

Meanwhile, as fast as her light runabout would carry her, Elaine whizzed over to Fort Dale.

As she entered the grounds, the sentry saluted her, though that part of the formalities of admission was purely perfunctory, for every one at the Fort knew her now.

"Is Lieutenant Woodward in?" she inquired.

"Yes ma'am," returned the sentry. "I will send for him."

A corporal appeared and took a message for her to Woodward. It was only a few minutes before Lieutenant Woodward himself appeared.

"What is the trouble, Miss Dodge?" he asked solicitously, noting the look on her face.

"I don't know what it is," she replied dubiously. "I've found something among the rocks. Perhaps it is a bomb."

Woodward looked at the package, studying it.

" Professor Arnold is investigating this affair for us,"
he remarked. " Perhaps you'd better take the package
to him on his yacht. I'm sorry I can't go with you, but
just now I'm on duty."

" That's a good idea," she agreed. " Only I'm sorry
you can't go along with me."

She started up the car and drove off as Woodward
turned back to the Fort with a lingering look.

.   .   .   .

Del Mar was hard at work in the library when, suddenly, he heard a sound at the panel. He reached over
and pressed a button on his desk, and the panel opened.
Through it came the diver still wearing his dripping
suit and carrying the weird helmet under his arm.

" That Dodge girl has crossed us again!" he exclaimed excitedly.

" How?" demanded Del Mar, with an oath.

" I saw her on the rocks just now. She happened to
stumble on the bomb which you left there to be placed."

" And then?" demanded Del Mar.

" She took it with her in her car."

" The deuce!" ejaculated the foreign agent, furiously. " You must get the men out and hunt the country thoroughly. She must not escape now at any cost."

The diving man dove back into the panel to escape
Del Mar's wrath, while Del Mar hurried out, leaving
his valet in the library.

Quickly, Del Mar made his way to a secret hiding-
place in the hills back of the bay. There he found his
picked band of men armed with rifles.

As briefly as he could he told them of what had happened. " We must get her this time—dead or alive,"

he ordered. "Now scatter about the country. Keep in touch with each other and when you find her, close in on her at any cost."

The men saluted and left in various directions to scour the country. Del Mar himself picked up a rifle and followed shortly, passing down a secret trail to the road where he had a car with a chauffeur waiting. Still carrying the rifle, he climbed in and the man shot the car along down the road.

.   .   .   .

On the top of a hill one of the men was posted as a sort of lookout. Gazing over the country carefully, his eye was finally arrested by something at which he stared eagerly. Far away, on the road, he could see a car in which was a girl, alone. Waving in the breeze was a red feather in her hat. He looked more sharply. It was Elaine Dodge.

The man turned and waved a signal with a handkerchief to another man far off. Down the valley another of Del Mar's men was waiting and watching. As soon as he saw the signal, he waved back and ran along the road.

As Del Mar whizzed along, he could see one of his men approaching over the road, waving to him. "Stop!" he ordered his driver.

The man hurried forward. "I've got the signal," he panted. "They have seen her car over the hill."

"Good," exclaimed Del Mar, pulling a black silk mask over his eyes. "Now, get off quickly. We've got to catch her."

They sped away again in a cloud of dust.

But even while Del Mar was speeding toward her,

another of his men had discovered her presence, so vigilant were they.

He had been keeping a sharp watch on the road, when he was suddenly all attention. He saw a car, through the foliage. Quickly, his rifle went to his shoulder. Through the sight he could just cover Elaine's head, for her hat, with a bright red feather in it, showed plainly just over the bushes.

He aimed carefully and fired.

.   .   .   .

I had been out for a tramp over the hills with no destination in particular. As I swung along the road, I heard the throbbing of a car coming up the hill, the cut-out open. I turned, for cars make walking on country roads somewhat hazardous nowadays.

As I did so, some one in the car waved to me. I looked again. It was Elaine.

"Where are you going?" she called.

"Where are *you* going?" I returned, laughing.

"I've just had a very queer experience—found something down on the rocks," she replied seriously, pointing to the square package on the floor of the car. "I took it to Lieutenant Woodward and he advised me to take it to Professor Arnold on his yacht. I think it is a bomb. I wish you'd go with me."

Before I could answer, up the hill a rifle shot cracked. There was a whirr in the air and a bullet sang past us, cutting the red feather off Elaine's hat.

"Duck!" I cried, jumping into the car, "And drive like the dickens!"

She turned and we fairly ricocheted down that road back again.

Behind us, a man, a stranger whom we did not pause to observe, rushed from the bushes and fired after us again.

Suddenly another rifle shot cracked. It was from another car that had stealthily sneaked up on us—coming fast, recklessly.

"There's her car," pointed one of the occupants to a man who was masked in black.

"Yes," he nodded. "Give her a little more gas!"

"Crouch down," I muttered, "as low as you can."

We did so, racing for life, the more powerful motor behind us overhauling us every instant.

We were coming to a very narrow part of the road where it turned, on one side a sheer hill, on the other a stream several feet down.

If we had an accident, I thought, it might be ticklish for us, supposing the square package really to be a bomb. What if it should go off? The idea suggested another, instantly. The car behind was only a few feet off.

As we reached the narrow road by the stream, I rose up. As far as I could, back of me, I hurled the infernal machine. It fell. We received a shower of dirt and small stones, but the cover of the car protected us. Where the bomb landed, however, it cut a deep hole in the roadway.

On came Del Mar's car, the driver frantically tugging at the emergency brake. But it was of no use. There was not room to turn aside. The car crashed into the hole, like a gigantic plow.

It took one header over the side of the road and down several feet into the stream, just as the masked man and the driver jumped far ahead into the water.

Safe now in our car which was slackening its terrific speed, I looked back. "They've been thrown!" I cried. "We're all right."

On the edge of the water, just covered by some wreckage, the chauffeur lay motionless. The masked man crawled from under the wreckage and looked at him a moment.

"Dead!" he exclaimed, still mechanically gripping a rifle in his hand.

Angrily he raised it at us and fired.

A moment later, some other men gathered from all directions about him, each armed.

"Don't mind the wreck," he cried, exasperated. "Fire!"

A volley was delivered at us. But the distance was now apparently too great.

We were just congratulating ourselves on our escape, when a stray shot whizzed past, striking a piece directly out of the head of the steering-post, almost under Elaine's hands.

Naturally she lost control, though fortunately we were not going so fast now. Crazily, our car swerved from side to side of the road, as she vainly tried to control both its speed and direction. On the very edge of the ditch, however, it stopped.

We looked back. There we could see a group of men who seemed to spring out of the woods, as if from nowhere, at the sound of the shots. A shout went up at the sight of the bullet taking effect, and they ran forward at us.

One of their number, I could see, masked, who had

been in the wrecked car, stumbled forward weakly, until finally he sank down.

A couple of the others ran to him. " Go on," he must have urged vehemently. " One of you is enough to stay with me. I'm going back to the submarine harbor. The rest—go on—report to me there."

As the rest ran toward us, there was nothing for us to do but to abandon the car ourselves and run for it. We left the road and struck into the trackless woods, followed closely now by two of the men who had out-distanced the rest. Through the woods we fled, taking advantage of such shelter as we could find.

" Look, here's a cave," cried Elaine, as we plunged, exhausted and about ready to drop, down into a ravine.

We hurried in and the bushes swung over the cave entrance. Inside we stopped short and gazed about. It was dark and gloomy. We looked back. There was no hope there. They had been overtaking us. On down a passageway, we went.

The two men who were pursuing us plunged down the ravine also. As ill-luck would have it, they saw the cave entrance and dashed in, then halted. Crouch-ing in the shadow we could see their figures silhoutted in the dim light of the entrance of the cavern. One stopped at the entrance while the other advanced. He was a big fellow and powerfully built and the other fellow was equally burly. I made up my mind to fight to the last though I knew it was hopeless. It was dark. I could not even see the man advancing now.

Quickly Elaine reached into her pocket and drew out something.

" Here, Walter, take this," she cried.

I seized the object. It was the searchlight gun.

Hastily I aimed it, the spot of light glowing brightly. Indeed, I doubt whether I could have shot very accurately otherwise. As the man approached cautiously down the passageway the bright disc of light danced about until finally it fell full on his breast. I fired. The man fell forward instantly.

Again I fired, this time at the man in the cave entrance. He jumped back, dropping his gun which exploded harmlessly. His hand was wounded. Quickly he drew back and disappeared among the trees.

We waited in tense silence, and then cautiously looked out of the mouth of the cave. No one seemed to be about.

"Come—let's make a dash for it," urged Elaine.

We ran out and hurried on down the ravine, apparently not followed.

Back among the trees, however, the man had picked up a rifle which he had hidden. While he was binding up his hand with a handkerchief, he saw us. Painfully he tried to aim his gun. But it was too heavy for his weakened arm and the pain was too great. He had to lower it. With a muttered imprecation, he followed us at a distance.

Evidently, to us, we had eluded the pursuers, for no one seemed now to be following, at least as far as we could determine. We kept on, however, until we came to the water's edge. There, down the bay, we could see Professor Arnold's yacht.

"Let us see Professor Arnold, anyhow," said Elaine, leading the way along the shore.

We came at last, without being molested, to a little

dock. A sailor was standing beside it and moored to it was a swift motor-boat. Out at anchor was the yacht.

"You are Professor Arnold's man?" asked Elaine.

"Yes'm," he replied, remembering her.

"Is the Professor out on his boat?" we asked.

He nodded. "Did you want to see him?"

"Very much," answered Elaine.

"I'll take you out," he offered.

We jumped into the motor-boat, he started the engine and we planed out over the water.

Though we did not see him, the man whom I had wounded was still watching us from the shore, noting every move. He had followed us at a distance across the woods and fields and down along the shore to the dock, had seen us talking to Arnold's man, and get into the boat.

From the shore he continued to watch us skim across the bay and pull up alongside the yacht. As we climbed the ladder, he turned and hurried back the way he had come.

.   .   .   .

Elaine and I climbed aboard the yacht where we could see the Professor sitting in a wicker deck chair.

"Why, how do you do?" he welcomed us, adjusting his glasses so that his eyes seemed, if anything, more opaque than before.

I could not help thinking that, although he was glad to see us, there was a certain air of restraint about him.

Quickly Elaine related the story of finding the bomb in the rocks and the peculiar events and our escape which followed. Once, at the mention of the searchlight gun, Professor Arnold raised his hand and coughed back of it. I felt sure that it was to hide an involuntary expression of satisfaction and that it must be he who had sent the gun to Elaine.

He was listening attentively to her, while I stood by the rail, now and then looking out over the water. Far away I noted something moving over the surface, like a rod, followed by a thin wake of foam.

"Look!" I exclaimed, "What's that?"

Elaine turned to me, as Arnold seized his glasses.

"Why, it seems to be moving directly at us," exclaimed Elaine.

"By George, it's the periscope of a submarine," cried Arnold a moment later, lowering his glasses.

He did not hesitate an instant.

"Get the yacht under way," he ordered the captain, who immediately shouted his orders to the rest.

Quickly the engine started and we plowed ahead, that ominous looking periscope following.

.   .   .   .

In the submarine harbor to which he had been taken, Del Mar found that he had been pretty badly shaken up by the accident to his car. His clothes were torn and his face and body scratched. No bones were broken, however, though the shock had been great. Several of his men were endeavoring to fix him up in the little submarine office, but he was angry, very angry.

At such a juncture, a man in a dripping diving-suit entered and pulled off his helmet, after what had evidently been a hasty trip from the land through the entrance and up again into the harbor. As he approached, Del Mar saw that the man's hand was bound up.

" What's the matter? " demanded Del Mar. " How did you get that? "

" That fellow Jameson and the girl did it," he replied, telling what had happened in the cave. " Some one must have given them one of those new searchlight guns."

Del Mar, already ugly, was beside himself with rage now.

" Where are they? " he asked.

" I saw them go out to the yacht of that Professor Arnold."

" He's the fellow that gave her the gun," almost hissed Del Mar. " On the yacht, are they? "

An evil smile seemed to spread over his face. " Then we'll get them all, this time. Man the submarine—the Z99."

All left the office on the run, hurrying around the ledge and down into the open hatch of the submarine. Del Mar came along a moment later, giving orders sharply and quickly.

The hatch was closed and the vessel sealed. On all sides were electrical devices and machines to operate the craft and the torpedoes—an intricate system of things which it seemed as if no human mind could possibly understand.

Del Mar threw on a switch. The submarine hummed and trembled. Slowly she sank in the harbor until she was at the level of the underwater entrance through the rocks. Carefully she was guided out through this entrance into the waters of the larger, real harbor.

Del Mar took his place at the periscope, the eye of the submarine. Anxiously he turned it about and bent over the image which it projected.

"There it is," he muttered, picking out Arnold's yacht and changing the course of the submarine so that it was headed directly at it, the planes turned so that they kept the boat just under the surface with only the periscope showing above.

Forward, about the torpedo discharge tubes men were busy, testing the doors, and getting ready the big automobile torpedoes.

"They must have seen us," muttered Del Mar. "They've started the yacht. But we can beat them, easily. Are you ready?"

"Yes," called back the men forward, pushing a torpedo into the lock-like compartment from which it was launched.

"Let it go, then," bellowed Del Mar.

The torpedo shot out into the water, travelling under her own power, straight at the yacht.

.   .   .   .

Elaine and I looked back. The periscope was much nearer than before. "Can we outdistance the submarine?" I asked of Arnold.

Arnold shook his head, his face grave. On came the thin line of foam. "I'm afraid we'll have to leave the yacht," he said warningly. "My little motor-boat is much faster."

Arnold shouted his orders as he led us down the lad-

18

der to the motor-boat into which we jumped, followed by as many of the crew as could get in, while the others leaped into the water from the rail of the yacht and struck out for the shore which was not very distant.

"What's that?" cried Elaine, horrified, pointing back.

The water seemed to be all churned up. A long cigar-shaped affair was slipping along near enough to the surface so that we could just make it out—murderous, deadly, aimed right at the heart of the yacht.

"A torpedo!" exclaimed Arnold. "Cast off!"

We moved off from the yacht as swiftly as the speedy little open motor-boat would carry us, not a minute too soon.

The torpedo struck the yacht almost exactly amidships. A huge column of water spurted up into the air as though a gigantic whale were blowing off. The yacht itself seemed lifted from the water and literally broken in half like a brittle rod of glass and dropped back into the water.

Below in the submarine, Del Mar was still at the periscope directing things.

"A hit!" he cried exultingly. "We got the whole bunch this time!"

He turned to the men to congratulate them, a smile on his evil face. But as he looked again, he caught sight of our little motor-boat skimming safely away on the other side of the wreck.

"The deuce!" he muttered. "Try another. Here's the direction."

Furiously he swore as the men guided the submarine and loaded another torpedo into a tube. As the tube came into position, they let the torpedo go. An instant later it was hissing its way at us.

"See, there's another!" I cried, catching sight of it.

All looked. Sure enough, through the water could be seen another of those murderous messengers dashing at us.

Arnold ran forward and seized the wheel himself, swinging the boat around hard to starboard and the land. We turned just in time. The torpedo, brainless but deadly, dashed past us harmlessly.

As fast as we could now we made for the shore. No one could catch us with such a start, not even the swiftest torpedo. We had been rescued by Arnold's quick wit from a most desperate situation.

Somewhere below the water, I could imagine a man consumed with fury over our escape, as the periscope disappeared and the submarine made off.

We were safe. But, looking out over the water, we could not help shuddering at the perils beneath its apparently peaceful surface.

CHAPTER XIV

THE LIFE CHAIN

EARLY one morning, a very handsome woman of the adventuress type arrived with several trunks at the big summer hotel, just outside the town, the St. Germain.

Among the many fashionable people at the watering-place, however, she attracted no great attention and in the forenoon she quietly went out in her motor for a ride.

It was Madame Larenz, one of Del Mar's secret agents who, up to this time, had been engaged in spying on wealthy and impressionable American manufacturers.

Her airing brought her, finally, to the bungalow of Del Mar and there she was admitted in a manner that showed that Del Mar trusted her highly.

"Now," he instructed, after a few minutes chat, " I want you to get acquainted with Miss Dodge. You know how to interest her. She's quite human. Pretty gowns appeal to her. Get her to the St. Germain. Then I'll tell you what to do."

A few minutes later the woman left in her car, so rapidly driven that no one would recognize her.

It was early in the afternoon that Aunt Josephine was sitting on the veranda, when an automobile drove

up and a very stylishly gowned and bonnetted woman
stepped out.

"Good afternoon," she greeted Aunt Josephine in-
gratiatingly as she approached the house. "I am
Madame Larenz of New York and Paris. Perhaps
you have heard of my shops on Fifth Avenue and the
Rue de la Paix."

Aunt Josephine had heard the name, though she
did not know that this woman had assumed it without
being in any way connected with the places she men-
tioned.

"I'm establishing a new sort of summer service at
the better resorts," the woman explained. "You see,
my people find it annoying to go into the city for
gowns. So I am bringing the latest Paris models out
to them. Is Miss Dodge at home?"

"I think she is playing tennis," returned Aunt
Josephine.

"Oh, yes, I see her, thank you," the woman murmured, moving toward the tennis court, back of the
house.

Elaine and I had agreed to play a couple of games
and were tossing rackets for position.

"Very well," laughed Elaine, as she won the toss,
"take the other court."

It was a cool day and I felt in good spirits. Just
to see whether I could do it still, I jumped over the
net.

Our game had scarcely started when we were interrupted by the approach of a stunning looking woman.

"Miss Dodge?" she greeted. "Will you excuse
me a moment?"

Elaine paused in serving the ball and the woman handed her a card from her delicate gold mesh bag. It read simply:

Mme. Larenz

Paris

Gowns

Elaine looked at the card a moment while the woman repeated what she had already told Aunt Josephine.

"You have them here, then?" queried Elaine, interested.

"Yes, I have some very exclusive models which I am showing at my suite in the St. Germain."

"Oh, how lovely," exclaimed Elaine. "I must see them."

They talked a few minutes, while I waited patiently for Elaine to start the game again. That game, however, was destined never to be finished. More weighty matters were under discussion.

I wondered what they were talking about and, suppressing a yawn, I walked toward them. As I approached, I heard scattered remarks about styles and dress fabrics.

Elaine had completely forgotten tennis and me. She took a couple of steps away from the court with the woman, as I came up.

"Aren't you going to play?" I asked.

"I know you'll excuse me, Walter," smiled Elaine. "My frocks are all so frightfully out of date. And here's a chance to get new ones, very reasonably, too."

They walked off and I could not help scowling at

the visitor. On toward the house Elaine and Madame Larenz proceeded and around it to the front porch where Aunt Josephine was standing.

"Just think, Auntie," cried Elaine, "real Paris gowns down here without the trouble of going to the city—and cheaply, too."

Aunt Josephine was only mildly interested, but that did not seem to worry Madame Larenz.

"I shall be glad to see you at three, Miss Dodge," she said as she got into her car again and drove off.

By that time, I had caught up with Elaine again. "Just one game," I urged.

"Please excuse me,—this time, Walter," she pleaded, laughing. "You don't know how sadly I'm in need of new frocks."

It was no use of further urging her. Tennis was out of her mind for good that day. Accordingly, I mounted to my room and there quickly donned my riding clothes.

When I came down, I found Aunt Josephine still on the veranda. In addition to my horse which I had telephoned for, Elaine's little runabout had been driven to the door. While I was talking to Aunt Josephine, Elaine came down-stairs and walked over to the car.

"May I go with you?" I pleaded.

"No, Walter," she replied laughing merrily. "You can't go. I want to try them on."

Properly squelched, I retreated. Elaine drove away and a moment later, I mounted and cantered off leisurely.

.   .   .   .

Near Del Mar's bungalow might have been seen

again the mysterious naturalist, walking along the road with a butterfly net in his hand and what appeared to be a leather specimen case, perhaps six inches long, under his other arm.

As Madame Larenz whizzed past in her car, he looked up keenly in spite of his seeming near-sightedness and huge smoked glasses. He watched her closely, noting the number of the car, then turned and followed it.

Madame Larenz drew up, a second time, before Del Mar's. As she got out and entered, the naturalist, having quickened his pace, came up and watched her go in. Then, after taking in the situation for a moment, he made his way around the side of the bungalow.

"Is Mr. Del Mar at home?" inquired Madame Larenz, as the valet ushered her into the library.

"No ma'am," he returned. "Mr. Del Mar is out. But he left word that if you came before he got back, you were to leave word."

The woman sat down at the desk and wrote hastily. When she had finished the short note, she read it over and folded it up.

"Tell Mr. Del Mar I've left a note here on his desk," she said to the valet.

A moment later she left the library, followed by the valet, who accompanied her to her car and assisted her in.

"The hotel," she directed to her driver, as he started off, while the valet returned to the bungalow.

Outside, the naturalist had come through the shrubbery and had been looking in at the library window, watching every move of Madame Larenz as she wrote. As she went out, he paused just a second to look about. Then he drew a long knife from his pocket, forced the window catch, and quickly climbed into the room.

Directly to the desk he went and hurriedly ran over the papers on it. There was the note. He picked it up and read it eagerly.

"My apartment—St. Germain—3 P. M.
                                          "Larenz."

For a moment he seemed to consider what to do. Then he replaced the note. Suddenly he heard the sound of footsteps. It was the valet returning. Quickly the naturalist ran to the window and jumped out.

A moment later, the valet entered the library again. "That's strange," he exclaimed under his breath, "I don't recall opening that window over there to-day."

He looked puzzled. But as no one was about, he went over and shut it.

Some distance down the road, the naturalist quietly emerged in safety from the bushes. With scarcely a moment's hesitation, his mind thoroughly made up to his course, he hurried along the road.

Meanwhile, at the St. Germain, Madame Larenz entered and passed through the rotunda of the hotel, followed by many admiring glances of the men.

Up in her room stood several large trunks, open. From them had been taken a number of gowns which were scattered about or hung up for exhibition.

As she entered, quickly she selected one of the trunks

whose contents were more smart than the rest and laid the gowns out most fetchingly about the room.

In the office of the hotel a few moments later, the naturalist entered. He looked around curiously, then went to the desk and glanced over the register. At the name " Mme Larenz, Paris, Room 22," he paused.

For some seconds he stood thinking. Then he deliberately walked over to a leather chair and took a prominent seat near-by in the lobby. He had discarded his net, but still had the case which now he had shoved into his pocket. From a table, he picked up a newspaper.

It was not long before Del Mar pulled up before the hotel and entered in his usual swagger manner. He had returned to the bungalow, read the note and hurried over to the St. Germain.

He crossed the lobby, back to the office. As he did so, the naturalist had his face hidden deeply in the open newspaper. But no sooner had Del Mar passed than the newspaper fell unappreciated and he gazed after him, as he left the lobby by the back way.

It was only a few minutes after she had completed arranging her small stock so that it looked quite impressive, that Madame Larenz heard a knock at the door and recognized Del Mar's secret code. She opened the door and he strode in.

" I got your note," he said briefly, coming directly to business and telling her just what he wanted done. " Let me see," he concluded, glancing at his watch. It is after three now. She ought to be here any minute."

Outside, Elaine drove up to the rather garish en-

trance of the St. Germain and one of the boys in uniform ran forward to open the door and take charge of
the car. She, too, crossed the lobby without seeing
the old naturalist, though nothing escaped him.

As she passed, he started to rise and cross toward
her, then appeared to change his mind.

Elaine went on out through the back of the lobby,
directed by a boy, and mounted a flight of stairs, in
preference to taking the lift to the second, or sort of
mezzanine floor. Down along the corridor she went,
hunting for number twenty-two. At last she found it
at the end, and knocked.

Del Mar and Madame Larenz were still talking in
low tones when they heard a light tap on the door.

" There she is, now," whispered Larenz.

" All right. Let her in," answered Del Mar, leaping
quietly to a closet. " I'll hide here until I get the signal. Do just as I told you."

Outside, at the same time, according to his carefully
concocted plans, Del Mar's car had driven up and
stopped close to the side of the hotel, which was on a
slight hill that brought the street level here not so far
below the second story windows. Three of his most
trusted men were in the car.

Madame Larenz opened the door. " Oh, I'm so glad
you came," she rattled on to Elaine. " You see, I've
got to get started. Not a customer yet. But if you'll
only take a few gowns, other people will come to me.
I'll let you have them cheaply, too. Just look at this
one."

She held up one filmy, creamy creation that looked
like a delicate flower.

"I'd like to try it on," cried Elaine, fingering it rapturously.

"By all means," agreed Madame. "We are alone. Do so."

With deft fingers, Larenz helped her take off her own very pretty dress. As Elaine slipped the soft gown over her head, with her head and arms engaged in its multitudinous folds, Madame Larenz, a powerful woman, seized her. Elaine was effectually gagged and bound in the gown itself.

Instantly, Del Mar flung himself from the closet, disguising his voice. Together, they wrapped the dress about Elaine even more tightly to prevent her screaming.

Madame Larenz seized a blanket and threw that over Elaine's head, also, while Del Mar ran to the window. There were his men in the car, waiting below.

"Are you ready?" he called softly to them.

They looked about carefully. There was no one on that side of the hotel just at the moment.

"Ready," responded one. "Quick!"

Together, Del Mar and Madame Larenz passed Elaine, ineffectually struggling, out of the window. The men seized her and placed her in the bottom of the car, which was covered. Then they shot away, taking a back road up the hill.

.   .   .   .

Hurriedly the naturalist went through the lobby in the direction Elaine had gone, and a moment later reached the corridor above.

Down it, he could hear some one coming out of room twenty-two. He slid into an angle and hid.

It was Del Mar and the woman he had seen at the bungalow. They passed by without discovering him, nor could he make out anything that they said. What mischief was afoot? Where was Elaine?

He ran to the door and tried it. It was locked. Quickly, he took from his pocket a skeleton key and unlocked it. There was Elaine's hat and dress lying in a heap on the bed. But she was not there. He was now thoroughly alarmed.

She could not have passed him in the hall. Therefore she must have gone or been taken out through the window. That would never have been voluntary, especially leaving her things there.

The window was still open. He ran to it. One glance out was enough. He leaped to the ground. Sure enough, there were automobile tracks in the dust.

"Del Mar's car," he muttered to himself, studying them.

He fairly ran around the side of the hotel. There he came suddenly upon Elaine's car standing alone, and recognized it.

There was no time for delay. He jumped into it, and let the swift little racer out as he turned and gathered momentum to shoot up the hill on high speed.

Meanwhile, I had been jogging along through the country, lonely and disconsolate. I don't know how it happened, but I suppose it was by some subconscious desire. At any rate I found myself at the road that came out across one leading to the St. Germain and it occurred to me that Elaine might by this time have

purchased enough frocks to clothe her for a year. At
any rate I quickened my pace in the hope of seeing her.

Suddenly, my horse shied and a familiar little car
flashed past me. But the driver was not familiar. It
was Elaine's roadster. In it was a stranger—a man
who looked like a " bugologist," as nearly as I can describe him. Was he running off with her car while
she was waiting inside the hotel?

I galloped after him.

.   .   .   .

Del Mar's automobile, with Elaine bound and
gagged in it, drove rapidly by back and unfrequented
ways into the country until at last it pulled up before
an empty two-story house in a sort of grove of trees.

The men leaped out, lifted Elaine, and carried her
bodily into the house, taking her up-stairs and into an
upper room. She had fainted when they laid her down
and loosened the dress from about her face so that she
could breathe. There they left her, on the floor, her
hands and feet bound, and went out.

How long she lay there, she never knew, but at last
the air revived her and she regained consciousness and
sat up. Her muscles were sore and her head ached.
But she set her teeth and began struggling with the
cords that bound her, managing at last to pull the dress
over herself at least.

In Elaine's car, the naturalist drove slowly at times,
following the tracks of the automobile ahead. At last,
however, he came to a place where he saw that the
tracks went up a lonely side road. To approach in a
car was to warn whoever was there. · He ran the car
up alongside the road in the bushes and jumped out

leaving it and following the tracks up the side road-way.

As he approached a single deserted house, he left even the narrow road altogether and plunged into the woods, careful to proceed noiselessly. Through the bushes, near the house, he peered. There he could see one of Del Mar's men in the doorway, apparently talking to others behind him.

Stealthily the naturalist crept around, still hiding, until he was closer to the house on the other side. At last he worked his way around to the rear door. He tried it. It was bolted and even the skeleton key was unavailing to slide the bolt. Seconds were precious.

Quickly, he went to the corner of the house. There was a water-leader. He began to climb it, risking its precarious support.

On the roof at last, the naturalist crawled along, looking for some way of getting into the house. But he could not seem to find any. Carefully, he crawled to the edge of the roof and looked over. Below, he could hear sounds, but could make nothing of them.

From his pocket, he took the leather case and opened it. There was a peculiar arrangement, like some of the collapsible arms on which telephone instruments are often fastened to a desk or wall, capable of being collapsed into small space or of being extended for some distance. On the thing was arranged a system of mirrors, which the naturalist adjusted.

It was a pocket periscope.

He thrust the thing over the edge of the roof and down, and looked through it. Below, he could see into the room from which came the peculiar sounds.

He looked anxiously. There he could see Elaine endeavoring still to loosen the cords and unable to do so. Only for a moment he looked. Then he folded up the pocket periscope into the case and shoved it back into his pocket. Quickly he crossed the roof again, and slid back down the rain-pipe.

At the door stood three of Del Mar's men waiting for Del Mar who had told them he would follow immediately.

The naturalist had by this time reached the ground and was going along carefully back of the house. He drew his revolver and, pointing it down, fired. Then he dodged back of an extension and disappeared for the moment.

Instantly, the three men sprang up and ran toward the spot where it seemed the shot had been fired. There was no one about the side of the house. But the wind had carried the smoke into some bushes beside the grove and they crashed into the bushes, beating about.

At the same time, the naturalist, having first waited until he saw which way the men were going, dashed about the house in the opposite direction. Then he slipped, unopposed and unobserved, in through the open front door, up the stairs and along to the room into which he had just been looking. He unlocked the door, and entered. Elaine was still struggling with the cords when she caught sight of the stranger.

"Not a word," he cautioned under his breath.

She was indeed too frightened to cry out. Quickly, he loosened her, still holding his finger to his lips to enjoin silence.

" Follow me," he whispered.

She obeyed mechanically, and they went out into the hall. On down-stairs went the naturalist, Elaine still keeping close after him.

He looked out through the front door, then drew back. Quickly he went through the lower hall until he came to the back door in the kitchen, Elaine following. He unbolted the door and opened it.

" Run," he said, simply, pointing out of the door. " They're coming back the other way. I'll hold them."

She needed no further urging, but darted from the house as he closed the door after her.

.   .   .   .

It was just at this point that Del Mar came riding along the main road on horseback. He pulled up suddenly as he saw a car run in alongside the road.

" That's Elaine's runabout," he muttered, as he dismounted and tied his horse. " How came it here? "

He approached the car, much worried by its unaccountable presence there instead of before the St. Germain. Then he drew his gun and hurried up the side road.

He heard a shot and quickened his pace. In the woods unexpectedly he came upon his three men still beating about, searching with drawn revolvers for the person who had fired the shot.

" Well? " he demanded sharply, " what's all this? "

" Some one fired a shot," they explained, somewhat crestfallen.

" It was a trick, you fools," he answered testily. " Get back to your prisoner."

19

Without a word they turned and hurried toward the house, Del Mar following. "You two go in," he ordered the foremost. "I'll go around the house with Patrick."

As Del Mar and the other man ran around the corner, they could just catch a fleeting glimpse on some one disappearing among the trees.

It was Elaine.

The man hurried forward, blazing away with his gun.

Running, breathless, Elaine heard the shot behind her which Del Mar's man had fired in his eagerness. The bullet struck a tree near her with a " ping!" She glanced back and saw the man. But she did not stop. Instead, she redoubled her efforts, running zigzag in among the trees where they were thickest.

Del Mar, a little bit behind his man where she could not recognize him, urged the man on, following carefully.

On fled Elaine, her heart beating fast. Suddenly she stopped and almost cried out in vexation. A stream blocked her retreat, a stream, swift and deep.

She looked back, terrified. Her pursuers were coming ahead fast now in her direction. Wildly she gazed around. There was a canoe on the bank. In an instant she jumped in, untied it, and seized the paddle.

Off she went, striking for the opposite shore. But the current was racing swiftly, and she was already tired and exhausted. She could scarcely make any headway at all in the fierce eddies. But at least, she thought hurriedly, she was getting further and further away from them down-stream.

Up above, Del Mar and his man came to the edge of the water. There they stood for a moment looking down.

" There she is," pointed the man.

Del Mar raised his revolver and fired.

Suddenly a bullet struck Elaine's paddle and broke it. Clutching the useless splintered shaft, she was now at the mercy of the current, swept along like a piece of driftwood.

She looked about frantically. What was that roaring noise?

It was the waterfalls ahead!

. . . .

In the meantime, Del Mar's other two men had entered the house and had run up-stairs, knowing well his wrath if anything had happened. As they did so, the naturalist poked his head cautiously out of the kitchen where he had been hiding, and saw them. Then he followed noiselessly, his revolver ready.

Headlong they ran into the room where they had left Elaine. She was gone!

Before they could turn, the naturalist locked the door, turned and took the steps down, two at a time.

Then he ran out of the front door and into the woods at an angle to the direction taken by Elaine, turning and going down hill, where a rapid, swollen stream curved about through a gorge. As he reached the stream, he heard a shot above, and a scream.

He looked up. There was Elaine, swept down toward him. Below he knew the stream tumbled over a tall cataract into the gorge below.

What could he do?

A sudden crackling of the twigs caused him to turn and catch sight of me, just coming up.

For, as best I could on horseback, I had followed Elaine's car until at last I saw that it had been abandoned. Thoroughly alarmed, I rode on, past a deserted house until suddenly I heard a shot and a scream. It seemed to come from below me and I leaped off my horse, making for it as fast as I could, racing toward a stream whose roar I could hear.

There on the bank I came upon a queer old codger, looking about wildly. Was he the automobile thief? I ran forward, ready to seize him. But as I did so, he whirled about and with a strength remarkable in one so old seized my own wrist before I could get his.

"Look!" he cried simply, pointing up the stream.

I did. A girl in a canoe was coming down toward the falls, screaming, her paddle broken and useless. My heart leaped into my mouth. It was Elaine!

"Come," he panted eagerly to me. "I can save her. You must do just as I say."

He pointed to an overhanging rock near-by and we ran to it.

By this time Elaine was almost upon us, each second getting nearer the veritable maelstrom above the falls.

From the rock overhung also a tree at the very edge of the water.

There was nothing to do but obey him. Above, though we did not see them, Del Mar and his man were gloating over the result of their work. But they were gloating too soon. We came to the rock and the tree.

"Here," cried the new-found friend, "I'll get hold of the tree and then hold you."

Instantly he threw himself on his stomach, hooking **his** leg about the tree trunk. I crawled out over the **ledge** of slippery rock to the very edge and looked over. It was the only chance.

The old naturalist seized my legs in his hands. I slid down the rock, letting myself go.

Literally, his presence of mind had invented what was really a life chain, a human rope.

On came the canoe, Elaine in it as white as death, crying out and trying to stop or guide it as, nearer and nearer through the smooth-worn walls of the chasm, it whirled to the falls.

With a grip of steel, the naturalist held to the tree which swayed and bent, while also he held me, as if in a vise, head down.

On came Elaine—directly at us.

She stood up and balanced herself, a dangerous feat in a canoe at any time, but doubly so in those dark, swirling, treacherous waters.

" Steady! " I encouraged. " Grab my arms! "

As the canoe reached us, she gave a little jump and seized my forearms. Her hands slipped, but I grasped her own arms, and we held each other.

The momentum of her body was great. For an instant I thought we were all going over. But the naturalist held his grip and slowly began to pull himself and us up the slippery rock.

A second later the canoe crashed over the falls in a cloud of spray and pounding water.

As we reached the bank above the rock, I almost lifted Elaine and set her down, trembling and gasping for breath. Before either of us knew it the queer old fellow had plunged into the bushes and was gone without another word.

"Walter," she cried, "call him back, I must tell him how much I owe him—my life!"

But he had disappeared, absolutely. We shouted after him. It was of no use.

"Well, what do you think of that?" cried Elaine. "He saved my life—then didn't wait even to be thanked."

Who was he?

We looked at each other a moment. But neither of us spoke what was in our hearts.

CHAPTER XV

'ALONE in the doorway before his rude shack on the shore of the promontory sat an old fisherman, gazing out fixedly at the harbor as though deeply concerned over the weather, which, as usual, was unseasonable.

Suddenly he started and would have disappeared into his hut but for the fact that, although he could not himself be seen, he had already seen the intruder.

It was a trooper from Fort Dale. He galloped up and, as though obeying to the letter his instructions, deliberately dropped an envelope at the feet of the fisherman. Then, without a word, he galloped away again.

The fisherman picked up the envelope and opened it quickly. Inside was a photograph and a note. He read:

FORT DALE

PROFESSOR ARNOLD,

J. Smith, clerk in the War Department, has disappeared. We are not sure, but fear that he has a copy of the new Sandy Hook Defense Plans. It is believed he is headed your way. He walks with a slight limp. Look out for him.

LIEUTENANT WOODWARD.

295

For a long time the fisherman appeared to study the face on the photograph until he had it indelibly implanted in his memory, as if by some system such as that of the immortal Bertillon and his clever " portrait parlé," or spoken picture, for scientific identification and apprehension. It was not a pleasant face and there were features that were not easily forgotten.

Finally he turned and entered his hut. Hastily he took off his stained reefer. From a wooden chest he drew another outfit of clothes. The transformation was complete. When he issued forth from his hut again, it was no longer the aged disciple of Izaac Walton. He was now a trim chauffeur, bearded and goggled.

.   .   .   .

In the library of his bungalow, Del Mar was pacing up and down, now and then scowling to himself, as though there flashed over his mind stray recollections of how some of his most cherished plans were miscarrying.

Still, on the whole, he had nothing to complain of. For, a moment later the valet entered with a telegram for which he had evidently been waiting. Del Mar seized it eagerly and tore open the yellow envelope. On the blank was printed in the usual way the following non-committal message:

> WASHINGTON, D. C.,
> August 12, 1915.

MR. DEL MAR,

What you request is coming. Answer to sign of the ring.—SMITH.

"Good," muttered Del Mar as he finished reading. "Strange, what a little gold will do—when you know how to dispose of it."

He smiled cynically to himself at the sentiment.

. . . .

At the little railroad station, they were quite proud of the fact that at least two of the four hacks had been replaced already by taxicabs.

It was, then, with some surprise and not a little open jealousy that they saw a new taxicab drive up and take its stand by the platform.

If the chauffeur, transformed from the lonely fisherman, had expected a cordial reception, he might better have stayed before his hut, for the glances the other drivers gave him were as black and lowering as the clouds he had been looking at.

The new chauffeur got off his seat. Instead of trying to brazen it out, he walked over to the others who were standing in a group waiting for the approaching train whose whistle had already sounded.

"I'm not going to locate here permanently," he said, pulling out a roll of bills as he spoke. "Leave any fare I claim to me," he added, passing a bill of a good denomination to each of the four jehus.

They looked at him curiously. But what business of theirs was it? The money felt good.

"All right, bo," they agreed.

Thundering down the platform came the afternoon train, a great event in the town life.

As the baggage was being tossed off, the passengers alighted and the five hackmen swarmed at them.

"Keb, sir, kerridge. Taxi, lady!"

From the Pullman alighted a widow, in deep mourning. As she got off and moved down the platform, it was apparent that she walked with a pronounced limp.

At the end of the platform, the chauffeurs were still calling, while the newcomer looked over the crowd hastily. Suddenly he caught sight of the face of the widow. He stepped forward, as she approached. The others held back as they had agreed and paid no attention. It was like forcing a card.

He held the door open and she entered the cab, unsuspecting. " Mr. Del Mar's," she directed, simply.

As the new taxicab driver cranked his engine and climbed into the seat, he was careful to let no action of his, however small, betray the intense satisfaction he felt at the working of his scheme.

He pulled away from the station. On through the pretty country roads the chauffeur drove the heavily veiled widow until at last they came to Del Mar's bungalow.

At the gate he stopped and ran around to open the door to assist his fare to alight.

" Wait for me," she said, without paying him yet. " I shall not be long and I want to be driven back to the station to catch the four twenty-nine to New York."

As she limped up the gravel walk, he watched her closely. She went to the door and rang the bell, and the valet admitted her.

Del Mar was still sitting, thinking, in the library.

" Mr. Del Mar? " she inquired.

The voice was not exactly soft, and Del Mar eyed her suspiciously. Was this the person he expected, or a " plant? "

"Yes," he answered, guardedly, "I am Mr. Del Mar. And you?"

The widow, too, evidently wished to make no mistake. As she spoke, she raised her hand. By that simple action she displayed a curious and conspicuous seal ring on her finger. It was the sign of the ring for which Del Mar had been waiting.

He extended his own left hand. On the ring finger was another ring, but not similar. As he did so, the widow took the ring from her own finger and placed it on the little finger of Del Mar.

"Good!" he exclaimed.

Every action of the sign of the ring had been carried out.

The woman raised her thick veil, disclosing the face of—a man!

It was the same face, also, that had appeared in the photograph sent to the old fisherman by Woodward.

Awkwardly, the man searched in the front of his shirtwaist and drew forth a paper which Del Mar almost seized in his eagerness. It was a pen and ink copy of a Government map, showing a huge spit of sand in the sea before a harbor, Sandy Hook and New York. On it were indicated all the defenses, the positions of guns, everything.

Together, Del Mar and Smith bent over it, while the renegade clerk explained each mark on the traitorous map. They were too occupied to see a face flattened against the pane of a window near-by.

The chauffeur had no intention of remaining inactive outside while he knew that something that interested him was transpiring inside. He had crept up by the side of the house to the window.   But he could see little and hear nothing.

A moment he strained every sense.   It was no use. He must devise some other way.   How could he get into that room?   Slowly he returned to his car, thinking it over.   There he stood for a moment revolving in his mind what to do.   He looked up the road.   An idea came to him.   There he saw a little runabout approaching rapidly.

Quickly he went around to the front of his car and lifted up the hood.   Then he bent over and pretended to be tinkering with his engine.

As the car was about to pass he deliberately stepped back, apparently not seeing the runabout, and was struck and knocked down.

The runabout stopped, the emergency brakes biting hard.

.   .   .   .

Elaine had asked me to go shopping in the village with her that afternoon.   While I waited for her in her little car, she came down at last, carrying a little hand-bag.   We drove off a moment later.

It was a delightful ride, not too warm, but sunny. Without realizing it, we found ourselves on the road that led past Del Mar's.

As we approached, I saw that there was a taxicab standing in front of the gate.   The hood was lifted and the driver was apparently tinkering with his engine.

"Let's not stop," said Elaine, who had by this time a peculiar aversion to the man.

As we passed the driver, apparently not seeing us,

stepped out and, before we could turn out, we had knocked him down. We stopped and ran back.

There he lay on the road, seemingly unconscious. We lifted him up and I looked toward Del Mar's house.

"Help!" I shouted at the top of my voice.

The valet came to the door.

Hearing me, the valet ran out down the walk. "All right," he cried. "I'll be there in a minute."

With his help I picked up the taxicab chauffeur and we carried him into the house.

Del Mar was talking with a person who looked like a widow, when they heard our approach up the walk carrying the injured man.

So engrossed had they been in discerning what the stolen document contained that, as we finally entered, the widow had only time to drop her veil and conceal her identity as the renegade Smith. Del Mar still held the plan in his hand.

The valet and I entered with Elaine and we placed the chauffeur on a couch near Del Mar's desk. I remember that there was this strange woman all in black, heavily veiled, in the room at the time.

"I think we ought to telephone for a doctor," said Elaine placing her hand-bag on the desk and excitedly telling Del Mar how we had accidently knocked the man down.

"Call up my doctor, Henry," said Del Mar, hastily thrusting the plan into a book lying on the desk.

We gathered about the man, trying to revive him.

"Have you a little stimulant?" I asked, turning from him.

Del Mar moved toward a cellarette built into the wall. We were all watching him, our backs to the chauffeur, when suddenly he must have regained consciousness very much. Like a flash his hand shot out. He seized the plan from between the leaves of the book. He had not time to get away with it himself. Perhaps he might be searched. He opened Elaine's bag, and thrust it in.

The valet by this time had finished telephoning and spoke to Del Mar.

" The doctor will be here shortly, Miss Dodge," said Del Mar. " You need not wait, if you don't care to. I'll take care of him."

" Oh, thank you—ever so much," she murmured. " Of course it wasn't our fault, but I feel sorry for the poor fellow. Tell the doctor to send me the bill."

She and Del Mar shook hands. I thought he held her hand perhaps a little longer and a little tighter than usual. At any rate Elaine seemed to think so.

" Why, what a curious ring, Mr. Del Mar," she said, finally releasing her own hand from his grasp.

Then she looked quickly at the woman, half joking, as if the ring had something to do with the strange woman. She looked back at the ring. Del Mar smiled, shook his head and laughed easily.

Then Elaine picked up her bag and we went out. A moment later we climbed back into the car and were off again.

.   .   .   .

Having left us at the door, Del Mar hurried back to the library. He went straight to the desk and picked up the book, eager now to make sure of the safety of the plan.

It was gone!

" Did you, Smith—" he began hastily, then checked himself, knowing that the clerk had not taken the plan.

Del Mar walked over to the couch and stood a moment looking at the chauffeur. " I wonder who he is," he said to himself. " I don't recall ever seeing him at the station or in the village."

He leaned over closer. " The deuce!" he exclaimed, " that's a fake beard the fellow has on."

Del Mar made a lunge for it. As he did so, the chauffeur leaped to his feet and drew a gun. " Hands up!" he shouted. " And the first man that moves is a dead one!"

Before the secret agent knew it, both he and Smith were covered. The chauffeur took a step toward Smith and unceremoniously jerked off the widow's weeds, as well as the wig.

At that very moment one of Del Mar's men came up to the secret panel that opened from the underground passageway into his library. He was about to open it when he heard a sound on the other side that startled him. He listened a moment, then slid it just a short distance and looked in.

There he saw a chauffeur holding up Del Mar and Smith. Having pulled the disguise from Smith, he went next around Del Mar and took his gun from his pocket, then passed his hands over the folds of Smith's dress, but found no weapon. He stepped back away from them.

At that point the man quietly slid the panel all the way open and silently stepped into the room, behind the chauffeur. Cautiously he began sneaking up on him.

As he did so, Del Mar and Smith watched, fascinated. Somehow their faces must have betrayed that something was wrong. For, as the newcomer leaped at him, the chauffeur turned suddenly and fired. The shot wounded the man.

It was a signal for a free-for-all fight. Del Mar and Smith leaped at the intruder. Over and over they rolled, breaking furniture, overturning and smashing bric-a-brac.

Del Mar's revolver was knocked out of the chauffeur's hand. With a blow of a chair, the chauffeur laid out Smith, entangled in his unfamiliar garments, shook himself loose from the two others, and made a rush at the door.

Del Mar paused only long enough to pick up the revolver from the floor. Instantly he fired at the retreating form. But the chauffeur had passed out and banged shut the door. Down the walk he sped and out to the gate, into his car, the engine of which he had left running.

Hard after him came Del Mar and the rest, joined now by Henry, the valet. One shot was left in the chauffeur's revolver and he blazed away as he leaped into the car.

" He's got me," groaned Smith as he stumbled and fell forward.

On kept Del Mar and the others. They caught up with the car just as it was starting. But the chauffeur knocked the gun from Del Mar's hand before he could get a good aim and fire, at the same time bowling over the man who had come through the panel.

Off the car went, now rapidly gaining speed. Del Mar had just time to swing on the rear of it.

Around the rapidly-driven car, he climbed, hanging on for dear life, over the mud-guard and toward the running-board. On sped the car, swaying crazily back and forth, Del Mar crouched on the running-board and working his way slowly and perilously to the front seat.

The chauffeur felt the weight of some one on that side. Just as he turned to see what it was, Del Mar leaped at him. Still holding the wheel, the chauffeur fought him off with his free hand, Del Mar holding on to some spare tires with one hand, also. Handicapped by having the steering-wheel to manage, nevertheless the chauffeur seemed quite well able to give a good account of himself.

.   .   .   .

Somehow, Elaine and I must have been hoodooed that day.

We had not been gone five minutes from Del Mar's, after the accident to the chauffeur, when we heard a mysterious knock in the engine.

"More engine trouble," I sighed. "Pull up along the road and I'll see if I can fix it."

We stopped and both got out. There was no fake about this trouble or about the dirt and grease I acquired on my hands and face, tinkering with that motor. For, regardless of my immaculate flannels, I had to set to work. A huge spot of grease spattered on me. Elaine laughed outright.

"Here, let me powder your nose, Walter," she cried undismayed at our trouble, gayly opening her bag. "Well—of all things—what's this, and where did it come from?"

I turned from the engine and looked. She was holding some kind of plan or document in her hand. In blank surprise she examined it. It looked like a fort or a series of forts. But I was sure at a glance that it was not Fort Dale.

"What do you think it is, Walter?" she asked, handing it to me.

I took it and examined it carefully. Incredible as it seemed, I figured out quickly that it must be nothing short of a plan of the new defenses at Sandy Hook.

"I don't know what it all means," I said. "But I do know that we won't get any dinner till I get this engine running again."

I fell to work again, eager to get away with our dangerous prize, Elaine now and then advising me. Finally I turned the engine over. For a wonder it ran smoothly. "Well, that's all right, at last," I sighed, wiping the grease off my hands on a piece of waste.

"What's the matter now?" exclaimed Elaine, turning quickly and looking up the road along which we had just come.

There, lurching along at full speed was a car. Two men were actually fighting on the front of it regardless of speed and safety. As it neared us, I saw it was the taxicab that had been standing before Del Mar's.

I looked closer at it. To my utter amazement, who should be driving it but the very chauffeur whom we had left at Del Mar's only a few minutes before, apparently unconscious. He could not have been hurt very badly, for he was not only able to drive but was fighting off a man clinging on the running-board.

On rushed the car, directly at us. Just as it passed us, the chauffeur seemed to summon all his strength. He struck a powerful blow at the man, recoiled and straightened out his car just in time. The man fell, literally at our feet.

It was Del Mar himself!

On sped the taxicab. Bruised though he must have been by the fall, Del Mar nevertheless raised himself by the elbow and fired every chamber of his revolver as fast as he could pump the bullets.

I must say that I admired the man's pluck. Elaine and I hurried over to him. I still had in my hand the queer paper which she had found so strangely in her hand-bag.

"Why, what's all this about?" I asked eagerly.

Before I could raise him up, Del Mar had regained his feet.

"Just a plain crook, who attacked me," he muttered, brushing off his clothes to cover up the quick recognition of what it was that I was holding in my hand, for he had seen the plan immediately.

"Can't we drive you back?" asked Elaine, quite forgetting our fears of Del Mar in the ugly predicament in which he just had been. "We've had trouble but I guess we can get you back."

"Thank you," he said, forcing a smile. "I think

anything would be an improvement on my ride here
and I'm sure you can do more than you claim."

He climbed up and sat on the floor of the roadster,
his feet outside, and we drove off. At last we pulled
up at Dodge Hall again.

"Won't you come in?" asked Elaine as we got out.

"Thank you, I believe I will for a few minutes,"
consented Del Mar, concealing his real eagerness to
follow me. "I'm all shaken up."

As we entered the living-room, I was thinking about
the map. I opened a table drawer, hastily took the
plan from my pocket and locked it in the drawer.
Elaine, meanwhile, was standing with Del Mar who
was talking, but in reality watching me closely.

A smile of satisfaction seemed to flit over his face
as he saw what I had done and now knew where the
paper was.

I turned to him. "How are you now?" I asked.

"Oh, I'm much better—all right," he answered.
Then he looked at his watch. "I've a very important
appointment. If you'll excuse me, I'll walk over to my
place. Thank you again, Miss Dodge, ever so kindly."

He bowed low and was gone.

.   .   .   .

Down the road past where we had turned, before a
pretty little shingle house, the taxicab chauffeur
stopped. One of the bullets had taken effect on him
and his shoulder was bleeding. But the worst, as he
seemed to think it, was that another shot had given
him a flat tire.

He jumped out and looked up the road whence he
had come. No one was following. Still, he was wor-

ried. He went around to look at the tire. But he was too weak now from loss of blood. It had been nerve and reserve force that had carried him through. Now that the strain was off, he felt the reaction to the full.

Just then the doctor and his driver, whom the valet had already summoned to Del Mar's, came speeding down the road. The doctor saw the chauffeur fall in a half faint, stopped his car and ran to him. The chauffeur had kept up as long as he could. He had now sunk down beside his machine in the road.

A moment later they picked him up and carried him into the house. There was no acting about his hurts now. In the house they laid the man down on a couch and the doctor made a hasty examination.

" How is he? " asked one of the kind Samaritans.

" The wound is not dangerous," replied the physician, " but he's lost a lot of blood. He cannot be moved for some time yet."

.   .   .   .

We talked about nothing else at Dodge Hall after dressing for dinner but the strange events over at Del Mar's and what had followed. The more I thought about it, the more it seemed to me that we would never be left over night in peaceful possession of the plan which both Elaine and I decided ought on the following day to be sent to Washington.

Accordingly I cudgelled my brain for some method of protecting both ourselves and it. The only thing I could think of was a scheme once adopted by Kennedy in another case. How I longed for him. But I had to do my best alone.

I had a small quick shutter camera that had belonged

to Craig and just as we were about to retire, I brought
it into the living-room with a package I had had sent
up from the village.

"What are you going to do?" asked Elaine curiously.

I assumed an air of mystery but did not say, for I
was not sure but that even now some one was eavesdropping. It was not late, but the country air made us
all sleepy and Aunt Josephine, looking at the clock,
soon announced that she was going to retire.

She had no sooner said good-night than Elaine began again to question me. But I had determined not to
tell her what I was doing, for if my imitation of Kennedy failed, I knew that she would laugh at me.

"Oh, very well," she said finally in pique, "then, if
you're going to be so secret about it, you can sit up
alone—there!"

She flounced off to bed. Sure as I could be at last
that I was alone, I opened the package. There were
the tools that I had ordered, a coil of wire and some
dry cells. Then I went to the table, unlocked the
drawer and put the plan in my pocket. I had determined that whether the idea worked or not, no one was
to get the plan except by overcoming me.

Although I was no expert at wiring, I started to
make the connections under the table with the drawer,
not a very difficult thing to do as long as it was to be
only temporary and for the night. From the table I
ran the wires along the edge of the carpet until I came
to the book-case. There, masked by the books, I
placed the little quick shutter camera, and at a distance
also concealed the flash-light pan.

Next I aimed the camera carefully and focussed it on a point above the drawer on the writing-table where any one would be likely to stand if he attempted to open it. Then I connected the shutter of the camera and a little spark coil in the flash-pan with the wires, using an apparatus to work the shutter such as I recalled having seen Craig use. Finally I covered the sparking device with the flash-light powder, gave a last look about and snapped off the light.

Up in my bedroom, I must say I felt like "some" detective and I could not help slapping myself on the chest for the ingenuity with which I had duplicated Craig.

Then I lay down on the bed with my clothes on and picked up a book, determined to keep awake to see if anything happened. It was a good book, but I was tired and in spite of myself I nodded over it, and then dropped it.

. . . .

In his bungalow, now that Smith had gone back again to New York and Washington, Del Mar was preparing to keep the important engagement he had told us about, another of his nefarious nocturnal expeditions.

He drew a cap on his head, well over his ears and forehead. His eyes and face he concealed as well as he could with a mask to be put on later. To his equipment he added a gun. Then with a hasty word or two to his valet, he went out.

By back ways so that even in the glare of automobile headlights he would not be recognized, he made his way to Dodge Hall. As he saw the house looming up in the moonlight he put on his mask and approached cautiously. Gaining the house, he opened a window, noiselessly turning the catch as deftly as a house-breaker, and climbed into the living-room.

A moment he looked around, then tiptoed over to the table. He looked at it to be sure that it was the right one and the right drawer. Then he bent down to force the drawer open.

"Pouf!" a blinding flash came and a little metallic click of the shutter, followed by a cloud of smoke.

As quick as it happened, there went through Del Mar's head, the explanation. It was a concealed camera. He sprang back, clapping his hands over his face. Out of range for a moment, he stood gazing about the room, trying to locate the thing.

Suddenly he heard footsteps. He dived through the window that he had opened, just as some one ran in and switched on the lights.

. . . .

Half asleep, I heard a muffled explosion, as if of a flash-light. I started up and listened. Surely some one was moving about down-stairs. I pulled my gun from my pocket and ran out of the room. Down the steps I flung myself, two at a time.

In the living-room, I switched on the lights in time to see some one disappear through an open window. I ran to the window and looked out. There was a man, half doubled up, running around the side of the house and into a clump of bushes, then apparently lost. I shot out of the window and called.

My only answer was an imprecation and return volley that shattered the glass above my head. I ducked

hastily and fell flat on the floor, for in the light streaming out, I must have been a good mark.

I was not the only one who heard the noise. The
shots quickly awakened Elaine and she leaped out of
bed and put on her kimono. Then she lighted the
lights and ran down-stairs.

The intruder had disappeared by this time and I had
got up and was peering out of the window as she came
breathlessly into the living-room.

"What's the matter, Walter?" she asked.

"Some one broke into the house after those plans,"
I replied. "He escaped, but I got his picture, I think,
by this device of Kennedy's. Let's go into a dark room
and develop it."

There was no use trying to follow the man further.
To Elaine's inquiry of what I meant, I replied by
merely going over to the spot where I had hidden the
camera and disconnecting it.

We went up-stairs where I had rigged up an im-
promptu dark room for my amateur photographic
work some days before. Elaine watched me closely.
At last I found that I had developed something. As
I drew the film through the hypo tray and picked it up,
I held it to the red light.

Elaine leaned over and looked at the film with me.
There was a picture of a masked man, his cap down,
in a startled attitude, his hands clapped to his face,
completely hiding what the mask and cap did not hide.

"Well, I'll be blowed!" I cried in chagrin at the out-
come of what I thought had been my cleverest coup.

A little exclamation of astonishment escaped Elaine.
I turned to her. "What is it?" I asked.

" The ring! " she cried.

I looked again more closely. On the little finger of the left hand was a peculiar ring. Once seen, I think it was not readily forgotten.

" The ring! " she repeated excitedly. " Don't you remember—that ring? I saw it on Mr. Del Mar's hand—at his house—this afternoon! "

I could only stare.

At last we had a real clue!

In his bungalow, Del Mar at that moment threw down his hat and tore off his mask furiously.

What had he done?

For a long time he sat there, his chin on his hand, gazing fixedly before him, planning to protect himself and revenge.

CHAPTER XVI

THE DISAPPEARING HELMETS

It was early the following morning that, very excited, Elaine and I showed Aunt Josephine the photograph which we had snapped and developed by using Kennedy's trick method.

"But who is it?" asked Aunt Josephine examining the print carefully and seeing nothing but a face masked and with a pair of hands before it, a seal ring on the little finger of one hand.

"Oh, I forgot that you hadn't seen the ring before," explained Elaine. "Why, we knew him at once, in spite of everything, by that seal ring—Mr. Del Mar!"

"Mr. Del Mar?" repeated Aunt Josephine, looking from one to the other of us, incredulous.

"I saw the ring at his own bungalow and on his own finger," reiterated Elaine positively.

"But what are you going to do, now?" asked Aunt Josephine.

"Have him arrested, of course," Elaine replied.

Still talking over the strange experience of the night before, we went out on the veranda.

"Well, of all the nerve!" exclaimed Elaine, catching sight of a man coming up the gravel walk. "If that isn't Henry, Mr. Del Mar's valet!"

The valet advanced as though nothing had happened

315

316 THE ROMANCE OF ELAINE

and, indeed, I suppose that as far as he knew nothing had happened or was known to us. He bowed and handed Elaine a note which she tore open quickly and read.

"Would you go?" she asked, handing the note over to me.

It read:

DEAR MISS DODGE,

If you and Mr. Jameson will call on me to-day, I will have something of interest to tell you concerning my investigations in the case of the disappearance of Craig Kennedy.

Sincerely,
M. DEL MAR.

"Yes," I asserted, "I would go."

"Tell Mr. Del Mar we shall see him as soon as possible," nodded Elaine to the valet who bowed and left quickly.

"What is it?" inquired Aunt Josephine, rejoining us.

"A note from Mr. Del Mar," replied Elaine showing it to her.

"Well," queried Aunt Josephine, "what are you going to do?"

"We're going, of course," cried Elaine.

"You're not," blurted out Aunt Josephine. "Why, just think. He's sure to do something."

But Elaine and I had made up our minds.

"I know it," I interjected. "He's sure to try something that will show his hand—and then I've got him."

Perhaps I threw out my chest a little more than was

necessary, but then I figured that Elaine with her usual intuition had for once agreed with me and that it must be all right. I drew my gun and twirled the cylinder about as I spoke. Indeed I felt, since the success of the snapshot episode, that I was a match for several Del Mar's.

"Yes, Walter is right," agreed Elaine.

Aunt Josephine continued to shake her head sagely in protest. But Elaine waved all her protestations aside and ran into the house to get ready for the visit.

Half an hour later, two saddle horses were brought around to the front of Dodge Hall and Elaine and I sallied forth.

Aunt Josephine was still protesting against our going to Del Mar's, but we had made up our minds to carry the thing through. "You know," she insisted, "that Mr. Kennedy is not around to protect you two children. Something will surely happen to you if you don't keep out of this affair."

"Oh, Auntie," laughed Elaine, a bit nervously, however, "don't be a kill-joy. Suppose Craig isn't about? Who's going to do this, if Walter and I don't?"

In spite of all, we mounted and rode away.

.   .   .   .

Del Mar, still continuing his nefarious work of mining American harbors and bridges, had arrived at a scheme as soon as he returned from the attempt to get back from us the Sandy Hook plans. Smith, who had stolen the plans from the War Department, was still at the bungalow.

Early in the morning, Del Mar had seated himself at his desk and wrote a letter.

"Here, Henry," he directed his valet, "take this to Miss Dodge."

As the valet went out, he wrote another note. "Read that," he said, handing it over to Smith. "It's a message I want you to take to headquarters right away."

It was worded cryptically:

A. A. L.
    N. Y.
    Closely watched. Must act soon or all will be discovered.—M.

Smith read the note, nodded, and put it into his pocket, as he started to the door.

"No, no," shouted Del Mar, calling him back. "This thing means that you'll have to be careful in your getaway. You'd better go out through my secret passage," he added, pointing to the panel in the library wall.

He pressed the button on the desk and Smith left through the hidden passage. Down it he groped and at the other end emerged. Seeing no one around, he made his way to the road. There seemed to be no one who looked at all suspicious on the road, either, and Smith congratulated himself on his easy escape.

On a bridge over a creek, however, as Smith approached, was one inoffensive-looking person who might have been a minister or a professor. He was leaning on the rail in deep thought, gazing at the creek that ran beneath him, and now and then flashing a sharp glance about.

Suddenly he saw something approaching. Instantly

he dodged to the farther end of the bridge and took refuge behind a tree. Smith walked on over the bridge, oblivious to the fact that he was watched. No sooner had he disappeared than the inquisitive stranger emerged again from behind the tree.

It was the mysterious Professor Arnold who many times had shown a peculiar interest in the welfare of Elaine and myself.

Evidently he had recognized Del Mar's messenger, for after watching him a moment he turned and followed.

At the railroad station, just before the train for New York pulled in, the waiting crowd was increased by one stranger. Smith had come in and taken his place unostentatiously among them.

But if he thought he was to be lost in the little crowd, he was much mistaken. Arnold had followed, but not so quickly that he had not had time to pick up the two policemen that the town boasted, both of whom were down at the station at the time.

" There he is," indicated Arnold, " the fellow with the slight limp. Bring him to my room in the St. Germain Hotel."

" All right, sir," replied the officers, edging their way to the platform as Arnold retreated back of the station and disappeared up the street.

Just then the train pulled into the station and the passengers crowded forward to mount the steps. Smith was just about to push his way on with them, when the officers elbowed through the crowd.

" You're wanted," hissed one of them, seizing his shoulder.

But Smith, in spite of his deformity, was not one to submit to arrest without a struggle. He fought them off and broke away, running toward the baggage-room.

As he rushed in, they followed. One of them was gaining on him and took a flying football tackle. The other almost fell over the twisted mass of arms and legs. The struggle now was short and sharp and ended in the officers slipping the bracelets over the wrists of Smith. While the passengers and bystanders crowded about to watch the excitement, they led him off quickly.

.   .   .   .

In his rooms at the St. Germain, cluttered with test tubes and other paraphernalia which indicated his scientific tendencies, Professor Arnold entered and threw off his hat, lighting a cigarette and waiting impatiently.

He had not as long to wait as he had expected. A knock sounded at the door and he opened it. There was Smith handcuffed and forced in by the two policemen.

"Good work," commended Arnold, at once setting to work to search the prisoner who fumed but could not resist.

"What have we here?" drawled Arnold in mock courtesy and surprise as he found and drew forth from Smith's pocket a bundle of papers, which he hastily ran through.

"Ah!" he muttered, coming to Del Mar's note, which he opened and read. "What's this? 'A. A. L.

N. Y. Closely watched. Must act soon or all will be discovered. M.' Now, what's all that?"

Arnold pondered the text deeply. "You may take him away, now," he concluded, glancing up from the note to the officers.. "Thank you."

"All right, sir," they returned, prodding Smith along out.

Still studying the note, Arnold sat down at the desk. Thoughtfully he picked up a pencil. Under the letters A. A. L. he slowly wrote "Anti-American League" and under the initial M the name, "Martin."

"Now is the time, if ever, to use that new telaphotograph instrument which I have installed for the War Department in Washington and carry around with me," he said to himself, rising and going to a closet.

He took out a large instrument composed of innumerable coils and a queer battery of selenium cells. It was the receiver of the new instrument by which a photograph could be sent over a telegraph wire.

Down-stairs, in the telegraph room of the hotel, [Arnold secured the services of one of the operators. Evidently by the way they obeyed him they had received orders from the company regarding him, and knew him well there.

"I wish you'd send this message right away to Washington," he said, handing in a blank he had already written.

The clerk checked it over:

U. S. WAR DEPARTMENT,
        Washington, D. C.
    Wire me immediately photograph and personal his-
21

tory of Martin arrested two years ago as head of Anti-
American League.—ARNOLD.

As the message was ticked off, Arnold attached his
receiving telaphotograph instrument to another wire.

It was a matter scarcely of seconds before a message
was flashed back to Arnold from Washington:

Martin escaped from Fort Leavenworth six months
ago. Thought to be in Europe. Photograph follows.
EDWARDS.

"Very well," nodded Arnold with satisfaction. "I
think I know what is going on here now. Let us wait
for the photograph."

He went over to the new selenium telaphotograph
and began adjusting it.

Far away, in Washington, in a room in the War Department where Arnold had already installed his system for the secret government service, a clerk was also
working over the sending part of the apparatus.

No sooner had the clerk finished his preparations and
placed a photograph in the transmitter than the buz-
zing of the receiver which Arnold had installed announced to him that the marvellous transmission of a
picture over a wire, one of the very newest triumphs
of science, was in progress. In the little telegraph
office of the St. Germain, the clerks and operators
crowded about Arnold, watching breathlessly.

"By Jove, it works!" cried one, no longer sceptical.

Slowly a print was being evolved before their eyes
as if by a spirit hand. Arnold watched the synchro-

nizer apparatus carefully as, point after point, the picture developed.   He bent over closely, his attention devoted to every part of the complicated apparatus.

At last the transmission of the photograph was completed and the machine came to rest.   Arnold almost tore the print from the receiver and held it up to examine it.

A smile of intense satisfaction crossed his face.

" At last! " he muttered.

There was a photograph of the man who had been identified with the arch conspirators of two years before, Martin.   Only, now he had changed his name and appeared in a new rôle.

It was Marcius Del Mar!

.   .   .   .

Already, in the library of his bungalow, Del Mar had summoned one of his trusted men and was talking to him, when Henry, the valet, reentered after his trip to see us.

" They're coming as soon as they can," he reported.

Del Mar smiled a cynical smile.   " Good," he exclaimed triumphantly, then, looking about at the electric fixtures, added to the man, " Let us see where to install the thing."

He walked over to the door and put his hand on the knob, then pointed back at the fixtures.

" That's the idea," he cried.   " You can run the line from the brackets to this door-knob and the mat. How's that? "

" Very clever," flattered the man, putting on a heavy pair of rubber gloves.

Taking a pair of pliers and other tools from a closet

in the library, he began removing the electric fixture from the wall. As Del Mar directed, the man ran a wire from the fixture along the moulding, and down the side of a door, where he made a connection.

In the meantime Del Mar brought out a wire mat and laid it in front of the door where any one who entered or left would be sure to step on it. The various connections made, the man placed a switch in the concealment of a heavily-curtained window and replaced everything as he found it.

Thus it was that Elaine and I came at last to Del Mar's bungalow, I must admit, with some misgivings. But I had gone too far to draw back now and Elaine was more eager even than I was. We dismounted, tethered our horses and went toward the house, where I rang the bell.

Preparations for our reception had just been completed and Del Mar was issuing his final instructions to his man, when the valet, Henry, ran in hastily.

" They're here, sir, now," he announced excitedly.

" All right, I'm ready," nodded Del Mar, turning to his man again and indicating a place back of the folds of the heavy curtains by the window. " You get back there by that switch. Don't move—don't even breathe. Now, Henry, let them in."

As his valet withdrew Del Mar gazed about his library to make sure that everything was all right. Just then the valet reappeared and ushered us in.

" Good morning," greeted Del Mar pleasantly. " I see that you got my note and I'm glad you were so prompt. Won't you be seated? "

Both Elaine and I were endeavoring to appear at

ease. But there was a decided tension in the atmosphere. We sat down, however. Del Mar did not seem to notice anything wrong.

"I've something at last to report to you about Kennedy," he said a moment later, clearing his throat.

.   .   .   .

Aunt Josephine turned from us as Elaine and I rode off on our horses from Dodge Hall considerably worried.

Then an idea seemed to occur to her and she walked determinedly into the house.

"Jennings," she called to the butler, "have the limousine brought around from the garage immediately."

"Yes, ma'am," acquiesced the faithful Jennings, hurrying out.

It was only a few minutes later that the car pulled around before the door. Aunt Josephine bustled out and entered.

"Fort Dale," she directed the driver, greatly agitated. "Ask for Lieutenant Woodward."

Out at Fort Dale, Woodward was much astonished when an orderly announced that Aunt Josephine was waiting in her car to see him on very urgent business. He ordered that she be admitted at once.

"I hope there's nothing wrong?" he inquired anxiously, as he noted the excitement and the worried look on her face.

"I—I'm afraid there may be," she replied, sitting down and explaining what Elaine and I had just done.

The Lieutenant listened gravely.

"And," she concluded, "they wouldn't listen to me,

Lieutenant. Can't you follow them and keep them out of trouble?"

Woodward who had been listening to her attentively jumped up as she concluded. "Yes," he cried sympathetically, "I can. I'll go myself with some of the men from the post. If they get into any scrape, I'll rescue them."

Almost before she could thank him, Woodward had hurried from his office, followed by her. On the parade grounds were some men. Quickly he issued his orders and a number of them sprang up as he detailed them off for the duty. It was only a moment before they returned, armed. An instant later three large touring cars from the Fort swept up before the office of Woodward. Into them the armed men piled.

"Hurry—to the Del Mar bungalow," ordered the Lieutenant, jumping up with the driver of the first car. "We must see that nothing happens to Miss Dodge and Mr. Jameson."

They shot away in a cloud of dust, followed hard by the other two cars, dashing at a breakneck speed over the good roads.

In the narrow, wooded roadway near Del Mar's, Woodward halted his car and the soldiers all jumped out and gathered about him as hastily he issued his directions.

"Surround the house, first," he ordered. "Then arrest any one who goes in or out."

They scattered, forming a wide circle. As soon as word was passed that the circle was completed, they advanced cautiously at a signal from Woodward, taking advantage of every concealment.

.   .   .   .

Around in the kitchen back of Del Mar's, Henry, the valet, had retired to visit one of the maids. He was about to leave when he happened to look out of the window.

"What's that?" he muttered to himself.

He stepped back and peered cautiously through the window again. There he could see a soldier, moving stealthily behind a bush.

He drew back further and thought a minute. He must not alarm us.

Then he wrote a few words on a piece of paper and tore it so that he could hold it in his palm. Next he hurried from the kitchen and entered the study.

Del Mar had scarcely begun to outline to us a long and circumstantial pseudo—investigation into what he was pleased to hint had been the death of Kennedy, when we were interrupted again by the entrance of his valet.

"Excuse me, sir," apologized Henry, as Del Mar frowned, then noted that something was wrong.

As the valet said the words, he managed surreptitiously to hand to Del Mar the paper which he had written, now folded up into a very small space.

I had turned from Del Mar when the valet entered, apparently to speak to Elaine, but in reality to throw them off their guard.

Under that cover I was able to watch the precious pair from the tail of my eye. I saw Del Mar nod to the valet as though he understood that some warning was about to be conveyed. Although nothing was said, Del Mar was indicating by dumb show orders of some kind. I had no idea what it was all about but I stood ready to whip out my gun on the slightest suspicious move from either.

"I hope you'll pardon me, Miss Dodge," Del Mar deprecated, as the valet retreated toward the door to the kitchen and pantry. "But, you see, I have to be housekeeper here, too, it seems."

Actually, though he was talking to us, it was in a way that enabled him by palming something in his hand, I fancied, to look at it. It was, though I did not know it, the hastily scrawled warning of the valet.

It must have been hard to read, for I managed by a quick shift at last to catch just a fleeting glimpse that it was a piece of paper he held in his hand.

What was it, I asked myself, that he should be so secret about it? Clearly, I reasoned, it must be something that was of interest to Elaine and myself. If I must act ever, I concluded, now was the time to do so.

Suddenly I reached out and snatched the note from his hand. But before I could read it Del Mar had sprung to his feet.

At the same instant a man leaped out from behind the curtains.

But I was on my guard. Already I had drawn my revolver and had them all covered before they could make another move.

"Back into that corner—by the window—all of you," I ordered, thinking thus to get them together, more easily covered. Then, handing the note, with my other hand, to Elaine, I said to her, "See what it says—quick."

Eagerly she took it and read aloud, " House surrounded by soldiers."

" Woodward," I cried.

Still keeping them covered, I smiled quietly to myself and took one step after another slowly to the door. Elaine followed.

I reached the door and I remember that I had to step on a metal mat to do so. I put my hand behind me and grasped the knob about to open the door.

As I did so, the man who had jumped from behind the curtain suddenly threw down his upraised hands. Before I could fire, instantaneously in fact, I felt a thrill as though a million needles had been thrust into all parts of my body at once paralyzing every muscle and nerve. The gun fell from my nerveless hand, clattering to the floor.

The man had thrown an electric switch which had completed a circuit from the metal mat to the door-knob through my body and then to the light and power current of high power. There I was, held a prisoner, by the electric current!

At the same instant, also, Del Mar with an oath leaped forward and seized Elaine by the arms. I struggled with the door-knob but I could no more let go than I could move my feet off that mat. It was torture.

" Henry! " called Del Mar to the valet.

" Yes, sir."

" Open the cabinet. Give me the helmets and the suits."

The valet did so, bringing out a number of queer looking head-pieces with a single weird eye of glass in

the front, as well as rubber suits of an outlandish design.   While he was doing so, Del Mar stuffed a handkerchief into Elaine's mouth to keep her quiet.

By this time, Del Mar, as well as the man from behind the curtains and the valet were provided with
suits, and one at a time holding Elaine, the others put
them on.

Del Mar moved toward Elaine, holding an extra helmet.   He strapped it on her, then started to force her
into a suit.

I struggled still, but in vain, to free myself from the
door-knob and mat.   It was more than I could stand,
and I sank down, half conscious.

I revived only long enough to see that Del Mar had
forced one of the suits on Elaine finally.   Then he
pressed a button hidden on the side of his desk and a
secret panel in the wall opened.   Picking up Elaine he
and the others hurried through into what looked like a
dark passage and the panel closed.

They were gone.   I put forth all my remaining
strength in one last desperate struggle.   Somehow, I
managed to kick the wire mat from under my feet,
breaking the contact.

I staggered toward the panel, but fell to the floor,
unconscious.

.   .   .   .

Outside, the iron ring, as Woodward had planned it,
of soldiers were looking about, alert for any noise or
movement.   Suddenly, two of them who had been
watching the grounds attentively signalled to each other
that they saw something.

From the shrubbery emerged a most curious and un-

couth figure, all in rags, with long, unkempt hair and
beard, sallow complexion, and carrying a long staff.
It might have been a tramp or a hermit, perhaps, who
was making his way toward the house.

The two soldiers stole up noiselessly, close to him.
Almost before he knew it, the hermit felt himself seized
from behind by four powerful arms. Escape was impossible.

"Let me go," he pleaded. "Can't you see I'm harm-
ing no one?"

But the captors were obdurate. "Tell it to the Lieutenant," they rejoined grimly forcing him to go before
them by twisting his arms, "Our orders were to seize
any one entering or leaving."

Protests were in vain. The hermit was forced to
go before Lieutenant Woodward who was just in the
rear directing the advance.

"Well," demanded Woodward, "what's your business?"

For an instant the hermit stood mute. What should
he do? He has reason to know that the situation must
be urgent.

Slowly he raised his beard so that Woodward could
see not only that it was false but what his features
looked like.

"Arnold!" gasped Woodward, startled. "What
brings you here? Elaine and Jameson are in the house.
We have it surrounded."

Half an hour before, in the St. Germain, Arnold
had no sooner received the telaphotograph than he
hurried up to his room. From a closet he had pro-
duced another of his numerous disguises and quickly

put it on. With scant white locks falling over his shoulders and long scraggly beard, he had made himself into a veritable wild man. Then he had put on the finishing touches and had made his way toward Del Mar's.

A look of intense anxiety now flashed over Arnold's face as he heard Woodward's words.

"But," he cried, "there is an underground passage from the house to the shore."

"The deuce!" muttered Woodward, more alarmed now than ever. "Come, men,—to the house," he shouted out his orders as they passed them around the line. "Arnold, lead the way!"

Together the soldier and the strange figure rushed to the front door of the bungalow. All was still inside. Heavy as it was, they broke it down and burst in.

"Walter, there's Walter!" cried Woodward as he saw me lying on the floor of the study when they ran in.

They hurried to me and as quickly as they could started to bring me around.

"Where's Elaine?" asked the strange figure of the hermit.

Weakly, I was able only to point to the panel. But it was enough. The soldiers understood. They dashed for it, looking for a button or an opening. Finding neither, they started to bang on it and batter it in with the butts of their guns.

It was only seconds before it was splintered to kindling. There was the passage. Instantly, Woodward, the hermit, and the rest plunged into it utterly regardless of danger. On through the tunnel they went until

at last they came, unmolested, to the end.   There they
paused to look about.

The hermit pointed to the ground.   Clearly there
were footprints, leading to the shore.   They followed
them on down to the beach.

"Look!" pointed the hermit.

Off in the water they could now see the most curious
sights.   Four strangely helmeted creatures were wad-
ing out, each like a huge octopus-head, without ten-
acles.

Only a few seconds before, Del Mar and his companions, carrying Elaine had emerged from the secret
entrance of the tunnel and had dashed for the shore
of the promontory.

Stopping only an instant to consider what was to be
done, Del Mar had seen some one else emerge from the
tunnel.

"Come—we must get down there quickly," he
shouted, hurriedly issuing orders, as all three, carrying
Elaine, waded out into the water.

At sight of the strange figures the soldiers raised
their guns and a volley of shot rang out.

"Stop!" shouted the hermit, his hair streaming
wildly as he ran before the guns and threw up as
many as he could grasp with his outstretched arms.
"Do you want to kill her?"

"Her?" repeated Woodward.

All stood there, wonderingly, gazing at the queer
creatures.

What did it mean?

Slowly, they disappeared—literally under the water.
They were gone—with Elaine!

CHAPTER XVII

THE TRIUMPH OF ELAINE

HALF carrying, half forcing Elaine down into the water, Del Mar and his two men, all four of the party clad in the outlandish submarine suits, bore the poor girl literally along the bottom of the bay until they reached a point which they knew to be directly under the entrance to the secret submarine harbor.

Del Mar's mind was working feverishly. Though he now had in his power the girl he both loved and also feared as the stumbling-block in the execution of his nefarious plans against America, he realized that in getting her he had been forced to betray the precious secret of the harbor itself.

At the point where he knew that the harbor was above him, hidden safely beneath the promontory, he took from under his arm a float which he released. Upward it shot through the water.

Above, in the harbor, a number of his men were either on guard or lounging about.

" A signal from the chief," cried a sentry, pointing to the float as it bobbed up.

" Kick off the lead shoes," signalled Del Mar to the others, under the water.

They did so and rose slowly to the surface, carrying Elaine up with them. The men at the surface were waiting for them and helped to pull Del Mar and his companions out of the water.

"Come into the office, right away," beckoned Del Mar anxiously, removing his helmet and leading the way.

In the office, the others removed their helmets, while Del Mar took the head-gear off Elaine. She stared about her bewildered.

"Where am I?" she demanded.

"A woman!" exclaimed the men in the harbor in surprise.

"Never mind where you are," growled Del Mar, plainly worried. Then to the men, he added, "We can't stay any longer. The harbor is discovered. Get ready to leave immediately."

Murmurs of anger and anxiety rose from the men as Del Mar related briefly between orders what had just happened.

Immediately there was a general scramble to make ready for the escape.

In the corner of the office, Elaine, again in her skirt and shirtwaist which the diving-suit had protected, sat open-eyed watching the preparations of the men for the hasty departure. Some had been detailed to get the rifles which they handed around to those as yet unarmed. Del Mar took one as well as a cartridge belt.

"Guard her," he shouted to one man indicating Elaine, "and if she gets away this time, I'll shoot you."

Then he led the others down the ledge until he came

to a submarine boat.   The rest followed, still making
preparations for a hasty flight.

. . . .

Woodward along with Professor Arnold, in his disguise as a hermit, stood for a moment surrounded by
the soldiers, after the disappearance of Elaine and Del
Mar in the water.

" I see it all, now," cried the hermit, " the submarine, the strange disappearances, the messages in the
water.   They have a secret harbor under those cliffs,
with an entrance beneath the water line."

Hastily he wrote a note on a piece of paper.

" Send one of your men to my headquarters with
that," he said, handing it to Woodward to read :

RODGERS,—
Send new submarine telescope by bearer.   You will
find it in case No. 17, closet No. 3.—ARNOLD.

" Right away," nodded Woodward, comprehending
and calling a soldier whom he dispatched immediately
with hurried instructions.   The soldier saluted and left
almost on a run.

Then Woodward turned and with Arnold lead the
men up the shore, still conferring on the best means
of attacking the harbor.

On a wharf along the shore Woodward, Arnold and
the soldiers gathered, waiting for the telescope.   Already Woodward had had a fast launch brought up,
ready for use.

. . . .

When Woodward, Arnold and the attacking party

had discovered me unconscious in Del Mar's study, there had been no time to wait for me to regain full consciousness. They had placed me on a couch and run into the secret passageway after Elaine.

Now, however, I slowly regained my senses and, looking about, vaguely began to realize what had happened.

My first impulse was to search the study, looking in all the closets and table drawers. In a corner was a large chest. I opened it. Inside were several of the queer helmets and suits which I had seen Del Mar use and one of which he had placed on Elaine.

For some moments I examined them curiously, wondering what their use could be. Somehow it seemed to me, if Del Mar had used them in the escape, we should need them in the pursuit.

Then my eye fell on the broken panel. I entered it and groped cautiously down the passageway. At the end I gazed about, trying to discover which way they had all gone.

At last, down on the shore, before a wharf I could see Woodward, the strange old hermit and the rest.

I ran toward them, calling.

.   .   .   .

By this time the soldier who had been sent for the submarine telescope arrived at last, with the telescope in sections in several long cases.

"Good!" exclaimed the old hermit, almost seizing the package which the soldier handed him.

He unwrapped it and joined the various sections together. It was, as I have said, a submarine telescope, but after a design entirely new, differing from the

22

ordinary submarine telescope. It had an arm bent at right angles, with prismatic mirrors so that it was not only possible to see the bottom of the sea but by an adjustment also to see at right angles, or, as it were, around a corner.

It was while he was joining this contrivance together that I came up from the end of the secret passage down to the wharf.

"Why, here's Jameson," greeted Woodward. "I'm glad you're so much better."

"Where's Elaine?" I interrupted breathlessly.

They began to tell me.

"Aren't you going to follow?" I cried.

"Follow? How can we follow?"

Excitedly I told of my discovery of the helmets.

"Just the thing!" exclaimed the hermit. "Send some one back to get them."

Woodward quickly detached several soldiers to go with me and I hurried back to the bungalow, while others carried the submarine telescope to the boat.

It was only a few minutes later that in Del Mar's own car, I drove up to the wharf again and we unloaded the curious submarine helmets and suits.

Quickly Woodward posted several of his men to act as sentries on the beach, then with the rest we climbed into the launch and slipped off down the shore.

The launch which Woodward had commandeered moved along in the general direction which they had seen Del Mar and his men take with Elaine. With the telescope over the side, we cruised about slowly in a circle, Arnold gazing through the eyepiece. All of us were by this time in the diving-suits which I had brought from Del Mar's, except that we had not yet strapped on the helmets.

Suddenly Arnold raised his hand and signalled to stop the launch.

"Look!" he cried, indicating the eyepiece of the submarine telescope which he had let down over the side.

Woodward gazed into the eyepiece and then I did, also. There we could see the side of a submerged submarine a short distance away, through the cave-like entrance of what appeared to be a great under-water harbor.

"What shall we do?" queried Woodward.

"Attack it now before they are prepared," replied the hermit decisively. "Put on the helmets."

All of us except those who were running the launch buckled on the head-pieces, wrapping our guns in waterproof covers which we had found with the suits.

As soon as we had finished, one after another, we let ourselves over the side of the boat and sank to the bottom.

On the bottom we gathered and slowly, in the heavy unaccustomed helmets and cumbersome suits, we made our way in a body through the entrance of the harbor.

Upward through the archway we went, clinging to rocks, anything, but always upward.

As we emerged a shot rang out. One of our men threw up his arms and fell back into the water.

On we pressed.

.   .   .   .

Elaine sat in a corner of the office, mute, while the

man who was guarding her, heavily armed, paced up
and down.

Suddenly an overwhelming desire came over her to
attempt an escape. But no sooner had she made a motion as though to run through the door than the man
seized her and drove her back to her corner.

"Take your positions here," ordered Del Mar to
several of the men. "If you see anybody come up
through the water, these hand grenades ought to set-
tle them."

Along the ledge the men were stationed each with a
pile of the grenades before him.

"See!" cried one of them from the ledge as he
caught sight of one of our helmets appearing.

The others crouched and stared. Del Mar himself
hurried forward and gazed in the direction the man indicated. There they could see Woodward, Arnold and
the rest of us just beginning to climb up out of the
water.

Del Mar aimed and fired. One of the men had
thrown up his arms with a cry and fallen back into the
water.

Invaders seemed to swarm up now in every direction
from the water.

On the semi-circular ledge about one side of the
harbor, Del Mar's men were now ranged in close order
near a submarine, whose hatch was open to receive
them, ready to repel the attack and if necessary retreat into the under-sea boat.

They fired sharply at the figures that rose from the
water. Many of the men fell back, hit, but, in turn, a
large number managed to gain a foothold on the ledge.

Led by Woodward and Arnold, they formed quickly and stripped off the waterproof coverings of their weapons, returning the fire sharply. Things were more equal now. Several of Del Mar's men had fallen. The smoke of battle filled the narrow harbor.

In the office Elaine listened keenly to the shots. What did it all mean? Clearly it could be nothing less than assistance coming.

The man on guard heard also and his uncontrollable curiosity took him to the door. As he gazed out Elaine saw her chance. She made a rush at him and seized him, wresting the rifle from his hands before he knew it. She sprang back just as he drew his revolver and fired at her. The shot just narrowly missed her, but she did not lose her presence of mind. She fired the rifle in turn and the man fell.

A little shudder ran over her. She had killed a man! But the firing outside grew fiercer. She had no time to think. She stepped over the body, her face averted, and ran out. There she could see Del Mar and his men. Many of them by this time had been killed or wounded.

"We can't beat them; they are too many for us," muttered Del Mar. "We'll have to get away if we can. Into the submarine!" he ordered.

Hastily they began to pile into the open hatch.

Just as Del Mar started to follow them, he caught sight of Elaine running out of the office. Almost in one leap he was at her side. Before she could raise her rifle and fire he had seized it. She managed, however, to push him off and get away from him.

She looked about for some weapon. There on the

ledge lay one of the hand grenades. She picked it up
and hurled it at him, but he dodged and it missed him.
On it flew, landing close to the submarine. As it exploded, another of Del Mar's men toppled over into
the water.

Between volleys, Woodward, Arnold and the rest
pulled off their helmets.

" Elaine! " cried Arnold, catching sight of her in
the hands of Del Mar.

Quickly, at the head of such men as he could mus-
ter, the hermit led a charge.

In the submarine the last man was waiting for Del
Mar. As the hermit ran forward with several soldiers
between Del Mar and the submarine, it was evident
that Del Mar would be cut off.

The man at the hatch climbed down into the boat.
It was useless to wait. He banged shut and clamped
the hatch. Slowly the submarine began to sink.

Del Mar by this time had overcome Elaine and
started to run toward the submarine with her. But
then he stopped short.

There was a queer figure of a hermit leading some
soldiers. He was cut off.

" Back into the office! " he growled, dragging Elaine.

He banged shut the door just as the hermit and the
soldiers made a rush at him. On the door they
battered. But it was in vain. The door was
locked.

In the office Del Mar hastily went to a corner, after
barring the door, and lifted a trap-door in the floor,
known only to himself.

Elaine did not move or make any attempt to escape,

for Del Mar in addition to having a vicious looking automatic in his hand kept a watchful eye on her.

Outside the office, the soldiers, led by the hermit and Woodward continued to batter at the door.

" Now—go down that stairway—ahead of me," ordered Del Mar.

Elaine obeyed tensely, and he followed into his emergency exit, closing the trap.

" Beat harder, men," urged the hermit, as the soldiers battered at the door.

They redoubled their efforts and the door bent and swayed.

At last it fell in under the sheer weight of the blows.

" By George—he's gone—with Elaine," cried the hermit, looking at the empty office.

Feverishly they hunted about for a means of escape but could find none.

" Pound the floor and walls with the butts of your guns," ordered Arnold. " There must be some place that is hollow."

They did so, going over all inch by inch.

Meanwhile, through the passage, along a rocky stairway, Del Mar continued to drive Elaine before him, up and ever up to the level of the land.

At last Elaine, followed by Del Mar, emerged from the rocky passage in a cleft in the cliffs, far above the promontory.

" Go on! " he ordered, forcing her to go ahead of him.

They came finally to a small hut on a cliff overlooking the real harbor.

" Enter! " demanded Del Mar.

Still meekly, she obeyed.

Del Mar seized her and before she knew it had her bound and gagged.

Down in the little office our men continued to search for the secret exit.

"Here's a place that gives an echo," shouted one of them.

As he found the secret trap and threw it open, the hermit stripped off the cumbersome diving-suit and jumped in, followed by Woodward, myself and the soldiers.

Upward we climbed until at last we came to the opening. There we paused and looked about. Where was Del Mar? Where was Elaine? We could see no trace of them.

Finally, however, Arnold discovered the trail in the grass and we followed him, slowly picking up the tracks.

.   .   .   .

Knowing that the submarine would cruise about and wait for him, Del Mar decided to leave Elaine in the hut while he went out and searched for a boat in which to look for the submarine.

Coming out of the hut, he gazed about and moved off cautiously. Stealthily he went down to the shore and there looked up and down intently.

A short distance away from him was a pier in the process of construction. Men were unloading spiles from a cable car that ran out on the pier on a little construction railway, as well as other material with which to fill in the pier. At the end of the dock lay a power-boat, moored, evidently belonging to some one interested in the work on the pier.

The workmen had just finished unloading a car full and were climbing back on the empty car, which looked as if it had once been a trolley. As Del Mar looked over the scene of activity, he caught sight of the power-boat.

" Just what I want," he muttered to himself. " I must get Elaine. I can get away in that."

The workmen signalled to the engineer above and the car ran up the wharf and up an incline at the shore-end.

The moment the car disappeared, Del Mar hurried away in the direction he had come.

At the top of the grade, he noticed, was a donkey engine which operated the cable that drew the car up from the dock, and at the top of the incline was a huge pile of material.

The car had been drawn up to the top of the grade by this time. There the engineer who operated the engine stopped it.

Just then the whistle blew for the noon hour. The men quit work and went to get their dinner pails, while the engineer started to draw the fire. Beside the engine, he began to chop some wood, while the car was held at the top of the grade by the cable.

.   .   .   .

In our pursuit we came at last in sight of a lonely hut. Evidently that must be a rendezvous of Del Mar. But was he there? Was Elaine there? We must see first.

While we were looking about and debating what

was the best thing to do, who should appear hurrying up the hill but Del Mar himself, going toward the hut.

As we caught sight of him, Arnold sprang forward. Woodward and I, followed by the soldiers also jumped out.

Del Mar turned and ran down the hill again with us after him, in full cry.

While we had been waiting, some of the soldiers had deployed down the hill and now, hearing our shouts, turned, and came up again.

Beside his engine, we could see an engineer chopping wood. He paused now in his chopping and was gazing out over the bay. Suddenly he had seen something out in the water that had attracted his attention and was staring at it. There it moved, nothing less than a half-submerged submarine.

As the engineer gazed off at it, Del Mar came up, unseen, behind him and stood there, also watching the submarine, fascinated.

Just then behind him Del Mar heard us pursuing. He looked about as we ran toward him and saw that we had formed a wide circle, with the men down the hill, that almost completely surrounded him. There was no chance for escape. It was hopeless.

But it was not Del Mar's nature to give up. He gave one last glance about. There was the trolley car that had been converted into a cable way. It offered just one chance in a thousand. Suddenly his face assumed an air of desperate determination.

He sprang toward the engineer and grappled with him, seeking to wrest the axe from his hand. Every

second counted. Our circle was now narrowing down
and closing in on him.

Del Mar managed to knock out the engineer, taken
by surprise, just as our men fired a volley. In the
struggle, Del Mar was unharmed. Instead he just
managed to get the axe.

An instant later a leap landed him on the cable car.
With a blow of the axe he cut the cable. The car began to move slowly down the hill on the grade.

Some of the men were down below in its path. But
the onrushing cable car was too much for them. They
could only leap aside to save themselves.

On down the incline, gathering momentum every
second, the car dashed, Del Mar swaying crazily but
keeping his footing. We followed as fast as we could,
but it was useless.

Out on the wharf it sped at a terrific pace. At the
end it literally catapulted itself into the water, crashing from the end of the pier. As it did so, Del Mar
gave a flying leap out into the harbor, struck the water
with a clean dive and disappeared.

On down the hill we hurried. There in the water
was Del Mar swimming rapidly. Almost before we
knew it, we saw him raise his hand and signal, shouting.

There only a few yards away was the periscope of a
submarine. As we watched, we could see that it had
seen him, had turned in his direction. Would they
get him?

We watched, fascinated. Some of our men fired, as
accurately as they could at a figure bobbing so uncer-
tainly on the water.

Meanwhile the submarine approached closer and rose
a bit so that the hatchway cleared the waves. It
opened. One of the foreign agents assisted Del Mar in.
He had escaped at last!

.   .   .   .

It was most heart-breaking to have had Del Mar so
nearly in our grasp and then to have lost him. We
looked from one to another, in despair.

Only Arnold, in his disguise as a hermit, seemed un-
discouraged. Suddenly he turned to Woodward.

"What time is it?" he asked eagerly.

"A little past noon."

"The Kennedy wireless torpedo!" he exclaimed.
"It arrived to-day. Burnside is trying it out."

Suddenly there flashed over me the recollection of
the marvellous invention that Kennedy had made for
the Government just before his disappearance, as well
as the memory of the experience I had had once with
the intrepid Burnside.

Woodward's face showed a ray of interest and hope
in the overwhelming gloom that had settled on us all.

"You and Jameson go to Fort Dale, quick," directed
Arnold eagerly. "I'm not fit. Get Burnside. Have
him bring the torpedo in the air-boat."

We needed no further urging. It was a slender
chance. But I reflected that the submarine could not
run through the bay totally submerged. It must have
its periscope in view. We hurried away, leaving
Arnold, who slowly mounted the hill again.

How we did it, I don't know, but we managed to
get to the Fort in record time. There near the aero-
plane hangar, sure enough, was Burnside with some

other men adjusting the first real wireless Kennedy torpedo, the last word in scientific warfare, making an aerial torpedo-boat.

We ran up to the hangar calling to Burnside excitedly. It was only a moment later, that he began to issue orders in his sharp staccato. His men swarmed forward and took the torpedo from the spot where they had been examining it, adjusting it now beneath the hydroaeroplane.

"Jameson, you come with me," he asked. "You went before."

We rose quickly from the surface and planed along out over the harbor. Far off we could see the ripple from the periscope of the submarine that was bearing Del Mar away. Would Kennedy's invention for which Del Mar had dared so much in the first place prove his final undoing? We sped ahead.

Down below in the submersible Del Mar was giving hasty orders to his men, to dip down as soon as all the shipping and the sand bars were cleared.

I strained my eyes through the glasses reporting feverishly to Burnside what I saw so that he could steer his course.

"There it is," I urged. "Keep on—just to the left."

"I see it," returned Burnside a moment later catching with his naked eye the thin line of foam on the water left by the periscope. "Would you mind getting that torpedo ready?" he continued. "I'll tell you just what to do. They'll try to duck as soon as they see us, but it won't be any use. They can't get totally submerged fast enough."

Following Burnside's directions I adjusted the firing apparatus of the torpedo.

"Let it go!" shouted Burnside.

I did so, as he volplaned down almost to the water. The torpedo fell, sank, bobbed up, then ran along just under the surface. Already I was somewhat familiar with the wireless device that controlled it, so that while Burnside steadied the aircraft I could direct it, as he coached me.

The submarine saw it coming now. But it was too late. It could not turn; it could not submerge in time.

A terrific explosion followed as the torpedo came in contact with the boat, throwing a column of water high in the air. A yawning hole was blown in the very side of the submarine. One could see the water rush in.

Inside, Del Mar and his men were now panic-stricken. Some of them desperately tried to plug the hole. But it was hopeless. Others fell, fainting, from the poisonous gases that were developed.

Of them all, Del Mar's was the only cool head.

He realized that all was over. There was nothing left to do but what other submarine heroes had done in better causes. He seized a piece of paper and hastily wrote:

> Tell my emperor I failed only because Craig Kennedy was against me.—DEL MAR.

He had barely time to place the message in a metal float near-by. Down the submarine, now full of water, sank.

With his last strength he flung the message clear of the wreckage as it settled on the mud on the bottom of the bay.

Burnside and I could but stare in grim satisfaction at the end of the enemy of ourselves and our country.

.   .   .   .

Up the hillside plodded Professor Arnold still in his wild disguise as the hermit. Now and then he turned and cast an anxious glance out over the bay at the fast disappearing periscope of the submarine.

Once he paused. That was when he saw the hydro-aeroplane with Burnside and myself carrying the wireless torpedo.

Again he paused as he plodded up, this time with a gasp of extreme satisfaction. He has seen the water-spout and heard the explosion that marked the debacle of Del Mar.

The torpedo had worked. The most dangerous foreign agent of the coalition of America's enemies was dead, and his secrets had gone with him to the bottom of the sea. Perhaps no one would ever know what the nation had been spared.

He did not pause long, now. More eagerly he plodded up the hill, until he came to the hut.

He pushed open the door. There lay Elaine, still bound. Quickly he cut the cords and tore the gag from her mouth.

As he did so, his own beard fell off. He was no longer the hermit. Nor was he what I myself had thought him, Arnold.

"Craig!" cried Elaine in eager surprise.

Kennedy said not a word as he grasped her two hands.

" And you were always around us, protecting Walter and me," she half laughed, half cried hysterically. " I knew it—I knew it! "

Kennedy said nothing. His heart was too happy.

" Yes," he said simply, as he gazed deeply into her great eyes, " my work on the case is done."

THE END